## KATHY JAY

I live in Cheshire with my family which includes a large dog and a cat. I love the changing seasons. I like pyjama days and cosy log fires in winter. In summer, my top things are strawberries and walking on beautiful beaches in North Wales. I started writing my first romance on a vintage typewriter. Writing got put on hold while I studied for a degree in Drama and French. I've been an office temp and a bilingual PA in London. Now I'm a member of the Romantic Novelists' Association, and thrilled to write fun, flirty romance for HarperImpulse.

# What If He's the One

## KATHY JAY

Harper*Impulse* an imprint of
HarperCollins*Publishers* Ltd
77–85 Fulham Palace Road
Hammersmith, London W6 8JB

www.harpercollins.co.uk

A Paperback Original 2015

First published in Great Britain in ebook format by Harper*Impulse* 2014

Copyright © Kathy Jay 2014

Cover images © Shutterstock.com

Kathy Jay asserts the moral right
to be identified as the author of this work

A catalogue record for this book is
available from the British Library

ISBN: 978-0-00-812277-5




Automatically produced by Atomik ePublisher from Easypress

*For Jake*

# Prologue

*Ten years ago in London*
"Tinseltown, here we come!"

The male voice reverberated through Magenta Plumtree's pounding head as she perched on the end of Alex Wells' bed, rolling a scarlet silk stocking up to her thigh.

Nick Wells burst into his twin brother's bedroom. "Get your act together, Bro. It's Christmas Eve," he yelled, then jumped out of his skin. "Well hello, Maggie! Looks like Santa filled Alex's stocking a day early."

Bleary-eyed, Maggie blinked at the blonde, brown-eyed version of the guy she'd woken up beside. Too hung over to blush she scanned the room for her other hold-up. She nodded at the boarded-up Victorian fireplace.

"There's no way Santa's going to make it down that chimney."

Nick grinned. He looked her up and down. "I'd suggest that Alex give Santa a key, but there's hardly any point."

"Quite." She shrugged. "Since the two of you are going to LA for the holidays." She bit her lip and wondered idly if there'd be any room in Alex's bag for a stowaway.

"And never comin' back! If things go according to plan." Nick rubbed his hands together, ostensibly because he was cold, but actually because he couldn't contain his glee.

The idea of Alex never coming back to London smarted. "Whose plan?"

"Mine," he said smugly.

"Don't count on it. You haven't even had the audition yet." Nick's shoulders tightened. He turned his back on Maggie, shuffled a few of his brother's things about randomly on his desk, more messing than tidying, and turned back abruptly to face her. He opened his mouth to say something. No sound came out. He was holding something back.

Alex, wearing only boxers, marched into the room, a mug of instant coffee in each hand. Tall and fabulous, he watched Maggie scrabble under the bed for her missing stocking with a suggestive twinkle in his bluer-than-blue eyes.

"Leaving so soon?"

"I've got a train to catch." She rolled the second indecently expensive silk stocking up her left leg and set about locating her shoes. Dressed as a sexy Santa in broad daylight on Christmas Eve? At best she looked like a festive kiss-o-gram. At worst? Best not go there.

"Great party last night. You pulled a cracker." Nick winked at his twin. "Where's my coffee?"

"He can have mine." Maggie took a mug from Alex's hand and shoved it at him. A tiny bow wave of milky coffee sloshed onto the threadbare carpet. The hideous pattern camouflaged the spill. Maggie shrugged. She slipped her feet into her sparkly red heels. "Gotta go."

Alex pushed a hand through his dark, disheveled hair. "Don't you have somewhere else to be?" He glowered at his brother.

Nick glanced at the alarm clock on Alex's bedside table. "Heathrow airport in about an hour." Everyone's eyes landed on the unopened foil condom package next to the clock.

Alex shot Nick a get-lost-now look and handed him the second cup of coffee. "Go and boost your caffeine level somewhere else."

Slurping coffee, Nick backed out into the hallway. "Alright,

alright, I'm gone already. I can take a hint." Alex glowered again and closed the door in his face.

Maggie scoured the messy room. "This place is a bombsite. What happened to my coat?"

"We lost it." Alex pulled an apologetic face. "Actually, I think I persuaded you to give it to a homeless guy."

Maggie groaned. "Thanks for that." Her head still hurt. The previous night's sequence of events was coming back to her. She didn't mind about the coat. It was a much-too-big impulse buy. Like much of her eclectic wardrobe it had come from a vintage shop. She'd only worn it because it drowned her enough to cover up her Sexy Santa outfit. Anyway, she and Alex had had a cozy room to go back to, whilst the guy on the street faced a bitterly cold night in a shop doorway with nothing but a sleeping bag and a makeshift cardboard tent. Alex had given him directions to a shelter, but he'd refused to go because he had a little scruffy dog with him. "She's all the family I have," he'd said. "They won't let me bring her in." She hoped her extra-large winter coat had helped the two of them keep warm.

He picked his sweater up off the floor. "Borrow this." She struggled into it. He dragged a preppy-ish scarf from under a pile of play scripts and clutter. He wrapped it around her neck, pausing to caress her nape.

His warm, firm touch put her into a reverie. It had been the weirdest night. Alex's mood had been hyper. Hadn't he stolen her antlers and performed a rendition of "Rudolph the Red- Nosed Reindeer" in the queue for the night bus? She vaguely remembered a "Jingle Bells" sing-along with the passengers on the top deck. Alex had been economical with the details even before they'd downed a festive quantity of alcohol, but something had happened with his dad.

From what Maggie could tell, he and Nick didn't see much of their actor father, but he'd come out with some scathing remarks in a newspaper interview about disowning his sons because their mother wanted them to audition for an American television drama. "A vampire is the last part on earth I'd choose for myself!" and "I wouldn't do *Mercy of the Vampires* if my life depended on it!" were the quotes from the "doyen of serious drama" that had upset Alex. The jibes said more about the legendary Drake Wells than his sons, and were most probably calculated to annoy his soap diva ex-wife, Maggie reckoned, but she could tell Alex was hurt. Having famous parents who were unabashed when it came to splashing their lives across the tabloids had to be hideous. No wonder he was stand-offish. So much so that when she'd first met him she'd thought he hadn't liked her. She'd been wrong on that one. Oh. So. Wrong.

"So…" His lovely rumbly voice filled the awkward silence. "Christmas with Grandma. How is the old dragon?"

"She'd have your …" She fired a twinkly look downwards. "… you-know-whats for Christmas-tree baubles if she knew about last night!"

"Um. Yeah. About last night …" Alex felled her with a sexy smile. "Rain check?"

"Sure." She pictured the "Tube journey of shame" that lay ahead. Technically, she didn't actually have anything to be ashamed of. More's the pity.

Alex pulled her close and forked his fingers into her hair. "Happy Christmas, Babe." His lips touched hers lightly, then he gathered her into his hold and deepened the kiss as if he'd never let her go. Head in a spin, her heart cartwheeled. This was it! They were tipping over the edge from friends into … What? She couldn't be sure what all of this meant. She and Alex had become fast friends when she'd moved to London to study fashion. They'd known each other for about a year, been part of a big group of artsy, thespiany students who hung out and went to the same parties. She'd kind of got close to him, as close as anyone could, given how aloof he could be. And, of course, she fancied him. Didn't everyone? In all honesty she'd been a teeny bit in love with him since the moment she'd first set eyes on him. She'd reconciled the feelings she had for her friend to being just the stuff of crushes, and then, bam! Practically out of nowhere it had flared up last night. She'd accidentally-on-purpose missed the last Tube home, and all of a sudden she had butterflies in her stomach and her head and her heart were in a lovely befuddled muddle.

*What if he's The One?*

She wished he didn't have to go. He had to spend Christmas with his crazy, mixed-up mother in LA. The Hollywood drama queen with the checkered past was at the top of her game, and about to pull off the nepotistic coup of landing her twin sons leading roles in a new vampire drama. Hence the furore with their disapproving father. Alex was stuck. She felt for him. Devoted to Nick and their mother, he'd walk through flames not to let either of them down. Even though he hated his father for publicly lambasting the family, he badly wanted to please him. Getting him to talk about it was impossible. Alex puzzled Maggie. He was positively taciturn about his dad. What she'd figured out was mostly guesswork.

Blow all that. She didn't want to think about it. She had faith in Alex. He wouldn't drop out of drama school. He wouldn't stay in LA. He wanted to be a serious actor. Maybe direct. That might be for the best, given how much he loathed the limelight. She pressed closer into his arms and got lost in his kiss. She closed her eyes and allowed herself to exist only in the moment, memorizing how good he felt, as if she was recording this perfect feeling to hold onto until he came back. A column of warmth and strong muscle, he tightened his hold on her melted body, and his lips crushed hers. Slowly, oh-so-deliciously slowly, they explored each other's mouths as though they had all the time in the world.

Nick hammered on the door. "I hate to break up the party, guys – but I don't want to miss my flight."

They broke from the delirious oblivion of each other. He rocked her world. His soft mouth and the rasp of his unshaven skin made her giddy. She remembered to breathe, and committed to memory his uniquely gorgeous scent of spicy guy.

Her impending Tube journey dragged her back to reality, as if she had lead feet instead of six-inch sequined heels. She had to go home and pack and get herself to Cornwall for what promised to be a traditional, but distinctly uneventful, Christmas break: just her and grandma, as per usual, same as every year in the ten or so since her mother had left.

"I don't want to go," she breathed in a whisper. "I wish we could just stay here for the holidays."

A low groan of frustration echoed from deep in Alex's throat. "Same." He brushed her lips in a final parting kiss. "Take these." He gave her his much-too-big gloves and she stuffed her hands into them.

Nick practically fell through the door as she opened it. "Bye Nick," she chirped, adding with a cheeky smile, "Good luck with the audition. You'd make a lovely vampire!"

She wanted to mean it. The opportunity meant everything to Nick, even if warring vampire brothers wasn't exactly Alex's cup of tea.

"Sayonara, Santa Girl." He sniggered at her fancy-dress costume. "I'd say thanks if I thought you meant it. Vamoose." He held the door wide open for her to make an exit. "Cheerio. Toodle-pip. Have a nice life."

Nick wanted her out of the picture and he wasn't making any effort to hide the fact. What did he think she might do? Abduct Alex and keep him prisoner in a beach cave so he couldn't go to LA for their big, life-changing audition. It was a tempting thought. She glared at Alex's younger twin and froze him out, pretended he had on an invisibility cloak and stood her ground.

She only had eyes for the dark-haired, blue-eyed twin. "Walk you to the Tube?" Alex offered.

Tongue jammed into her cheek, Maggie arched a brow and razed nearly-naked-Alex with a top-to-toe look. She shook her head. "I. Don't. Think. So." Despite her ridiculous appearance she was aiming for a sophisticated vibe, like she was terrifically cool with the fact that at some point in the previous twelve hours the world had tilted on its axis and they had become something that was a whole heap of fabuliciousness more than friends. Only her composure cracked and she bubbled over with a fit of the giggles. "Arrivederci. I'll see myself out."

"I'm glad you see the funny side." His drawl echoed in the stairwell. "I'll call you in Cornwall."

"Be warned." She managed to sound nonchalant, even though her heart was racing, "The signal's rubbish down there. Most of my grandmother's texts get lost in cyber space for days on end."

Outside on the London street snow had started to fall, coating everything in a thin layer of white, like frosting on a Christmas cake. Maggie shivered. Tottering to the Underground station, she fumbled her toasty fingers out of Alex's gloves and texted him. "*GBFN.*"

A second later his reply pinged onto her phone. Her heart jumped. She missed everything about him already – his strong arms, the touch of his big hands. Suddenly she felt bizarrely isolated. She stopped stock-still on the busy street, a lone eccentric figure in red silk, sequins and oversized knitwear. A skinny black cat with white paws had been watching her from its perch on top of a rubbish bin. It jumped down and twisted itself against her legs. Purring loudly, it circled her, almost knocking her off balance. "Give me a break, Puss-in-Boots," she muttered through chattering teeth. "It's hard enough to walk in these stupid shoes as it is. Black cats are supposed to bring good luck," she scolded chirpily. "I'll not be feeling very lucky if you trip me up and I break my ankle!"

A sharp tap on the shoulder made her jump. She spun round to find Nick smiling down at her, holding a shoe box. "You can't go home in those things," he said, nodding at her feet, and whipping the lid off the box with a flourish. "Ta-dah ..." He held out a pair of brand-new boots. "... I'm the health-and-safety guy."

"I can't take those."

"You can and you will," he joked. "They're a present."

"For someone else," she insisted.

"Yeah, but your need is greater." He shrugged. "I can get something else."

Steadying herself on his shoulder she swapped her heels for the flat, sheepskin boots. They were about a size too big but she wasn't complaining.

"Thanks, Nick."

"No problem."

He turned and fled. She bit her lip and checked the screen on her phone.

*I'll call you when I get back. :-) Promise. Alex XXX*

She hoped he'd be okay. He hated his parents lashing out at each other in the press. Publicity usually sent him retreating behind a wall of steely silence. Last night had been different. His barriers had come down like never before. If only she could rewind the clock and not fall asleep in his bed. What a twit!

She'd giddily tumbled into bed with Alex, a hot tangle of limbs, breath, skin. The rasp of a zip, feeling her sexy Santa dress fall to the floor, stayed fresh in her mind, even if the rest was hazy. She'd blown her budget on stockings and high heels, but not having anticipated revealing her undies to anyone, let alone Alex, they'd been on the ever-so-slightly unsightly side of things, grey from too many laundry days. Frankly her lingerie – if it qualified to be called that – had seen better days. She cringed, remembering the pause for condoms, uncertainty setting in. Having fruitlessly turned his room upside down, Alex had gone off to see if he could cadge one off a house mate. In a house shared by four guys, a stash had eventually been found. But by then, hit by a wave of embarrassment and beaten by the alcohol, she'd started drifting off to sleep. He'd held her, her hair tangled with his, her head in the curve of his neck, and they'd fallen asleep in each other's arms, waking in the cold grey dawn to the realization that in a drunken frenzy they'd almost gone too far.

Except he'd kissed her again and now she was on cloud nine.

Flakes of snow swirled around her. She was having a snow-globe moment. Inside her own little bubble Nick's words hit home. "Have a nice life." Alex didn't realize it yet, but as sure as lucky black cats didn't wear white boots, the Wells twins were leaving London for good.

They wouldn't be coming back from LA.

She'd fallen asleep and blown the only chance she'd ever have of making love to the gorgeous guy she'd been really more than a little bit in love with since the moment she'd first looked flirtily into his seductive eyes, and said, "My name's Magenta, but my friends call me Maggie."

# Chapter One

*Oh my giddy aunt! He's actually on the flight!*

What had possessed her when she'd accepted this last-minute styling job? Apart from itchy feet and the promise of a healthy paycheck, there was the decidedly unhealthy curiosity she still harbored over the big what-might-have-been-and-wasn't-meant-to-be factor.

Secretly, she'd always kicked herself that she hadn't had sex with Hot Vampire Guy when she had the chance. Frankly, she should be over all that. And she was. Really, she was.

Magenta Plumtree, fashion-stylist-on-a-mission, boarded the flight from London Heathrow to Boston clutching her cabin baggage so tight that her knuckles turned white. A British magazine had hired her to fly out and style twin celebrities, Alex and Nick Wells, in two fashion shoots scheduled to coincide with the promo for the final series of their top-of-the-ratings television show, *Mercy of the Vampires*. It was all very last-minute and a bit of a shock.

The flight attendant, a blonde bombshell with a candy-pink pout, checked her boarding card.

"You've been upgraded to Business."

To her right, bursting at the seams, Economy buzzed with passengers stowing carry-ons.

"I have? How come?" She almost high-fived Blondie. She'd lucked in. For once. Delighted to be moving up in the world, she turned left.

*Yay.*

Then again. Not so yay. Of course there was a drawback. The empty seat was smack-bang next to super-sexy vampire actor Alex Wells. In this position many women would have imagined they'd died and gone to heaven. Not so Magenta. She winced. She'd braced herself for working with him in Boston. She hadn't planned on travelling with him, or being bowled over by his fabulousness. These days he was just another celebrity clothes hanger. It was her job to pick him out some knock-out fashion items. Unusually for her she was lost for words.

He flicked her an arrogant glance up and down from behind dark glasses.

"Hey."

She reeled. One rumble was enough to make her heart drop into her freebie, perk-of-the-job designer boots. "Hey." Her terse echo masked intense, self-conscious attraction. With a perfunctory smile, she sat down and snapped on her seatbelt.

*Big comfy seat. Masses of leg room. Nice.*

They ignored each other through the spiel about life jackets and no smoking in the toilets. She picked up the emergency-procedure leaflet and gave it the benefit of her undivided attention for longer than was strictly necessary.

After take-off a star-struck flight attendant batted her eyelashes at Alex with a dose of not-so-professional allure. "Complimentary champagne, Sir?"

He removed his sunglasses. "Don't mind if I do," he quipped, infamous Wellsian charm much in evidence. How did he manage to pull off that cool twinkle? He turned his penetrating gaze on Magenta. "Join me?"

"No thanks." She declined the bubbly, and the flight attendant substituted champagne with orange juice.

Alex's eyebrows shot up. "What happened to your party-girl tendencies?"

She tried him with a couple of lame excuses. "I'm detoxing. Anyhow, alcohol and jetlag don't mix."

He was having none of it. "Go on. Be a devil. You used to be fun," he joked. "A. Lot. Of. Fun." She hadn't seen him for donkey's years and here he was, large as life, all flirty and fabulous. She gritted her teeth. She wasn't about to tell him the truth, so she needed another excuse for not drinking. She could hardly claim to be a recovering alcoholic. That would be insensitive given his mother's history of stints in rehab.

"I've just finished a course of antibiotics and, anyway, I'm counting calories." She tipped her head to one side, exuding fake nonchalance.

Alex sipped from his flute. "No champagne for you, huh? That's tough." He checked that the flight attendant was out of earshot and whispered so she wouldn't hear. "It's not properly chilled. It pretty much tastes like fizzy bath water – if that's any consolation, Maggie."

The mini champagne bottle looked perfectly chilled. Was this Alex being considerate? She didn't know what she'd expected from the man who'd walked away without saying goodbye, but it definitely wasn't quips about tepid champagne.

His incendiary eyes ignited a touch paper of acute embarrassment topped off with a sprinkling of nostalgia. Her heartbeat skipped, like an awkwardly timed hiccup. She laughed, jittery. His voice was all actorly. Posh – sort of. Not marbles – more velvety, like rich, dark, melted chocolate. So much for having got over the effect he'd had on her in their student days.

He sounded kind of mid-Atlantic, half-Brit, half-American. De-lish. And altogether too smooth. What was it about that soft rumble? He made the tiny hairs on the back of her neck stand to attention.

"No one's called me Maggie since …" She stopped abruptly.

*Um. You did. Way back when.* "… It's Magenta now."

"Magenta Plumtree – fashion stylist to the stars." Did she detect a hint of cynicism?

"I wouldn't go quite that far." A lump formed in her throat. "Until now, that is."

He snared her gaze. The moment lasted a second too long. Even after all this time, she could lose herself in his dreamy eyes.

"You're still just plain Maggie to me." His delectable drawl gave her tingles. The orange juice sloshed. She set it down on the tray table, eyes fixed on it as if she'd just found a fly floating in there. Avoiding Alex's roguish face, she studied her blue nails, the only soupçon of color in her meticulously monochrome appearance. She pinched the skin on the back of her hand, though a little bit harder than she intended. "Ouch."

"What are you doing?" he asked.

"Checking you're not a nightmare."

He frowned and pinched the back of his own hand. "Well, what do you know? Neither are you."

A bubble of emotion burst. He compelled her to smile despite her inclination to send him frosty, couldn't-care-less-about-you vibes.

*You're ridiculously dreamy actually!*

The Wells twins' celebrity status was stratospheric. They had the bad-boy reputations to go with it. Less inclined to publicly flaunt his love life than his scandal-prone brother, Alex maintained an air of mystery. Even so, he'd been the subject of his fair share of gossip over the years.

"So. Long time, no see. How the hell are you?"

She must be hearing things. He'd said "long time, no see". Despite her annoyance at his cheek, sparks of their once-upon-a-time chemistry flickered. "I'm good. Grr-reat. You?"

"Fine. Busy. Doing promo for the final series of *Vampires*. She took another hit of his blue eyes and spine-tingly voice, barely listening to the actual words he was saying. "And working on a new project in London."

Fidgety, she picked up her drink, took a sip and waited for the next question.

"What about you, Maggie? What are you up to these days? Not married or anything?"

*Right on cue. More cheek!*

"Nope. Not married."

Maggie met his magnetic stare full on. She sizzled. She had to tough this out. She couldn't in all honesty add "Or anything", but she certainly wasn't about to share her personal life with him. The eyes that wowed women all over the planet from the safety of their TV screens slid to her left hand. No wedding ring.

*Flipping flippity flip.*

Why couldn't they be on a posh new plane? Then he'd have his own personal first-class pod to chillax in? Instead of spoiling her upgrade.

"How do you like your upgrade? Shame about the champagne. I hope you don't mind, Maggie, but I took the liberty of having you moved to Business. It's been a long time, I thought it might be good to meet, clear the air, ahead of working together."

Maggie gulped, only just managing not to splutter juice all down her front.

"You upgraded me?" she squeaked. *How dare he interfere with her travel arrangements?* "There was really no need. I'll reimburse you."

He downed his champagne. His eyes scintillated. "It's a tight schedule. I thought you'd be more comfortable in Business. And I get the pleasure of your company. We can have a catch-up."

*Awkward!*

"A catch-up? It's been ten years, Alex. How long have you got?"

He glanced at his watch and laughed. "About seven hours."

Even after a decade, he unnerved her with a sense that he could see inside her soul with those penetrating blue irises.

*Outrageous.*

That was silly. Deluded. It was the TV-star effect. Guys like Alex shouldn't be allowed in confined spaces – like airplanes. Much too distracting. Flight attendants should be issued with Hot Man Alert signs. By law, or something.

*Keep calm and carry on.*

Her professional preparedness for the prospect of working with him after all these years had taken on an unexpected turn now that she was sitting next to him. Polite chit-chat she could do. The last thing she wanted was to start spilling out an over-share of personal details as if they'd never lost touch.

"There's not much to tell. I know transatlantic travel is boring, but I'm not the in-flight entertainment."

Okay, so long ago in a forgotten land, Alex had been her friend … And they'd fallen into bed together – that one time. She winced. That was before he went off and became famous and dropped her like a hot potato. She fumed. If they were on a bus, she'd hop off at the next stop. Seeing him like this had catapulted her back in time, and she was suddenly a tad out of her depth.

"Go on. Indulge me. Tell me all about it. How did my old mate Maggie become fashion guru Magenta Plumtree?" Alex's mid-Atlantic voice hypnotized her, weakening her wariness.

*His old mate! Really?*

"I have my dippy mother to thank for the la-di-da name. The rest, I guess, is down to a lot of good luck and hard work."

"Not to mention an instinct for style and a flair for all things fashion. Don't be modest. You're good and you know it."

"The truth is I sort of fell into it. I've loved fashion since I was a little girl. I guess I like playing dress-up."

"Good for you for doing what you love."

He was more heart-stoppingly attractive than he'd ever been, but there was an aura of distance about him. Was this his celebrity bubble? She couldn't make up her mind if she was annoyed with him for quizzing her, or pleased that he still thought of her as having been a friend. She was intrigued by him, that was for sure.

"I like helping people express their sense of style – whether it's a special event or a makeover." She was off. "I love it all. I like putting together looks that are bang on trend, or quirky ones that are a bit of a mash-up, the way we're doing for these shoots with you and Nick. I love catwalk shows, fashion weeks, shoes – oh my lucky stars – how I love shoes." She dipped her glance towards her beloved designer boots, wiggled her toes and clicked her feet together in the mode of *The Wizard of Oz's* red-shoed Dorothy. "Then there's the shopping – need I say more? I get to go wild in great cities. New York. London. Paris. I pick up accessories. I find little boutiques off the beaten track. Just last week I found a vintage shop to die for in Montmartre. It's the best!" He watched her intently. Was he actually interested? He'd always been kind of unreadable. Her heart hammered. The more her pulse raced, the faster she burbled. "I've worked with designers and big high-street chains. I don't have a preference. I can't get enough of it all." She forced herself to draw breath. "Sorry." She sensed the spread of a blush rising up her neck and setting her face ablaze. "I'll get down off my soap box now. I suppose you could say I'm incredibly shallow."

"I wouldn't say that." She couldn't believe that he wasn't completely indifferent, like he'd spotted a vaguely intriguing but ultimately forgettable relic on a between-takes boredom-busting visit to the studio prop store. "There's nothing wrong with making people feel good about themselves."

The heat in Maggie's face began to subside. She'd pulled her hair back into a ponytail for travelling. On autopilot she undid and re-fixed it. "I guess I'm just a free spirit. Fashion styling suits me. I like working freelance." She hated that she felt such a strong need to justify her lifestyle. If things went according to plan, she'd have to stop travelling, settle down and try something different. She'd already started putting out feelers, thinking about new directions. "If you must know, I'm planning to make some changes. I've been a bit of a rolling stone since uni. I did this and that for the first few months, then I got hired as a temporary Girl Friday for a designer at London Fashion Week. I worked my socks off for her and she gave me recommendations. Before I knew it I was building a reputation as a stylist. And voilà."

"What kind of changes?"

He'd zapped her cool, if she'd ever had any. Although she'd taken this styling job because she'd felt compelled to find out about the man Alex had become, it hadn't occurred to her for one moment that he'd want to know about her. He was fabulously good-looking and then some. These days she'd have been happy to put it all down to air-brushing. Seeing him in the flesh reminded her it was so not. He was off-the-charts gorgeous.

"Oh, you know," she said evasively, brushing her hand through the air as if she could sweep her words away. "I want to settle down. Find something a bit more permanent."

Fidgety, she pretended to pluck a non-existent piece of fluff off the sleeve of her black designer sweater.

Miles above the Atlantic Ocean, there were hours to go. How was she going to damp down the disastrous fireworks that she thought had died long ago? With any luck it was down to sky-high hormones, and the plan she was hell bent on not sharing with him. She hadn't told anyone yet. Not even Layla, her lovely BFF since age zilch. She hadn't wanted people to try and dissuade her from her decision.

"Your meal, sir." Alex accepted his tray from the flight attendant turned swoony bimbo.

Maggie identified with her wholeheartedly. Being on the flight with Alex was too surreal – more like riding a rollercoaster. She'd expected to meet him at the shoot and adopt an air of professional distance. Instead the memory of tumbling into bed with him wouldn't get out of her head. It mortified her.

He'd gone to LA. And he'd never called. She'd forgotten him – kind of not. The problem was that his alter ego loomed everywhere. Hot Vampire Guy, as Layla called him, adorned the walls of Tube stations. His eyes blazed from the sides of red, double-decker London buses. Co-workers at coffee breaks bandied his name around. Alex had been replaced by Jago. And Jago was not a man who went unnoticed.

She was more than a smidge curious about getting a call out of the blue asking her to style Alex and Nick. It was extremely short notice and very unusual. The editor was about to put the magazine to bed when she got the green light for these photo shoots, so the pressure was on to get it right. Maggie was beginning to think that she should have said no. Still, she planned to tack an extra day onto her stay in Boston and go on a whale-watch. It was something she'd always wanted to do. Added to that, her bank balance was healthy enough, but she was in no position to turn down work; especially well-paid editorial work for a top magazine.

The funny timing coincided with a new phase in her life. Some kind of karma? Alex had gone off to a new life and hadn't contacted her. It wasn't so much the one-night-flop, although she could have kicked herself about that. It was the silence that hurt. She'd called him half a dozen times, but he hadn't answered his phone or followed up the message she'd finally left with Nick. Basically, she hadn't mattered enough for him to say goodbye. She'd been dumped. So she did what she always did. She glossed over it, put on a smile, and moved on. After all, being left behind was Magenta Plumtree's normal.

She was proud of her life, excited for the future. She needed to keep that in her head, up front and center. She'd power through the awkwardness and focus on her work.

"Your meal." The flight attendant made to set a tray down in front of Maggie. As she did so the knife, fork, and spoon wrapped in a linen napkin wobbled and dropped off. Alex held out one large hand and caught it in mid-air. Sleeve rolled back, tanned arm dusted with dusky hairs, an understated platinum watch sat on his wrist. He passed the cutlery to Maggie. Their fingers brushed. Attraction danced in her veins and shimmied to the tips of her fingers and toes. She trembled, discombobulated beyond belief.

"It's really good to see you, Maggie."

He challenged her with his wicked eyes. If only just sitting beside him didn't take her breath away. Blast his blatant sex appeal. Everything about his body language screamed an invitation to play. He made her want to smile in spite of herself.

"You too." She lowered her eyes only to find herself making a study of his muscular thighs in dark denim. He exuded masculine vitality from every single pore. "I'm looking forward to working with you," she blurted, adding a second too late "and Nick."

Alex turned back and gave her one of his rare smiles. He was devastating when he did that. Not that people got to see him smile much. He was way too cool. She'd done an internet search to check out the looks that they used on the show. She'd unearthed infinite pages of Alex channeling his vampire character Jago – all dark and compelling and smileless. His smile was infectious. Maybe that's why he didn't do smile-for-the-camera. Perhaps he'd spent ten years perfecting an image of supreme indifference to save women from themselves. On the receiving end of Alex's wicked, wide smile she might as well be weightless, as if she'd boarded a rocket for Mars and flown off into space. All rationale eliminated, she had mush for a brain.

Wound-up, spaceship Maggie returned from outer orbit. Alex Wells had been on planet La La Land for ten years. She'd be crazy to wonder if they could go back to square one – on any level, never mind the events of that last night. He wanted to get up to speed. Make sure she had enough experience for the styling job. She'd worked with celebrities, even a handful of really big names, but mostly she got hired by a well-heeled social elite, who desperately wanted to look like A-listers. She'd be fooling herself if she imagined Alex, with his "old mates" interrogation and his upgrade, was interested in her beyond the end of this week. He was all fake charm and chumminess because he wanted her to make him look good. She wondered how he handled the publicity, given that he'd loathed being its focus before he got famous.

"Come on. Out with it, Maggie. Spill the beans. What have you got in the pipeline?"

She tensed and bit down on her bottom lip, aching to tell him to mind his own business and literally clamping her mouth shut. Alex did not need to know about her recent visit to a private fertility clinic.

"I can't say," she said evasively. "Nothing's finalized yet. But I can tell you that if it works out, it's going to totally change my life."

# Chapter Two

High-voltage silence reigned while they ate. Even after they'd been served coffee and things had been cleared, electricity still thrummed in the air. Alex shifted in his seat. He stared out the window at the vast, empty sky. He should choose a movie, freeze out the atmosphere by plugging in his headset.

He'd wanted to break the ice ahead of working together. He hadn't expected to be affected by her. Something about her had changed. Her business-like appearance was a surprise, but it wasn't that. She was different beneath the surface. Perhaps she still felt strange about that night they'd spent together. He certainly did. There'd been that awkwardness when he'd taken too long to find a condom. In truth, the delay was deliberate. He'd known he and Nick wouldn't fail the audition. He shouldn't have been starting something with Maggie. When he'd kissed her the morning after, he'd hoped with all his heart that he'd be back after Christmas and that life would continue like before. Cutting her off seemed obvious at the time, kinder than stringing her along. He couldn't go back to London, and her coming to LA was out of the question. She was a year and a term into her degree. Remembering the girl from a dot on the map, who grew up with her mess-with-my-Maggie-and-you'll-have-me-to-answer-to grandma made him smile. More than once she'd got on the Underground heading in the wrong direction. That's what had drawn him to her. She'd belonged to a place completely outside his world and she was better off not getting dragged into it.

Seven hours on a plane was too much ice-breaking time. Why hadn't he suggested a breakfast meeting? She was fixating on a magazine as if she had to memorize it.

Maggie read the in-flight magazine from cover to cover. Including the horoscope page. All twelve star signs. Irritatingly, the cover story was about Drake Wells, Alex's father, and how at the age of sixty-four he'd reinvented himself and discovered new-found fame starring as the villain in a hit sci-fi movie. In the duty-free section she picked out a new fragrance, which promised to be "beyond zingy". Its apple-green bottle appealed to her. She made a mental note to try some at the airport on the way home. A preserving jar bursting with rainbow-colored jelly beans gave her a hankering for peachy-pie flavor. She'd definitely get some of those. Disgruntled, she stuffed the magazine into the seat pocket. Drake's face, handsome, but not in the least bit like Alex's, stared back at her.

On edge, she stared into space and caught sight of Nick Wells. Her eyes popped open. She hadn't realized he was on the flight. There seemed to be no getting away from Wells men. He was schmoozing a flight attendant; the one with the candy-pink pout. A moment later he vanished behind the curtain, with the pretty woman in hot pursuit. The toilet-occupied light popped on. Maggie glanced around the cabin. Had anyone else noticed?

Alex had. He rolled his eyes, implying he hadn't seen a thing.

It was impossible to ignore him.

"Please tell me they're not doing what I think they're doing. People don't, do they? Not in the real world?"

"That depends what you're thinking." He was just the right amount of unshaven. His white shirt accentuated his tan. With some of the top buttons undone the fabric fell open in a loose vee. Her eyes were drawn to his broad chest. Amazing pecs hid under that designer shirt – she'd watched the TV show. She'd seen the evidence. "I guess they're renewing their membership."

"Sorry? What?" Maggie's cheeks glowed. The burning memory in the back of her head had come out of storage despite her efforts to contain it. It was in the front part of her brain. It wasn't likely to go away anytime soon.

Her one-night-flop with Alex had given her more to daydream about than most fans of *Mercy of the Vampires* could lay claim to. Shame the night of giving in to temptation had faded into a fiasco.

"Keep up, Maggie. Nick and his pick-of-the-day are fulfilling the terms and conditions of the mile-high club." He narrowed his eyes, studying her carefully. "Have you become a bit of a prude?"

"Certainly not." She wasn't about to let him make her feel like a fuddy-duddy. "Sex plus a toilet cubicle don't add up to fun times in my book."

"Perhaps we should put that theory to the test. I might be able to change your mind."

*Is he for real?* The mile-high club seemed more fantasy than reality. Dead set on proving that she was as worldly as the next person, she raised a brow and blurted, "Bet you're a fully paid-up member already, right?"

His seductive eyes sparkled. "Is that a proposition?" His ve-ry sexy drawl sent party poppers of attraction bursting through her. She was absolutely not going to repeat her past mistake with this guy. A faint smile twisted his lips. "Relax, Maggie. I'm kidding. Anyway, we've kinda been there, nearly done that. Minus the altitude factor. Remember?"

He'd mentioned the unmentionable night.

"How could I forget?" Oh the shame. The embarrassment! Was that what this upgrade had been about? Getting things out in the open. She was none too sure how much air-clearing she could handle. Her throat was dry. She'd better get a grip. Her night with Alex didn't matter anymore. Except – she'd gained an immensely unforgettable one-night-disaster, and she'd lost a friend. Instant unfriending! Alex smiled his potent smile. Did he have to bring this up? "Our one night non-event. The least said about that the better."

"You couldn't keep your hands off me."

*Oh no!* She wasn't taking that. *The impertinence!* In defiance of her newly acquired coyness with Alex the TV personality, she challenged Alex, her once-upon-a-time friend.

"We couldn't keep our hands off each other." She cleared her throat. "Best not go there."

"You fell asleep."

She assessed the eaves-dropping potential of the passengers around her, and hissed through gritted teeth, "You couldn't find a condom." The corners of Alex's mouth twitched.

"Um – how are we even having this conversation?" His silence forced her to fill the void. "It was a long time ago. About a hundred years."

"Ten, actually. Before I became a dropout."

"Before you became television's most popular vampire."

"I think you'll find that's Nick."

"Not according to what I've read. I've done my research. Allegedly, women the world over go weak at the knees for – and I quote ..." She made annoying squiggles in the air with her fingers. "... The complicated twin." Their eyes locked in combat. "That's you."

"I'm not complicated. That's PR. Nobody pays any attention to that stuff."

"So what are we doing in Boston – if no one pays any attention?"

Alex shrugged. "Work. The last part of my contract, before I shake off Jago for good, and get on with my life." Something electric fizzed between them. "Where were we? Let's get back to debating the mile-high club. I like that topic better." He trained his eyes intensely on her neck. "What does it take to qualify, do you reckon? Does this count?"

He took her hand in his, turned it over and touched the inside of her wrist, firmly tracing a figure of eight with the pad of one finger. Awareness prickled her skin. He pushed back her sleeve and drew a line with his finger to the indent of her elbow. He marked out another invisible figure of eight on her skin. It was his character's trademark gesture when seducing women in the vampire show. It gave her goose bumps of pure pleasure.

His mouth was kissingly close. She trembled.

He lowered his head and his mouth grazed her neck, his heat injecting lava into her veins. She breathed in his scent of spice. His shiny black hair brushed her skin, oh so softly. "Alex," she breathed, aiming for mock stern. "If that's your party trick, I think it's time to get a new one."

He touched her neck very gently, pushed back a wave of hair that had escaped her ponytail and moved his thumb in sensuous figures of eight around her pulse point. Her heart raced.

"I'm not up for being practiced on like some kind of seduction technique guinea-pig," she burbled. "I can't play your game. It might work on the zillion other women in your life. But it doesn't do anything for me. I knew you before you were television's sexiest vampire …" She was aiming for sarcasm. It was a struggle. "In case you'd forgotten."

"Ohhhhh, I've definitely not forgotten," he rumbled. Before she could respond he silenced her, feathering her lips with his for a fraction of a nano-second.

"Alex!" She exhaled his name and sucked in a breath, almost fighting for air. There was no confusion. Vampires were fiction. This was real. He'd hijacked her controls and she was tipsy on a cocktail laced with one hundred per cent temptingly awesome man.

He settled back into his own seat. Leaning on the cushiony headrest, he taunted, "It's no good. If you want to make me a club member there's only one thing for it." He nodded towards the front of the aircraft. "We'll have to join the queue."

"Ha flipping ha." She smirked at him caustically. "Very funny. Like that's going to happen." Apparently fashion stylist Magenta had put on a parachute and jumped, leaving the teenager she'd been when she first met him in her place.

Maggie was in a crazy spin. She wasn't going to let Alex know it. He was only flirting with her. Even so, he was sinfully hard to resist.

She glanced around the cabin. In the low light the other passengers either worked on laptops or dozed. Luckily.

Her heart squeezed. Her life plan didn't include a man to share it. She'd convinced herself that she didn't need one. Alex's provocative half a heartbeat of an almost kiss told her in no uncertain terms that men had their uses. For some things they were indispensable, even.

That was by the by. There was still no such thing as The One. He didn't exist. For one sugary moment ten years ago she'd wondered if Alex might be her One. As it turned out – he wasn't. She got over it – eventually. She hadn't seen it at first, but the writing had always been on the wall for Maggie. Her dad hadn't stuck around for her mum. And no guy was going to stick around for her. Even her grandfather hadn't been a long-haul guy. He'd gone off with an ahead-of-her-time cougar from the village fish-and-chip shop.

In spite of the evidence, Maggie had remained positive. She'd truly believed she could find her Mr. Right and beat the family curse. Only things had changed when Marcus came along and burst that bubble. Men were fickle creatures. And as if she needed any more proof. Here was Hot Vampire Guy, charming the life out of her, just to pass the time.

The plane juddered. The seatbelt lights pinged on. "Ladies and gentleman – we are experiencing some turbulence. Please return to your seats and refrain from moving about the cabin."

Nick was ejected from the toilet; followed after about thirty none-too-discreet seconds by the petite flight attendant.

Nick ignored the instruction to sit. He stopped beside Maggie.

"Maggie Plumtree – we meet again." He raked his gaze over her. "Last time I saw you, you were wearing a fetching little Santa Girl number," he teased. "I'm glad to see your dress sense has improved."

She laughed off his jokey remark. It dawned on her, somewhat belatedly, that the fashion shoot had the makings of the old friends' reunion from hell. Why hadn't she seen that coming? She needed a thick skin.

Alex glared at his brother.

Nick crossed his arms over his broad chest. "I've heard a lot about your work – all good, of course."

"Of course." She looked him up and down, hoping the looks she had planned were going to work. "It's good to see you too, Nick." She pointed to the fasten seatbelts lights. "Shouldn't you go back to your seat?"

Nick had been a bit-part actor when she'd known the brothers in London. Unlike Alex, he'd avoided drama school, scoring roles mostly through luck and the helping hand of a famous name. It opened doors and got him into TV medical dramas and whodunits. The way she remembered it, Nick and their mother had more or less kidnapped Alex when *Mercy of the Vampires* came along. It would have been crazy not to go for the once-in-a-lifetime opportunity. But, ultimately, TV in Hollywood had been Nick's dream, not Alex's. Seeing the brothers together now, she wondered what direction Alex's life might have taken if he hadn't gone to LA. Before he'd dropped out of drama school to play Nick's evil vampire twin in the pilot series of *Mercy* he'd talked about getting into theater, serious stuff like directing and Shakespeare.

Nick pinned her with his sparkly almond gaze and didn't budge.

"So, what have you got planned for us? Or is it top secret?"

Maggie snapped into professional mode, reminding herself that she needed to let bygones be bygones.

"Day one we're in downtown Boston. We're planning something rural meets urban – with fresh produce." Nick frowned. "Apples. Flowers. Helium balloons." She bubbled with enthusiasm. "I'm aiming for a kitsch vibe with pretty girls in retro florals. And you guys in country tweeds."

"Tweeds?" Alex and Nick echoed in sync. They exchanged a skeptical look.

"It'll be fab. Trust me. The magazine wants something cute. A farmers' market in the heart of the city feel. I'm going to work with a devil within theme to keep the focus on the vampire premise of the show."

"Brainy as well as beautiful. No wonder you've done so well for yourself."

Nick's playboy reputation was as legendary as Alex's mystery. Lately the tabloids couldn't get enough of his allegedly on-off affair with his on-screen love interest Ella Swift. Going by what she'd just witnessed, it was more off than on.

In contrast, scandal about Alex rarely appeared in the gossip magazines. Even so, the paparazzi frequently photographed him with some glitterati girl glued to his side. Only last week she'd seen his name on a list of the world's top twenty most-eligible bachelors.

The show had been a huge success, running for almost ten years and making them household names. It helped that their mother was the flamboyant Cassandra Wells, and being real-life twins didn't hurt either. It added to the hype that surrounded the Wells brand.

"We're at Cape Cod the second day. Doing something atmospheric in the dunes."

"Tell me more. I'm intrigued." Alex butted into the conversation.

"Leather and lace. Anyone?" *Oops.* She wasn't doing very well on the act-professional-absolutely-no-flirting front.

"Just as long as it's you in leather and Alex wearing the lace. Or should it be the other way around?" A cheeky grin spread across Nick's face.

"Well, no." She feared that working with Alex and Nick might require the bringing out of her inner schoolmarm – if she had one. "We've booked some lovely willowy girls to do something a bit Victoriana meets boho chic. We're going to blend that with sea, sand, and a sexy biker-boy look." She gave a little shrug. "That's where you guys come in."

"Cool." Nick's grin widened at the approach of the flight attendant, smiling pinkly.

"Sit down, please – um, sir."

The seatbelt lights pinged off, but Nick was bored now. He made a move to go back to his seat. "Catch you later," he said loudly, drowning out the disembodied voice of the co-pilot regaling passengers with details of the cruising height and the ground temperature in Boston.

Towards the end of the flight Alex looked down at Maggie. She'd fallen asleep. Her head had dropped onto his shoulder, but he hadn't dared wake her.

Where had the Maggie who wore bright colors gone? She'd been replaced by a sophisticated looking interloper. Alex gritted his teeth, trapped in his seat by a gently snoring Maggie.

Ten years ago she had made a big crack in the armor he wore like a theatrical mask. He'd chosen LA over following his heart. He'd blocked out everything he loved about London when he'd given up on his dream. That included Maggie.

He looked at her face, her long lashes. Her wavy hair had escaped from its ponytail. It brushed softly against his cheek. She smelt delicious. Every time he inhaled, her wild-flower-meadow fragrance floated up his nose. Her mouth was full. In a good way. Not an LA trout pout. Her skin glowed.

*Awkward!*

He couldn't help thinking about the last time she'd slept right next to him. She belonged to a time and place pre-TV. Before things had changed completely. He'd lived and breathed *Mercy of the Vampires* for ten years – and loved every minute of it. But ten years was enough. When he'd pulled the plug on the show, Nick had been incandescent. He still hadn't got over it. Too bad. Alex intended to move on, lead his own life – not a default version of his brother's.

Nick had been depending on him since the miserable night Drake had left their mother twenty-four years ago. Older by just twelve minutes, Alex had gradually become more like a substitute dad to his twin. They'd been alone watching a cartoon while his parents argued, shouting at the top of their lungs. Alex had protected Nick, getting him to stick his fingers in his ears, until he could find the remote and turn the volume up full. He'd drowned out the frightening sound of his parents' anger. He'd been putting Nick first ever since.

Maggie shifted in her sleep. She still rated ten out of ten on his hot-ometer. He'd happily pick up right where they'd left off. It would make the next couple of days a lot more interesting.

Being near her was like breathing fresh air. It had to be down to her impossible-to-ignore curves. The gentle rise and fall of her breasts drove him crazy. This close, and at this angle, he had an attractive view of her cleavage. Her black top gaped slightly and he caught an unintentional glimpse of deep-pink shimmering silk. *Lovely.* Who'd have thought that the new understated Maggie would be wearing pulse-raising underwear in a magenta shade that matched her name?

With his free arm he stretched down and picked up Maggie's in-flight blanket, which had slipped into a scrunched-up ball between their feet. Awkwardly, he tried to cover her without disturbing her.

He dragged his eyes back to her face. She had freckles, as if someone had dipped a paintbrush in caramel and flicked it across the bridge of her nose. He didn't remember that about Maggie. A stab of shame lanced him. He didn't remember because he'd blanked her out.

The cabin crew announcement ping sounded. "Ladies and gentlemen, the captain has started our descent into Boston Logan International Airport, please fasten your seatbelts, make sure your seats and tray tables are in the upright position and switch off any electronic equipment."

The saccharin voice shook Maggie out of her sleep. Her creamy skin turned pink. Alex watched the blush travel up her neck from the dip of her top.

*Sexy.*

"I nodded off."

"Am I that boring?"

Her lips curved teasingly. "Yes, very." Her hazel eyes shone. She removed the elastic holding what was left of her ponytail and shook loose her hair. "Sorry."

"Don't worry about it. It's no big deal." He deliberately held back a smile. "It was just like old times – apart from the snoring."

"Flipping Nora. I didn't, did I?" Maggie sat up straight and clicked on her seatbelt. "Alex Wells. I do not snore, and you know it."

"I only have limited experience of your sleeping habits, Maggie." Exactly that kind of meaningless banter had landed them in bed together once before.

Maggie's mysterious eyes shot him down. For the first time in several hours she didn't have the perfect reply on the tip of her tongue.

He'd better snap out of it. He weighed up the possibilities. Temptress Maggie? Professional Maggie?

*Face it, Wells. She's way off limits.*

Flirting with her was a mistake. He'd been bored. It was what he did. Playing on the vampire thing. Still, he shouldn't have gone there with Maggie.

He'd better come up with an action plan. He quickly formulated a strategy, of sorts.

Be civil.

Put up with wearing tweed.

No flirting – definitely no flirting.

Wish her luck and wave goodbye.

5? There was no number 5. Four points should cover it.

What would he do if he'd never met stylist Magenta Plumtree

before? Truthfully? He'd be tempted to explore her possibilities. She'd be just the thing to take his mind off Nick and the promo treadmill.

"I've got a driver waiting at the airport. Can I offer you a ride to the hotel?"

Her freckly nose wrinkled. "Oh … no … Don't worry about me. I'm fine. I'll get a taxi." She waved a neatly manicured hand dismissively. The new Magenta had a neutral image. The peculiar-shade-of-blue nails, and the enticing underwear, reminded him of sparkly Maggie. The rest of her sophisticated appearance – all designer black and grey – slapped him in the face like a cold kipper; a reminder, although he didn't need one, that time had changed everything.

"Don't argue, Maggie. Just say yes."

# Chapter Three

*I. Am. Actually. With. Him.*

Alex took control at the airport. He heaved Maggie's bags off the carousel. "Good grief. You've got a lot of baggage." She really did. Literally – because she'd brought things with her for the shoot. And figuratively. She trembled inside, wondering if her procedure at the clinic had worked, and if today would be too soon to test.

He queued with her in the passport check lines, placing a hand in the small of her back and ushering her forward in a way that made her feel like she wasn't just with him by accident. The pressure of his hand meant more than it should. He'd branded her with his delicious heat.

Turning heads every step they took, he towered over Maggie. His stop-you-in-your-tracks eyes were masked with dark sunglasses, but people recognized him anyway; and even if they didn't they still looked. Recognition didn't fizz on Alex. But awkwardness prickled through Maggie. She noted the stares, the admiring glances, the nudgings and finger pointings. Not to mention the phone-photo moments.

In the arrivals hall a young woman thrust a camera into Maggie's hands. She and her mother draped themselves either side of a stony-faced Alex.

"Take a photo! Would you mind?"

Maggie raised an eyebrow. "Do you mind?"

"Be my guest." He hooked his sunglasses into the top pocket of his jacket and looked into the camera, suppressing a scintilla of a smile. It was the look he was famous for. The fans expected it. Maggie's legs turned to jelly. She took the picture and handed the camera back.

"Thank you so much," the women chorused. "You've made our day." They raced off, dragging their cases with nippy little wheels behind them, ready to waylay Nick and repeat the photo opportunity.

Through the flurry of attention Alex located his driver and whisked Maggie out of the airport. He held the car door for her while the driver dealt with the bags.

"Nick and I have different drivers. In theory we attract less attention that way."

"If all the drooling damsels and general purpose nut-jobs back there are anything to go by, different cars isn't going to do it. What you guys need is separate planets!"

Lips set in an unflinching line, a muscle twitched in his cheek. "We're working on it."

His body brushed hers when he slid into the car. Being around Alex over the next few days would be so much easier to cope with if he came with a button and an instruction manual telling her how to turn his infernal sex appeal off.

She couldn't afford to indulge in swoony fan moments. She had a job to do. This Boston shoot was nothing more than a slot blocked off in her diary. Styling Alex would be easy. He'd rock any look she threw at him.

Maggie tugged at her seatbelt. It had jammed. She tugged again.

"Need a hand?" Alex leaned across. *Mmm… Spiced man.* His unshaven jawline was so close she wondered how it would feel against her skin. Any more of these moments, or – heaven forbid – incidents like the one on the plane and she would melt like micro-waved chocolate. She needed to come up with a self-preservation plan, something to keep her one step ahead of Hot Vampire Guy.

One deft movement unjammed the seatbelt and he passed it into her hands, his fingers brushing hers as he did so. There was a knowing quirk of an almost-smile on his lips when he pulled back and settled into his half of the back seat to snap on his own seatbelt.

Her heart fluttered, hormones sky-high. If she could roll back time she'd make sure her one not-so-stellar night with television's dreamiest man played out very differently. That Christmas, before Alex went off and got famous, Layla had teased her about her missed opportunity and bought her a pack of fluorescent, glow-in-the-dark condoms to keep handy just in case she ever got so lucky again. She didn't. She'd been wearing blinkers when she met Marcus, moved in with him, started making long-term plans. What a mistake. The words "man" and "plan" might rhyme, but they were otherwise utterly incompatible.

The car pulled away from the terminal. Boston didn't look very welcoming. A misty rain was falling, wrapping the whole place in gloom; the streets, the sea, the sky and everything in between looked grey.

Now that he wasn't being scrutinized by any members of the public, a flirty smile lit up Alex's features. His much-too-blue eyes twinkled, the corners creased.

"When do you start ripping my clothes off, Maggie? Tomorrow, is it?"

His deep voice did things to her that a girl in the back of a chauffeur-driven car should be ashamed of. How in heaven's name was she going to get through the next few days if she couldn't get her berserk hormones under control? She fidgeted, smoothing the grey fabric of her skirt under her palms. To stop herself, she locked her hands, as if she was praying, only to end up rubbing one thumb over the blue varnish on the other as if doing so might erase the color.

"The day after," she replied primly. "And the general idea is to get you in clothes, not out of them. If it was a naked photo shoot you'd hardly need a fashion stylist."

Alex laughed. He ploughed the fingers of one big hand into his jet-black hair. There was silence and then he hit her with a bombshell. "For the record, I'm sorry I didn't call you."

She gulped. Her throat felt tight as if she'd tried to swallow a peach stone. "Oh, it's no biggie." She whooshed a hand through the air, as if sweeping his words away. Her heart thudded as if it had been surgically removed and replaced with a piece of rock. She wanted to kick herself. Not a biggie? Of course it was a biggie. It was the biggest biggie of all time. She'd been crushed.

"I should have called," he insisted.

"I really truly didn't expect you to." She babbled out the brush-off. "I mean, I rang your mobile a couple of times." *Six – at least.* "You had things to do." She'd got voice mail and hadn't known what to say. When she'd tried him that final time, Nick had answered Alex's phone. She'd told him to give Alex her love and wish him luck. He'd promised he would.

A shiver ran through her as though someone was trailing icy fingers along her spine. When he hadn't called back, she shouldn't have been surprised. Her grandmother had warned her to keep her expectations of the male species extra low. It was safer than having shattered hopes. She hadn't believed her. She'd gone into the adult world with an open heart. And she'd been hurt. Twice.

Although she was controlled on the surface, her mind was paddling like a duck's feet underneath. She'd thought she and Alex shared something special. They almost had. Only he'd kept his feelings locked away. Maybe allowing her to get that close had been a step too far. He'd always been out of reach.

After the holidays everyone was buzzing with the news that he'd dropped out to make *Mercy of the Vampires.* At the time she'd ached, knowing that he wasn't coming back to London. The disappointment had been excruciating, but she'd clung on to a thread of consolation. He hadn't just dropped her. He'd dropped his entire life.

"It's ancient history." She gave a nonchalant shrug and a bright smile. She'd had an airy- fairy notion that, in spite of her grandma's professed wisdom on the non-existence of soul mates, she might prove her wrong. She and Alex simply weren't meant to be.

Then along came Marcus and she'd had the stuffing knocked out of her. She'd come back a day early from working away, turned the key in the lock, and walked into her home to discover her fiancé getting down and dirty with someone he'd picked up at the pub. She wasn't even that attractive and she was at least ten years older than Maggie. Maybe twelve. The gut-wrenching shock had turned her cold.

"Anyway, I called you, remember? You were busy and Nick answered. I told him to wish you all the luck in the world, and … well, anyway … c'est la vie, as they say."

One hand on his perfectly hewn-in-granite chin, an inscrutable shadow darkened his gaze.

"I apologize," he rumbled. "It was inconsiderate."

"It's okay."

She'd been miserable. She'd felt cut off and abandoned, but she'd understood. Like she'd understood why her dad had left her mum pregnant, and why her mum had left for Spain without her when she was only eight years old. Understanding why people left each other behind was what she did. It was practically a talent. And one that had come in handy when she'd walked away from Marcus. Bouncing back from the heartache was another matter, but she'd become quite good at that too. She'd dreamed up a fool-proof method for guaranteeing that she'd never have to bounce back again.

The car sped towards downtown Boston. She turned away, feigning interest in the grey city they'd landed in, all the while scraping at one nail with another so that some of the blue peeled away revealing a pale streak. It was high time they put this clearing the air of Alex's behind them. She decided to steer the conversation onto safer ground.

"I gather *Mercy of the Vampires* is going out with a bang."

"About time too. The show has been running my life for a decade."

"Tell me about it. I've caught episodes in hotels all over place. I've watched Jarvis and Jago wreak havoc in German, French, Italian, and Spanish."

"You're a fan of the show?"

"It's kind of impossible to avoid it, frankly."

"Well, it all ends in hellfire just before Christmas, you'll be glad to know." Maggie refused to let herself look at him. She kept on staring out of the car window.

"Rumor has it you go out in the sunlight with a string of garlic wrapped around your neck and Nick, I mean Jarvis, strangles you and then rams a stake through your heart, just to be sure he's finished you off."

"It could happen," he joked. "And I don't mean in the TV world. Nick's not best pleased with me at the moment. In fact, that's an understatement. He's furious. We've got a day of back-to-back promo here in Boston tomorrow. And the same again in New York next week. If he can find a string of garlic that's long enough, I think he'd happily throttle me."

Maggie knew she'd detected an atmosphere between the brothers. "Best strike Paris off your promo tour list. They use a lot of garlic there."

"Nick had better watch it. It might turn out that Jago's the one who can't be trusted with a string of garlic."

The deep rumble of his laugh gave her tingles. When she'd agree to style Alex and Nick, she'd been fascinated, and a smidge nostalgic. Part of her had wanted to prove that he was just someone she used to know. Only he was turning out to be a whole heap of fantasticness more than that, and she wasn't at all sure how to deal with that.

*Play. It. Cool.*

She splayed her fingers and looked at her hands. She'd paint her nails sunshine yellow next.

Alex steeled himself the minute the car pulled up in front of the hotel. The driver opened the car door and he stepped out, throwing a quick glance about to see if Nick had arrived yet. Knowing him, he'd probably taken a spur-of-the-moment detour. Loyalty to his family came first, but the conversation he'd just had tugged at the frayed edges of his stoicism. He'd gone to LA for Nick, put his own life on hold, and forgotten all about Maggie. Something inside him sparked the moment she stepped onto the plane. She was lovely – with hints of the bubbly, colorful girl who stood out from the crowd he used to know. She'd changed, though. He couldn't put his finger on it, exactly, but she'd become sort of buttoned-up.

He automatically glued on his sunglasses, despite a heavy sky and grey pavements slick with rain. He summoned a bellhop to take care of the luggage and stood back to play the gentleman, guiding Maggie into the all-mirrors-and-marble lobby with his palm placed protectively in the curve at the base of her spine. Despite the long flight he crackled with energy at her scent of wild flowers. A wicked knot tightened his gut. It would be tempting to see if he could unbutton her, prove that he could have the exact opposite of the soporific effect he'd had on her ten years ago.

The hotel was old and elegant with a smooth, marble floor, a grand carpeted staircase, and a glittering chandelier, which cast a welcoming glow over the lobby, where a clutch of smart Japanese tourists had gathered on bygone chic sofas and chairs, chatting animatedly over their cameras and shopping bags.

Ignoring Maggie completely, the immaculately groomed receptionist went to check Alex in. He took off his sunglasses and slid a glance in Maggie's direction, gesturing with one hand. "You can take care of the lady first." He only slightly growled. The receptionist's face reddened.

"I'm sorry, sir. I thought you were together." Recognizing what she'd just implied, her face burned some more.

She tore her eyes away from him and checked Maggie in, tapping manically at her computer keyboard, in case her colleague, who was answering the phone, finished talking and got to deal with him before she finished with Maggie. Normally he'd have been amused, tempted to play the game.

He was so ready to drop the whole Jago and Jarvis thing, couldn't wait for the promo to be over. And right now he was more interested in Project Magenta. Shamefully, when he'd learned that Maggie was the highly rated stylist who'd been booked to work with him in Boston his first reaction had been "Magenta Who?" It hadn't taken him long to figure out exactly who she was and curiosity kicked in. Regretful curiosity that he'd left things unfinished with Maggie.

When it was Alex's turn to check in the receptionist switched from ultra-speedy to incredibly slow. She finally gave him his cardkey and he turned to speak to Maggie, but she was already attempting to push the big gold trolley laden with her baggage in the direction of the elevators. She was having trouble. One of the wheels was spinning in useless circles and instead of going in a straight line the trolley kept veering off to the left. A smile that started somewhere in his chest burst onto Alex's face and cracked his superficial mask.

He strode across the lobby with purpose and caught her up.

"Where's your bellhop?"

"Gone for a tea break, or something."

She gave a shove. The dodgy wheel wobbled and the trolley didn't budge.

"This is all I need," she gasped. "To get stuck with no bellhop and the trolley-from-hell with a doolally wheel and a mind of its own." She rolled her eyes. "Yay."

"Don't be such a drama queen. There are enough of them in my world already." The comment earned him a withering look.

"What do you suggest?"

"Chill out, Maggie." Since there was absolutely no sign of the bellhop, he hauled her small mountain of baggage off the less-than-useless trolley. "I'll bring your stuff to your room."

He picked up a heavy bag in each hand and headed for the elevators.

Maggie grabbed the handle of his compact case and wheeled it off, hurrying ahead to press the button.

"Haven't you ever heard of travelling light?" He stepped into the elevator and dumped her bags on the floor.

"Not when I've got handmade bespoke tweed jackets to tote across the Atlantic because the Wells brothers can't fit a UK photo shoot into their busy schedules and only have a two-day window in Boston that will work for them."

She fixed him with her doe-eyed gaze. He always had been a sucker for the appeal of those come-to-bed eyes of hers. It was amazing he'd resisted her for so long when they were friends.

"Point taken." The doors slid closed. "Which floor?"

"Two." His fingers collided with hers as they both made to press the button. She pulled back as if he'd given her a static shock.

Was this what they called a blast from the past? She was certainly a temptation. Perhaps he should add something more watertight than "no flirting" to his action plan, like a temporary celibacy clause, for example. Technically, it should be a "no action" plan. What he should be doing over the next few days was getting to know her again, not weighing up her fling-potential. She wasn't fling material. He looked down at the big bags at his feet.

"Strictly speaking I guess some of this is my baggage," he mused.

A puzzled smile twisted her rosy lips. Her eyes sparkled. Even after seven hours on a plane, she looked very kissable.

"I guess," she agreed, crossing her arms defensively.

Back when he'd landed *Mercy*, he'd wanted to call her. Badly. But he'd been afraid that if he did, he might turn down a golden opportunity and disappoint his mother and Nick. Maggie might have been the girl who'd rather sleep than have sex with him, but she'd also been the friend who could read him like a play script. He couldn't talk to her, because if he had done, he'd have risked convincing himself to fly back to London, finish drama school, and audition for serious roles; something that met with his father's approval.

That would have been out of the question, no matter how badly he wanted to do it. Their mother pulling strings only got them so far. The studio required both Wells twins, and the publicity mileage that came with them thanks to their parents' celebrity. Without Alex, there'd have been no contract for Nick. No way would Alex have let his brother down, but with each new series, each new contract signed, he'd become more entrenched in a role he'd been lukewarm about at the outset.

Now that he was standing next to Maggie, his blinkers were off. His crassness ate at him. He should have said goodbye. Saying sorry, like it was only last week and he'd just forgotten to call, seemed inadequate. Leaving everything behind to follow his brother's dreams had been tough, so he'd confined her to a compartment labeled 'past', along with all the other stuff he'd failed to deal with.

The elevator stopped and the doors opened with a ping. Maggie stepped quickly into the corridor, looking down the line of numbered doors. Alex strode out after her, carrying the baggage.

"Which room?"

She glanced at her key. "It's right here." She pointed to the door in front of her. "This one. You can go, I can manage now." She tilted her head and smiled up at him. "Thanks."

Did she have to have such a sexy smile?

"Open up and I'll lift this lot in for you. I don't want you rupturing something and failing to turn up to the shoots. I need you."

Maggie huffed out a breath and did as she was told. She was loaded with the irresistibility factor.

"You've gone all chivalrous knight," she laughed. There was a smoky glint in her hazel eyes and curls of amusement tweaked the corners of her mouth.

"What were you expecting? I haven't turned into my TV character. Jago might be mysterious and moody, but that isn't me." He hesitated. He wanted to add, "I shouldn't need to tell you that", except he thought better of it. The way he'd treated her was distinctly unchivalrous.

Maggie waved a dismissive hand. "I know that," she said. "Please promise me you won't forget to channel a smattering of mean and menacing for the shoots, though, because I'm quite sure the magazine isn't expecting me to stick you in a suit of armor."

"Vampires in shining armor?" he chuckled.

"That's what I'd call a drastic makeover," she laughed, "And one guaranteed not to get me any follow-up calls. I'd like to raise my profile, not bury it without trace. Anyway, you needn't worry, the looks I've got planned are very cool."

He captured her gaze and the urge to play with her reeled him in. "I'm yours to do with as you please."

The devil in him wanted to feel her blue-nailed fingers tear his clothes off, and make stupid, crazy love to her with the finesse their last encounter had lacked. These rogue thoughts weren't helping his no-action plan.

She looked him up and down slowly. "Now there's an offer I bet not many stylists would refuse," she joked. "I just might have to take you up on it and give you a revamp!"

"Funny one! I like what you did there."

She smirked and he grinned back, itching to press his mouth to her smile. He wanted to crush her lips, feel her mouth open beneath his, their bodies meld like molten metal. Forget the tea party. Boston could turn out to be Party Central. She was a whole decade more attractive right now than ever. Perhaps she'd turn out to be his party girl after all.

*His? Where had that come from?*

Arms crossed, she chewed her bottom lip, measuring him up. Was it wishful thinking to imagine she was mentally undressing him?

Reason set in and he grasped his case. "I'd better go. See you anon."

Outside, on the safe side of Maggie's door, Alex stepped quickly back into the elevator. He needed to find his room, and then he'd find the gym. Every muscle in his body had tensed. He hadn't expected to have feelings for Maggie, good, bad or indifferent. He'd been hoping to make sure their almost-sex-disaster-fest incident was all in the past. There was more than enough animosity between him and Nick without adding awkwardness with the stylist into the mix. The attraction that had flared up between him and Maggie was infernally inconvenient.

*Chapter Four*

"Madly busy" summed up Maggie's first day in Boston, which was just as well because it took her mind off Alex. Far from clearing things up and proving that they were both entirely different people at different places in their lives, meeting him again had given her an uneasy feeling that he wasn't out of her system. She could fight it all she liked, but she'd been craving a little bit of Alex's amazing sexual energy ever since he'd arranged her upgrade on the plane. That was ridiculous. She needed to focus on making him look great. Not that it would be a stretch. He was altogether too dreamy.

At noon she met Hannah, the photographer, at her converted warehouse studio, which was the base for the city shoot. After they'd discussed the brief, she put together the outfits, took Polaroid photos of them, and left everything ready on hanging rails.

She spent the rest of the day dashing around Boston picking up last-minute bits and bobs. Finally, she had a meeting with Natalie, the make-up artist, for a coffee and a quick chat about the looks she and Hannah were aiming for.

Anchored in a leather tub chair in a downtown coffee shop Maggie fought the buzz in her head planted there by Alex. The low hum of chatter filled her ears, and fresh aromas of newly ground beans swirled in the air. Normally she loved the smell, but she felt queasy. The prospect of working with the Wells brothers had

45

turned into a witch's brew of craziness that had set her nerves jangling.

"The magazine wants something dark and mysterious in keeping with the actors' TV characters." She took a quick sip of her decaf skinny latte. It tasted yuck, like she'd been chewing copper pennies. "It needs to be subtle," she advised, setting down her cup and pushing it away. "Nothing too over-the-top."

"Aw," the make-up artist objected. "Let's make 'em real spooky."

"If you mean a trickle of fake blood dribbling from the corner of Alex Wells' mouth, then no, I'm afraid not." Maggie and Natalie laughed. "Pale and interesting is good, though. I have to warn you, it might be a bit of a challenge. I've met them already and they were both looking very tanned."

Natalie was bursting with curiosity. "So what are they like? Have you worked with them before? I can't wait."

"I – um. No, I haven't worked with them." Natalie was so sweet and friendly that Maggie was tempted to tell her everything – all about how she knew Alex in a previous life.

Before he became famous.

Before she got a career as a fashion stylist.

Before she came to the conclusion that falling in love was much too risky, and that if she wanted a happy family, she was going to have to go it alone.

A sparkly, curvy twenty-something with flawless skin and a halo of dark corkscrew curls, Natalie popped a spoonful of froth from her cappuccino into her mouth. "Which one's your favorite? Nick or Alex? I mean they're both hot as hell, right? But if you had to choose?"

Maggie's stomach did a somersault. Since this spur-of-the-moment styling job had come up she'd been preoccupied with work. So much so she'd lost track of days. It was over two weeks since she'd been to the clinic for the medical procedure that could change her life. She'd had artificial insemination with donor sperm. She had half a dozen pregnancy tests in her handbag and she hadn't had the courage yet to do one. She was itching to find out the result. Was she pregnant, or wasn't she? She had more important things to think about than discussing which of the Wells twins was the hotter.

"Oh I don't know, Nick, I guess." She mentally crossed her fingers against the white lie.

"No way!" Natalie picked up her coffee cup. She'd left a red lipstick print on the porcelain. "It's Alex any day of the week for me. I'm dying to meet him."

Maggie bit her tongue. Hitting the make-up artist with the details of her past connection with Alex would be ill-advised. She clearly had a bit of a crush on him. And as for announcing, "Excuse me, I just need to pop off and do a pregnancy test"? Well, that would be unprofessional in the extreme, and probably a bit off-putting.

Maggie steered the conversation back on topic, discussed colors, the clothes, the models, and the theme for the first shoot. Then she headed back to the hotel, feeling inappropriately light-hearted at the prospect of possibly running into Alex in the lobby.

Alex was nowhere to be seen. Maggie ended the day ordering room service and crashing out ready for an early start the next morning. She had a night of fractured sleep. Three times she woke up sprawled in the king-size bed thinking she should get up and do the pregnancy test. She didn't. She had a mental block so strong it was as if something physical was preventing her from doing what she needed to do.

If the insemination was a success, it was because her donor had knowingly made a decision to create a life without being there. Her father hadn't made that choice. He'd been a summer romance. Her mum was sixteen when she'd fallen in love with the golden-haired surfer boy from Australia. By the time she realized she was pregnant he'd left, and by the time she tried to tell him he was a dad, it was too late.

Her mother's pregnancy had been a minor scandal in their

seaside village. By the time her grandmother had got over the embarrassment, got used to the idea of her daughter being a teen mum, and decided that they should track down surf-boy Sam, he was dead. A seventeen- year-old adrenaline junkie, happy-go-lucky Sam had surfed a notorious point break two days after he arrived home. Taken out by a freak wave, he'd drowned on the reef. His parents sent a clipping from their local newspaper reporting his death. Maggie's mum kept it in a shoebox under her bed with a load of photos and a heart-shaped pebble he'd given her. When she went to work in Spain she left the box behind, along with Maggie.

Technically, her father had been a sperm donor. So why shouldn't a donor-sperm baby grow up to be as strong and independent as she'd learned to be?

Finally she fell into deep sleep. She always dreamed when she was jet-lagged, but usually she had a vague sense that she was asleep and only dreaming. This time the dream was so real that she woke up all spaced-out and it took a minute or so to register that the blissful scenario she'd been so immersed in hadn't actually happened.

And she thanked her lucky stars it hadn't. Because in her dream she'd slept with Alex, and her heart thudded, wondering if that embarrassing little gem was going to be written on her face the minute she set eyes on him. He'd stirred up a mess of emotions. She hadn't just been a little bit in love with him, she'd been head over heels, and right when she'd not been able to resist him a second longer, he'd upped and gone and vanished from her world. She'd thought she was oh-so-over him, but the deep down, buried truth was that she'd gone on being hooked on him for much too long after he'd left. No one measured up to him. The guys she'd dated never stood a chance by comparison, because she didn't allow them to. When she got anywhere near starting a relationship she let it fizzle out. Fearing rejection somewhere down the line, she pushed men away. Until Marcus. Marcus had taken her over, organized her, a self-appointed personal drill sergeant. She'd trusted him completely.

She felt raw. It didn't help that her hormones had begun to whoosh around uncontrollably like fallen leaves being whizzed into the air on a gust of autumn wind. She wasn't just as susceptible to the charms of Alex Wells as every other fan of the show, she was more so. She'd known him before he shot to fame – that was the trouble.

Awkwardness set in the moment Alex arrived at the studio. Hannah popped out for some takeout coffees, leaving Maggie to dress Alex ahead of Nick and the two models who hadn't shown up yet.

The dream memory returned. It seared her mind's eye with an image of hot, tangled bodies, obliterating reasonable thought processes. A sensuous picture of soft, warm skin and hard muscles filled her imagination; her lips seeking his, his mouth devouring hers, hands clasped, bodies entwined.

Trapped in tongue-tied silence, Maggie forced herself to focus on the brick walls and wood floors of Hannah's warehouse studio. They helped ground her. Samples of photographic work dotted about the place gave her something more appropriate to visualize. She picked out a photo of white sailboats afloat on glassy water against the Back Bay skyline with powder-puff clouds in an azure sky, and honed in on that.

Outside, Boston basked under just such a perfect blue sky.

"Great day for it." He oozed confidence. His drawl set off those hopping hormones again. He could make reading aloud from the telephone directory sexy without even trying.

"Couldn't be better." She ignored the fact that he was attempting to snare her gaze. She resolved to avoid looking him in the eye, if at all possible. If she did, he'd be bound to see all the things she'd dreamed in the night swimming in her head. Utter torture.

"Good day yesterday?"

"Um. Busy. Getting this lot ready." She turned her back to him and stood at the hanging rail shuffling the clothes about a bit on their hangers, pretending to be absorbed in her work. "You?"

"The usual. Interviews. The final series airs here next week. And the big question on everyone's lips is "How does Jago die?"."

"What did you say?" Maggie grabbed a pencil and over-acted the need to score off a couple of items on her to-do list.

"I told them Nick – sorry, Jarvis – ties me up in a string of garlic, and shoves me out in the sunlight with a stake through my heart."

Maggie turned to face him. "So it was you that started the rumor?"

"Actually – it was you! But I liked it, so I borrowed it."

She wrinkled her nose. "So what does happen to Jago? Maybe I've lost the plot, but I thought he was the bad guy in this set-up?" Her tone was deliberately blasé, as if she wasn't really that interested.

"Nice try, Maggie. I'm afraid I can't let you in on that secret."

"Not strangled by your brother in the sunshine with the garlic, after all? Someone should invent a board game. I bet there'd be a market for it. Great merchandising opportunity. It's sounding more like a whodunit and less like warring vampire twins every minute."

Wry tension twitched in the corners of Alex's mouth. "It's war. Make no mistake."

Maggie guessed he wasn't talking about their TV characters. "What's up?"

"It's no secret that Nick wasn't ready for *Mercy* to finish. But I was. My leaving was okayed with the powers that be. They told the writers to write me out. Then the studio did an about face and cancelled the show."

"I suppose it's a question of balance. Without the good-vampire-twin-bad-vampire-twin thing going on there wouldn't be much drama left." Maggie chewed on the end of her pencil.

Alex's shoulders tensed. He watched Maggie with deep concentration, mesmerizing her with his eyes, and lowered his voice, "I'll swear you to secrecy. There's a big twist in the final episode. Turns out Jago isn't evil after all. He's the good vampire and Nick's character is the one that's mad, bad, and dangerous to know."

"I'm guessing he's not very happy with that."

"Let's just say that's an understatement." He sucked in a sharp breath and scraped his fingers through his hair. "It was time the series ended. It had a good run. If we'd gone on any longer the characters would have dried up. People would have lost interest. It's better this way. We're ending on a high."

Alex's tension filled the air in the empty studio. He stared off into space. "Nick doesn't agree with you on that?"

He let out a grating laugh. "Nick blames me for the show being cancelled. He's livid."

"He'll come round."

"He has no choice. He's going to LA to talk movies. I'm going to London to do theater."

"Cool."

"It's time for us both to move on with our lives, and he knows it. Even if he's not ready to admit it."

Alex's moodiness and her wayward pheromones produced a terrible combination of angst and attraction. She wished Hannah would come back with the coffee, although she still had that weird metallic taste in her mouth. She didn't want to be so interested, but she was itching to know if Alex had managed to find a way back into serious acting. She couldn't picture him headlining a West End musical, somehow. "What theater are you doing?"

"*Hamlet*."

"Wow. Shakespeare in London. That's a far cry from vampires in LA."

"That's the general idea."

"To be or not to be." She put on a tone of ominous gravity.

Suddenly she blushed, thinking about her own date with destiny. She hadn't done the pregnancy test. She told herself she'd been way too busy, but she was putting it off.

"To be honest, I'm ready to disassociate myself from the vampire gig. It's been a blast, but it wasn't part of my plan. I did it because

Nick wanted me to, and because I didn't want him to miss out on his big chance."

"You went along for the ride."

Alex let his breath go in a long sigh. "Enjoy the ride while you're on it?" He paused and fixed Maggie with his gaze. "It hasn't been all bad. Far from it. But Nick needs to get over himself. He's much too into this promo tour. *Vampires* is over."

"It's over for you, but the fans are looking forward to the final series. It can't hurt to big it up for a few more days," she coaxed. Alex harrumphed. "And now you're getting to do Shakespeare, like you always wanted to, so it's all good." Nick might be going to discuss a movie, but it didn't sound like he had anything definite lined up. It was little wonder he was having more difficulty than Alex letting go of the series that had made him famous. "You got your dream."

"You remember that about me?"

"Sure I do." She looked down at her bright-yellow nails for a second. "Why wouldn't I?"

His sexy mouth spread into a wide smile. He started to undo his buttons. And suddenly he was stripped to the waist.

"How do you want me?"

Maggie picked her jaw up off the floor. "Um." She focused on the row of clothes on the rail. The hangers tinkled as she faffed. "Here," she said, as if she was actually concentrating on her job. Really she was busy enjoying the view. His broad, bronze chest and honed muscles blew her away. His hands went to his belt buckle and she couldn't help but notice the dark line that arrowed downwards into his jeans. "I need you to change into this lot." She pushed a well-laden hanger into his hands before he could strip off completely.

Clearly he'd been around enough wardrobe girls not to feel bashful. Why would he? With that body! He was way too hot to handle, a one-hundred-and-ten per cent sexy fireball of a man. His fingers brushed hers as he took the clothes. The contact ignited fierce heat inside her. She wished the floor would open up and swallow her. She had to remind herself that it would have been insane to turn this job down.

A hot, half-naked Alex must feature in a high percentage of women's fantasies. And she was living the dream.

*Might as well enjoy it!*

Everyone arrived together. Hannah with the coffee, Natalie with the make-up, and Nick with the two stunning flame-haired, pre-Raphaelite-style models. From then it was all go. Run off her feet, Maggie clicked into super-efficient mode, making changes to the clothes to suit Hannah, keeping a tight rein on Natalie to make sure that she didn't do anything too scary with the make-up, generally trouble-shooting, and making sure that everything was absolutely fab.

At lunch they all went to a bustling café-bar near Faneuil Hall. The walls were covered with Boston Red Sox memorabilia. The place was packed. It made Maggie smile to see how the lunching office workers and shoppers made a production out of acting like they hadn't noticed the famous Wells brothers. Not to mention the striking six-foot models they were with. Before she joined the others at the table Hannah's assistant had reserved, Maggie ducked into the Ladies. She bolted the cubicle door, took a deep breath and dived into her handbag to dig out a pregnancy test.

"Maggie, is that you in there?"

*Oh flip*. It was Natalie. She thought about putting on a very deep voice and pretending to be a transvestite to get her to leave, but she liked Natalie and she didn't want to freak her out.

"Yes," she squeaked.

"Oh. My. Gosh. I think I'm in love. Don't tell my fiancé, but Nick Wells is the most delicious thing on this earth."

Maggie abandoned her mission to establish if she was or wasn't pregnant and exited the toilet cubicle.

"Didn't you tell me that Alex was the vampire for you – any

day of the week?"

"That was yesterday, before I'd met them. Today ..." Natalie sighed dreamily. "It's Nick."

Maggie nudged her with her elbow. "Fight you for him."

"No way." Natalie slicked on a generous layer of her signature red lipstick. "You can have Alex." She paused with a minxy grin on her face. "Judging by the way his eyes were following you all morning, I'd say you have a better chance with him. And I don't mean in your dreams."

Maggie froze. Unless Natalie had supernatural powers, there was no way she knew what Maggie had been dreaming. Even so her words had an uncanny effect on her resolve to appear unaffected by Alex.

"You leave my dreams out of this," she joked. "Come on, let's get some lunch. I'm starving."

Paralysis set in the moment she walked into the bar. The compelling rumble of Alex's smooth-as-the-most-exquisite-chocolate voice resonated off the baseball-themed walls. The group was hanging on his every word – and so was everyone else in the café-bar.

"Maggie and I are old, old friends," he said. "We knew each other in London, right before Nick and I moved to LA." He stared directly at Maggie, and she stopped, hands hanging weakly at her sides. "Things moved pretty fast back then. I guess we lost touch."

As his words trailed off Nick cut in. "The last time we saw Maggie she was wearing sparkly stilettos, red silk stockings and a verrrrry cute Santa suit! Alex had to lend her his best sweater so that she could go home on the London Underground without drawing too much attention to herself."

"And reindeer antlers." Alex's cool Jago face brightened into a wide, winning smile. "Don't forget the reindeer antlers."

There were guffaws of laughter. All eyes turned on Maggie. The picture Nick and Alex painted didn't exactly tally with her current blend-into-the-background image. In smart black designer jeans and black ankle boots, with a businessy white shirt, unbuttoned at the neck where she'd hooked her big, black oversized sunglasses into the vee, she aimed to look unremarkable. The laughing triggered a blush the color of a London bus – a glowing contrast to her monochrome look.

*Great!*

"And to avoid freezing," she chipped in. "I'd like to point out that it was one of the coldest Decembers on record."

"It was Christmas Eve, actually." Alex spoke slowly. The piercing glimmer in his eyes sent shivers up and down her spine. She wished he would stop looking at her like that.

"Hence the Santa ensemble." She made a face, shrugged, and held her palms out apologetically to the group.

Sitting on a bench seat at the opposite side of the table between the two models, Nick leaned forward and moved the things in front of him about randomly – the salt pot, his sunglasses, a coaster. He seemed to be watching his brother for a reaction. Alex didn't say anything more. He stopped looking at her and stared off into the distance.

Maggie sat down at the table, picked up a couple of menus and handed one to Natalie, who suddenly closed her gawping mouth, as if for a fraction of a second she'd lost control of her features. Almost faint, not with hunger, but embarrassment at being scrutinized by every woman within earshot, and most of the men, Maggie's fingers trembled. "So," she announced, eager to close the subject. "Enough of the boring friends reunited stuff." She rolled her eyes. One of the models sent her a sympathetic smile across the sea of drinks, menus and cutlery littering the rustic table top. "Should we order? What's everyone having?"

The memory of her Underground journey wrapped in his sweater, scarf and oversized gloves gave her butterflies. His student house had been in North London, hers South. She pictured herself sitting on the Tube in her barely-there Santa suit and scarlet silk stockings, squished amongst the bag-laden Christmas shoppers, hung-over and smarting from her night of doomed passion with Alex. Her heart fluttered. The stops had seemed never-ending – Leicester Square, Charing Cross, Waterloo. On and on, until Clapham Common, where she shared a down-at-heel terraced house with five friends. Had she been too much of a coward to step into the danger zone and get full-on physical with Alex? Had she allowed herself to fall asleep on purpose? She'd been procrastinating, shying away from her feelings. Even so she'd been elated at the prospect of hooking up with Alex after the holidays. Friend to boyfriend. Result.

Except her grandmother's instinct that no man was to be trusted had been right. No matter how much she'd hoped to love and love back, Alex wasn't The One. There was no such thing. Marcus had proved that beyond a shadow of a doubt. His antics with the woman from the pub had got rid of any rubbish notions she'd had about forever love. At least he'd cheated before she'd been dumb enough to marry him. The one positive that she'd clung onto was that they hadn't had a baby. It was a plus – no child to get hurt.

Maggie pasted a chipper smile on her face and forced herself to stay afloat. She hadn't expected to react so strongly to Alex. His aura was intoxicating. She was all out of kilter. Her body going on a bender every time she took a hit from those eyes was one thing. His magnetism sending her emotions into free fall was quite another. She'd learned to protect her heart the hard way. Letting people go was easier than complex feelings, and safer – much less risky. So how come she was sitting there wondering "what if"?

She was over that we-were-almost-an-item thing, really she was. And she was at a new place in her life – ready to have a baby, a child whose feelings she could safeguard, the same way she shielded her own emotions.

She ordered a New England crab roll. Then she sat quietly in the corner of the table and let herself drift out of the conversation. Push men away. It was the best way she knew of putting up barriers. The last thing she needed was Alex waltzing back into her life and stealing her heart again, so she closed him out.

She had a knot in her gut from wading through a quagmire of feelings. When the food arrived she only picked at it. She felt nauseous. With one more day to get through, she'd play along in her role of old friend from way back when, and then she'd wave bye-bye to the Wells brothers, this time for good.

After lunch, back at the studio, she threw herself into preparations for day two. Everyone else had gone, except for Hannah who was working on her photographs.

"Hey Maggie, come see," she beckoned. The petite thirty-something had shiny brown hair in a boyish crop and legs that were made for skinny jeans. With a big grin on her face she looked like a cute and happy pixie.

Maggie watched as she scrolled through the pictures on her laptop. "They're amazing," she gasped. "Well done you."

Maggie loved the photos. Alex and Nick looked fabulous in the bespoke Harris Tweed jackets she'd commissioned for them. Tall and aloof, they were pictured with the red-headed models against a backdrop of perfect blue sky. In the foreground it was a market scene. There were crates of apples and tomatoes and one of the girls was holding a huge bunch of helium balloons. Behind them a steel and glass skyscraper was silhouetted against the blue.

"Well done us," Hannah corrected. "I'm loving the colors in those Scottish tweeds. The guys' look is awesome."

"Some might argue that the guys are always awesome," Maggie quipped.

"Sure," Hannah smiled. "But in our photos, they're beyond awesome. They'll love this at the magazine. These pictures are going to knock their readers' socks off."

Hannah folded her arms and studied Maggie with a shrewd look on her face. "That was some story Nick and Alex told at lunch. You could have cut the atmosphere with a knife. What's the deal with you and Alex? Do I detect a hint of romance in the air? Were you two more than just friends back then?"

Now that she was over the embarrassment, she quite liked that Alex had fessed up to having been friends. The difficult part was that she'd failed spectacularly to prove to herself that, ten years on, she was no longer affected by him. She wasn't handling her attraction at all well, but Hannah didn't need to know that.

Maggie chewed on her bottom lip and shook her head. "Nope," she said with conviction. She curled the fingers of her left hand into her palm. "Just friends."

# Chapter Five

Alex sat in the hotel cocktail lounge watching for Maggie. He had a perfect view across the lobby to the elevators. He looked at his watch. Where was she?

He took a slug of mineral water. And waited. This stake-out was probably a bad idea. He'd give it five more minutes, then he'd quit. Knowing she was around here someplace felt good. The prospect of seeing her again turned him stupidly cheerful.

He spotted her, dressed in black, kitten heels clicking on the marble floor. Stroke of luck, she was heading for the cocktail bar – alone.

"Maggie," he called. She spun on her heels and her hazel eyes met his for an nth of a second. "Where've you been? You're a workaholic!"

"I've been returning the things I borrowed for today's shoot. I got a bit of a rollicking. One of the models got make-up on her collar and we lost a button." She dumped her bags on the floor and sank into a chair, frazzled. "Then I was going through the clothes for the Cape Cod shoot tomorrow and realized I'd forgotten leather belts. So, I've been talking nicely to a PR in one of the other big stores."

"Like I said, you work too hard. Nick and I could have worn our own belts."

"Models' own!" Maggie laughed. "Why didn't I think of that? Anyway, it's sorted now. The PR was lovely." She gave a knowing smile. "Naturally, when she heard they were for Jarvis and Jago she let me borrow exactly what I needed."

"Buy you a drink?" A shadow crossed Maggie's face.

"I shouldn't really. I should just grab a bottle of mineral water and run. I'm really busy. I need to look over the brief for tomorrow."

Was she making excuses? He could swear she was avoiding making eye contact with him. "Go on. Live dangerously." She grimaced. "Chill and have a cocktail. You deserve it."

She bit her glossy bottom lip. He hoped she was contemplating caving.

"Since you're offering …" She arched a brow. "…Why not?" She held up a finger and sucked in a breath as if something important had just occurred to her. "Can we make it alcohol-free? I – um – need to stay off the booze."

A strip of pink neon light illuminated the wall behind the bar. A pop of contemporary color in the midst of the otherwise Edwardian elegance, it sent a glow into the room. In the far corner a pianist effortlessly played something jazzy on a baby grand. The wood on the piano's lifted lid shone with a mirror-like polish. Waiting for the barman to pour the cocktails, Alex took a mental snapshot. Being here with Maggie was like being lifted out of his life and dropped into another world. Not the past exactly. That was a closed door. But somewhere familiar.

He signed for the drinks and took Maggie her cocktail.

"I got you this. Try not to be too under-whelmed." He set a Martini glass down in front of her. It included a cocktail stick with a row of multi-colored gummy bears impaled upon it. "Passion fruit and pomegranate."

Maggie stared. "Wow, a gummy-bear cocktail?" She picked it up, turned the stem of the glass between her fingers, and admired the little bears like pretty jewels. "You know the way to a girl's heart."

"Don't blame me if it's awful," he added, "The barman

recommended it. It's his teen special." He sat down next to her. He'd like to get to know her. She'd been part of a carefree time when the only real problem was finding two clean socks that matched; no difficult choices. His parents' fights had stopped for a while, and he'd been left to his own devices. Things had been easier. "I'd go easy on the gummy bears if I were you."

"Ohhh-kay."

She stretched out the syllables and stared off in the direction of the music. Why wouldn't she look him in the face? She seemed spiky. Maybe it was the jetlag.

"Cheers. I'm glad we're here." He clinked her glass and captured her gaze, determined not to let her look away. "Doing this."

She drew in an indignant breath. "About that Santa costume stuff. In future I'd appreciate it if you didn't regale my co-workers with the details of your trip down memory lane." She was looking at him with raised eyebrows and she'd somehow managed to set her lips in a thin, disapproving line.

"It was a very sexy Santa costume, if my memory serves me well." Was she blushing? She'd gone all buttoned-up again.

"Frankly, it was a little bit slutty. I wouldn't be seen dead in anything like that these days."

*Pity!*

Maggie bit the head off a gummy bear. "It may be news to you, but I have a professional image to maintain."

So, that's what this was about? Her image? She glared fixedly at her hands. He'd spotted her bright-yellow nails and caught himself wondering if there was a set of brightly colored underwear lurking under her clothes. All her outfits were in black, white and grey. The hint of deep-pink silk he'd inadvertently seen on the plane was enticing, but black was good, white too. He was inappropriately preoccupied with her lingerie possibilities. And the laid-back, colorful person she used to be. What had happened to her? She'd moved on. It was time he got his head around that. "I'm sorry," he said, "We didn't mean to embarrass you. Nick and I got carried away. The last thing I want to do is offend you."

Finally, she met his eyes.

He held her gaze again, determined not to be the first one to look away. "It was a long time ago. I doubt anyone paid much attention. Things like that go in one ear and out the other. It's not like I told them we slept together."

"Yes – about that." She pulled the remaining gummy bears off the cocktail stick and arranged them in a neat little row in her palm. "A line needs to be drawn. First off, we didn't sleep together. We fell asleep together. There's a difference." The cool exterior intrigued him. His vibrant friend had morphed into Monochrome Magenta, all-purpose style adviser. He shouldn't be the least bit affected by her. But the hot hints of color beneath the surface turned out to be impossible to ignore. The pop of silky pink he'd accidently glimpsed on the plane had fired his imagination. "Since we're working together, and there are twenty-four more hours to go …" she continued, all hoity-toity, talking as if not to him, but to an audience in general, and looking like a TV fashion presenter about to introduce a lineup of models. She'd be good at that! "I think we should agree that what happened was a ve-ry forgettable, ve-ry regrettable drunken night."

*Ouch!*

"Don't pull any punches."

"Honestly. If I could go back to that night and not not-sleep with you, that's exactly what I'd do." Her voice was convincingly couldn't-care-less.

*Double Ouch!* There'd been a time when he'd wondered what would have happened if he hadn't left London when he did. She'd given him the answer. If he'd fantasized that they'd almost been more than friends, he'd been mistaken.

Except – he wasn't entirely clear about what she was actually saying. Was it that she wished they had slept together? Or that she was glad they didn't? The gist of it seemed to be that she'd rather the episode had not occurred. All the same, he couldn't resist winding her up a bit. "For the record," he said. "If I could rewind the clock I'd definitely still sleep with you."

She didn't even crack a smile. Instead, she fired daggers at him with her eyes. Another gummy bear disappeared into her mouth. Slicked with a coating of natural, shiny gloss, her lips were magnetic. Tempted to kiss her, he ran a hand across his jaw. The prickle of stubble grated against his fingers.

Hands planted on his knees, he slowly shook his head. "Fine," he conceded. "Let's pretend it never happened. We're two friends who lost touch. End of story."

"Okay." Did she flinch? He must have imagined it.

"Okay." He held out a hand to her. "Shake on it?" She put her small hand in his. He clasped her fingers, his eyes drawn to her nails and the glaring contrast the splashes of yellow made against her clothes.

She downed her fruit cocktail much too quickly and stood up. "I've got to go," she said. "There's something I need to do."

"What's the rush?"

Was she crossing the fingers of her left hand? What was that about? There was a noticeable vacancy on the ring finger. She appeared so available – and yet there was a shut-offness about her that he didn't get. One minute he got sparks of the old Maggie, the next she was giving him the cold shoulder.

She gathered her bags together. "Bye Alex. Thanks for the drink."

This was a first. Women in hotel bars weren't usually so keen to get away from him. She was about to make her escape when she wobbled on her heels, her face woozy. "Maggie!" He jumped up and caught her as she started to crumple. "Are you okay?"

"I stood up too quickly. That's all. I'm fine." She sat down again, all of a sudden wan. "Actually, I'm not fine," she admitted. "I feel queasy."

"It'll be those damn gummy bears. I knew they looked like trouble. I'll get you some iced water." He strode quickly to the bar.

Maggie sucked in a few deep breaths. She felt okay-ish again. The cocktail had been a tad on the sickly-sweet side but it hadn't made her ill. She had the distinct feeling that her artificial insemination procedure had worked. She should do that pregnancy test and check. Ought she to tell Alex the truth? Try as she might to put up her defenses, she was drawn to him, and she was desperate to confide in someone. He was so much more than a familiar face. He reminded her of a time when grown-up life was new and fresh and fun. Before he left. Before Marcus cheated. Choices weren't difficult then – everything was as easy as choosing a nail color.

As she sipped the water he sat watching her, concern etched on his face. The pianist had taken a break. The bar was empty and silent apart from the clinking of ice cubes in her glass.

"That something I was talking about," she started. "The thing I have to do."

Alex's concern deepened. "Whatever it is, it can wait."

"I think I might be pregnant." The hopelessly blabber-mouthed admission was out there, and the wave of nausea had gone, almost as quickly as it had hit.

"What do you mean – you think? It's not my place, but shouldn't you do a test?"

"I plan to."

The penny dropped. "That's the thing?"

"Uh-huh."

"So-o, you're with child … Maybe?" He gulped. She nodded, and bit down on her lip.

"Who's the lucky guy?"

"There isn't one."

Proud to be going it alone, she waggled her ringless fingers. "This is the twenty-first century. I don't need a man to have a baby."

"So what do you need? Pray tell." He was looking at her in disbelief, as if she'd told a joke with a surprisingly rude punch line. "A magic wand? You can't conjure up a baby out of thin air!" Judging by his tone, he was going to have difficulty getting his head around her decision to eliminate the man factor from the baby-making process.

"I could raid a cabbage patch," she joked, trying to make light of her confession. "Or kidnap a passing stork!"

Silence.

"Here's the thing. I'm having a baby on my own. I've – um." She stopped in midstream. "I've had artificial insemination."

"Good grief," Alex gasped, his impossibly perfect face shocked. "I've heard it all now." He fired words at her. "Are you stark-staring mad? You can't have hit thirty yet! How old are you?"

"Twenty-nine," she supplied. "Didn't anyone ever tell you it's rude to ask a woman's age?"

She began to regret telling all. This was nothing to do with Alex. She'd felt wobbly and allowed herself to get too comfortable with him.

He ignored her question and shot another one right back at her, aghast. "Surely you could have waited for the right guy to come along?"

She neither wanted nor needed a permanent man in her life. And she'd done her research. Her fertility would start to decline once she was in her thirties. She was spontaneous about pretty much everything in life, but the possibility of there never being a right time to start a family, let alone a reliable Mr. Right, was something she didn't want to leave to luck. She'd blindly believed she'd have it all with Marcus – the perfect marriage, the perfect home, the chance to have the family of her dreams. The night she'd walked into the apartment filled with flickering candles, she'd thought for a minute that he'd found out she was coming back a day early, made the place beautiful to welcome her home. Her heart turned to stone as she spotted the empty wine bottle, the trail of discarded clothes leading to the bedroom – her bedroom. Her bed!

"I'm risk averse. That's not a chance I wanted to take."

A muscle in his jawline flickered. "DIY conception, Maggie? Isn't that a bit drastic?"

His words hit her like a stomach blow.

"Apparently not. You can buy a kit on the internet," she said bravely. Her eyes held his, facing him off, trying to push him away, sorry she'd said anything. "And yes, before you ask, the turkey baster is an urban myth." This conversation would have been so much easier if she hadn't been an eensy bit in love with him once. "The kit contains a syringe, a thermometer, an ovulation test …" She hesitated for a micro-second, then ploughed on, "… And a collection pot – if you're interested." She composed herself, resisting the urge to leap up and head for the elevators. "That's not what I did, though. I thought about it, but I couldn't find a friend who was willing to donate me his sperm."

*Oops. Perhaps I shouldn't have said that!*

Maggie thanked the heavens he'd finished his drink. Otherwise he'd have snorted it out his nostrils and ruined his cool image.

"You're not kidding, right?" Disbelief tinged his sexy voice.

"I didn't do it on a whim," she answered quietly. "I went to a fertility clinic. A doctor did the procedure."

Undiluted tension swirled in the atmosphere between them.

"With *donor* sperm?"

"You should keep the laconic sneers for when you're in character. They don't suit you in real life."

Alex shook his head. "I'm not sneering, Maggie." Her heart skipped a beat at the way he softly rumbled her name. "I'd never do that."

*Was he in shock?*

She drew in a breath, self-conscious of her every move, as if breathing was no longer something she did on automatic. "I want a baby," she said solemnly. "Do you have a problem with that?"

"I'm being objective." He didn't sound it. "I mean, what do you know about this donor guy?"

She didn't understand him. He seemed aggrieved, like she'd inflicted some sort of pain on him. She'd been feeling all over the place, a little bit lonely, and dying to tell someone. Now she was getting the Alex Wells inquisition. It was her own fault for over-sharing. She'd let her guard down and it was out there, so she steeled herself, ready to defend her decision.

"Enough." She'd known more about the donor than she knew about her own dad. "Quite a lot, actually. I picked him out online."

Alex's face froze. "Such as?"

"The essential stuff. The donor guy's profession, his medical history – all the nitty-gritty."

"Sounds like baby pick-and-mix," he teased. "What's his favorite sport? Is he good at math? Did he go bald at fifteen?"

*The impudence!* They'd been strangers for years and he had the gall to question her choice of sperm donor.

"That's it exactly." She warmed to her theme. "Not forgetting the obvious. Hair color – dark. Height – five eleven and a half. Eyes ..." Her voice dropped to a throaty whisper. Apart from several more inches height-wise the description pretty much covered the super-hot man in front of her. "... Blue."

Alex stayed stonily silent for a long moment. He narrowed his famous eyes and scrutinized her. A shivery frisson weaved through Maggie to each and every nerve ending. Suddenly it wasn't Donor Guy's eyes she was thinking about, but Alex's.

*Yikes.*

She was his stylist. She needed to remember that. She'd prattled like a runaway train about her biggest-ever decision. Alex taking her to task about it – as if he'd never stopped being her friend – floored her.

"What type of guy would do that anyway?"

Her heart lurched. "Do what?"

"Give babies away?"

"An unselfish one." She glared at him. She used to be on the same wavelength as Alex. Right now his over-reaction was mystifying. "You're like a dog at a bone. Can't you drop it? I only told you because I didn't want you to think you'd made me sick with that fruit cocktail."

That wasn't exactly true. She'd told him because the wave of nausea had hit her so unexpectedly that she'd suddenly felt vulnerable, and a tiny bit scared. It was a blip. She needed to get back on track. She'd taken control of her future. She wanted a baby more than anything. She had everything she could wish for and she'd worked hard for it – a career, a crash pad in London, a never-a-dull-moment lifestyle … But at the end of the day she was alone in the world. She'd inherited the family cottage in Cornwall when her grandma died, and dreamed up the plan of creating a family to go with it. An uncomplicated, no-ties, no-commitment, guaranteed-hurt-free designer family. No man required. She'd been raised without a dad, and she was certain that she could make a success of family life all on her own. Best of all, there'd be no false hopes and no broken promises.

The last thing she needed was second thoughts. Especially ones put into her head by a testosterone-loaded actor who'd ignored her for ten years and then popped into her life to play her nemesis – like he'd never left. Like he'd never promised to call. Like his kiss had never made her weak with spine-tingling desire …

"Aren't you even just a bit weirded-out by the genetic randomness of it all?" His words rankled, and all the while his deep voice made her fizz like a can of shaken-up cola.

Was he incapable of letting the subject drop? She hadn't done this on impulse. She'd thought it through meticulously. She tensed her shoulders, bristling with the strength of her resolution.

"I'm sorry I mentioned it. It's very early days. I might not even be pregnant." She bit her lip and reined herself in. She needed to retain a veneer of polite detachment in order to work with Alex. Instead she'd blabbed about her personal life, and things were going horribly wrong. So much for the outwardly calm, sophisticated image she normally projected in her professional life. Her feathers were well and truly ruffled.

"It's your life. Go for it," he said, his tone loaded with censure.

"I don't need your blessing."

"Look, Maggie. I've got to be honest with you." His jaw clenched. "I hope Donor Guy doesn't have a winner on his sperm team."

"You have no right ..."

"No." He cut her off. "I have none." He watched her thoughtfully. "I'm no expert, but a dad should come with a lifetime guarantee. When you look at your baby's face you should know whose smile he's going to have. You shouldn't have to go on guess work."

"And you'd know all about that?" Her heart squeezed. She had a photo of her dad. A teenage surfer boy with sparkling eyes, fair hair bleached streaky blonde by sun and sea salt, and a carefree smile. Apart from that the tiny amount she knew about him could be written on a square sticky note. Alex had overstepped the mark. "You're talking out of your ..."

He butted in, saving her from an expletive.

"I know more than you might think." A note of defense in his voice warned her off asking him what exactly that meant. "If you ask me, if the insemination hasn't worked, then you should find The One – the guy who makes your heart sing – and have a baby with him."

"Oh puh-leeeese! My heart sing?"

"You know what I mean."

*I might if I thought he'd be along any time before the turn of the next millennium.*

"I don't believe in The One. It's a fundamentally flawed concept." His interference offended her. "Believe it or not, my plans don't require your seal of approval."

"Donor insemination might be right for some people. But not you, Maggie. You're putting the cart before the horse."

"Nonsense. Horses and carts are very last century."

She fought the urge to pick at her nail polish.

"Don't settle for second best. You deserve better than that."

She'd taken enough criticism. She drank in his cool exterior, the hard lines of his much- too-handsome face. Opinionated, sure of himself, his objections hurt more than she dared admit. She needed Alex-proofing.

Defensive, she let fly. "You're not in my life anymore. You don't have any part in this – not even the right to an opinion." She kept her tone measured. She'd die if he realized that he'd wounded her. "Don't you get it?" She hesitated for a zillionth of a second and blasted him with the basic fact. "You're just somebody I used to know." A shadow crossed Alex's face as Maggie blustered on. "As far as I can tell genes are a lottery," she insisted. She didn't care if she sounded smug. "It's what you make of what you get that counts. Look at you and Nick."

A muscle twitched uncomfortably in Alex's cheek. "What about me and Nick?"

*Flipping heck.* Did she have to spell it out? She shrugged. With their talent, their hot bodies and to-die-for looks, they were the epitome of watchability, wrapped up in a package of naturally sculpted masculinity. If there were any winners in the genes lottery it was the Wells twins. They'd taken the television world by storm.

"You got lucky in the genes lottery. That's my point. No matter what way it happens, life's genetic bingo. Besides, my baby will be legally entitled to contact "Donor Guy" …" She made air squiggles. "…When he – or she – is eighteen, so it's all good."

"I respect your decision," he said, his face hard set. "But I don't have to like it. As I see it, your bingo game is missing an essential piece."

She seethed. "Oh? And what's that?"

Alex's lips almost tipped up into a smile for half a second. "Love," he said simply.

She cursed herself for having started this conversation. She had enough love for a crèche full of babies. It was guys she couldn't handle.

"Thankfully, I don't have to consult you about how to ruin my life." She struggled to keep her cool, and out came a Freudian slip. "Run, I meant run my life," she corrected. "What's it to you anyway? I don't have a problem with AI. Why should you?"

Alex's granite expression darkened some more. With a long finger he touched the furrow between his knitted brows. "It's irrelevant – I know. And I have no right to an opinion – I agree." His voice dropped to a husky whisper. "I *used* to care about you, Maggie."

"Well, for your information, this is my baby and nobody else's." She hesitated. "And if I'm pregnant ..." She held back, desperate to avoid a rant. She couldn't help herself. "And only if, because according to the clinic there may be a sperm motility problem, and I might have to try again." She drew breath. "If it doesn't work first time, when it does happen, I'm going to love my child for who they are on the inside."

Alex held up the palms of his hands. "You're absolutely right. It's none of my business. It's your life. I'll butt out." Silent for a moment he suddenly bowled her over with his elusive smile. "And I know you'll love your baby unconditionally. Even if you get one with pointy elf ears!"

The tension evaporated. They looked straight into each other's eyes and burst out laughing. Her insides melted. Electricity hummed in the air between them.

"Yes, even then," she agreed. "Although, you're being completely ridiculous. And you know it."

Whatever misgivings he'd had about her announcement she appreciated his lightening up. Her maybe-baby plan was out in the open and it felt good that she wasn't keeping a secret from him. She might be his stylist but she'd spiraled into territory that was way beyond old friends picking up where they left off. She'd have to be careful with that. Really, they were different people now. She'd changed inside. He didn't know that. And she didn't know the faintest thing about him. In a moment of weakness she'd leaned on him as if he was still the person she knew a decade ago, when actually, he was a stranger. Relaxing into their old familiarity could only lead to trouble.

After she'd gone, Alex went to the bar and perched on a stool. He ordered single malt Scotch, no ice, and sat swirling the amber liquid around in the glass. Eventually, he knocked a mouthful back. He inhaled the smoky aroma just before the whiskey hit his taste buds; its heat burned his throat.

Maggie's news blind-sided him. She knew next to nothing about her dad and yet she wanted to bring a child with only half an identity into the world. He didn't know who his biological father was, but it sure as heck wasn't Drake Wells. Another gulp slid fierily into his stomach. Just because he was hung up about not knowing who he was, it didn't give him the right to judge Maggie.

"Hey Bro!" Alex looked up to see Nick standing there, all blonde hair and easy smile, and still wearing the tweed jacket from the fashion shoot. He ordered a beer and pushed a coaster about on the bar while the barman uncapped the bottle. "I talked to my agent. She reckons it's a done deal for this action movie in the spring. The big name they had lined up baled. The part's mine if I want it."

"Cool." The muscles in Alex's neck and shoulders relaxed. His jaw unclenched. If Nick was over blaming him for the studio axing *Mercy*, there'd be less tension on tomorrow's shoot; not to mention the weekend they had scheduled, the New York premiere of a movie they had cameos in, and their mother's annual charity gala. At the Empire State Building this year, it promised to be an extravaganza on a scale that should just about keep their mother happy.

"It looks like Thursday's meeting in LA is a formality. I fly out tomorrow night after the Cape Cod shoot."

"Just make sure you're in New York on Friday. You'll only have a studio to answer to if you miss the premiere of *The Magician of Arden*, but fail to turn up at Cassandra's charity gala on pain of death." He rolled his eyes, made a gruesome sound, and ran a finger across his throat.

They both laughed guardedly.

"She'll be auctioning us off as instant kiss-o-grams again this year, I presume."

"Uh-huh." Alex nodded slowly, relieved that the tension between him and his brother was finally easing. "You presume right."

Nick picked up his beer and drank in long slugs straight from the bottle, which glistened with ice-cold condensation. He set his half-quaffed beer firmly down on the bar. "I just saw Maggie in the lobby. Man, is she ten years hotter, or what?" His almond eyes were trained on Alex. "So what's the score? Any chance of you two picking up where you left off?"

Alex felt a stab of protectiveness towards Maggie. For all that he'd been tempted to finish what they'd started with a fling, it wasn't going to happen. They'd shaken on it. He wouldn't be bending his rules.

"Absolutely not. It's out of the question."

"Shame." Nick picked up his beer, set it down again, and pushed the bottle about on the bar. He abruptly changed tack. "Everyone loved the looks she came up with today. I have to admit I wasn't keen on the tweed at first, but hey ..." He held his arms out in a ta-dah way, "It's grown on me. I'm keeping the jacket. Might even wear it in LA tomorrow."

Alex laughed. He couldn't help it. He and Nick had been different peas from the same pod their whole lives.

He fixed on the strip of pink light behind the bar. Maggie had touched a nerve. He buzzed with nostalgia. He'd thought about her for a long time after he'd left London, wished he'd seen her one last time to say goodbye. If he had, he might have caved, gone back, finished his degree, tried his luck in the theater, fallen for her ... After a while he'd thought about her less often, until finally he'd blocked her out completely. When he'd deleted Maggie from his phone he'd deleted her from his life. He had a chance to change that. Would she give him a makeover? He'd like to lose the Jago connection. He could use a cool new image. There'd be no harm in asking.

Nick tightened his fist around his beer bottle. "I guess things are working out for the best after all," he admitted. "I know it's some other actor's cast-off action hero part, but it's progress."

"You'll be stellar. They'll forget they ever asked the other guy."

Nick let out a tense laugh. "I still don't think you were right about *Mercy.* The vampires hadn't run out of steam."

"You get to be an action man and I'm going back to what I really wanted to do in the first place." Alex fought his rising hackles. He clinked his glass against the green bottle in Nick's hand. "It's win-win!"

He could see that something was playing on Nick's mind. His brother stood bristling, a tower in tweed. Features taut, he went for it, spilling out what was bugging him, unable to keep it in a second longer.

"The thing is, Bro. I went to London for you. I talked you up on a morning chat show and two radio interviews over there. And what did you do? You played Jago and Jarvis down, like *Mercy of the Vampires* has been written out of history. The trouble with you is you won't admit that *Mercy* was good for you. It was good for us both."

Alex's heart lurched. He disagreed with Nick.

"You want my honest opinion, Alex? If you hadn't done Jago in *Mercy* there's no way you'd be about to play the lead in *Hamlet.*"

Nick stormed out of the cocktail lounge leaving his unfinished beer on the bar, and the trickle of early-evening customers who'd begun to arrive with their ears twitching. Alex sighed. *Great!* Right when he thought he and his brother were starting to see eye to eye he'd thrown a temper tantrum.

So what if he'd talked about *Vampires* in hushed tones? Sure, the series had been fun to make, but it wasn't serious acting, the kind of work that would make Drake Wells proud.

A final mouthful of smoky whiskey scalded his mouth. Thank heavens Maggie was here, with her can-do take on life. Though, even she was riddled with complications, taking her styled-up life to the extreme of planning a designer family. Her announcement had caught him off guard. He didn't doubt that she'd thought it all through. His remarks had been too strong. He should have kept his opinion to himself.

He'd meant it when he'd said he respected her decision. It was the genetically dad-shaped hole in his own identity that got his blood boiling, but there was no need to make that Maggie's problem. It was a well-kept family secret that although Drake Wells' name was on his birth certificate, he wasn't his biological father.

He froze. He'd reacted as if they'd never stopped being friends. Since when did it matter a damn what his stylist planned to do with her life? He shouldn't give a toss. She was in a totally different place in life to him. Settling down, starting a family. That was somewhere he'd never be headed. It was actually pretty brave that she wanted to do it on her own. He shouldn't care. But curiously he did. He cared – a lot.

She'd said it herself – she was just someone he used to know. So how come he felt like he might spontaneously combust?

# Chapter Six

"What's the verdict? Are congratulations in order?"

Maggie blanked out Alex's question. She didn't want to answer because she still hadn't done the pregnancy test.

She'd been up since stupid o'clock. They'd driven down from Boston to a beach on Cape Cod. The location was fab. There was a lighthouse and they were using a clap-board, picket-fenced seaside vacation cottage as their base.

The weather had turned horrible. Grey-black storm clouds were gathering with appalling speed. The pressure was on. Because of the heavy sky the light was poor and the forecast was for rain. Hannah wanted to get the pictures and wrap it up as quickly as possible.

Maggie threw herself into the job. It was up to her to be eagle-eyed. She had to make sure that everything was spot-on for the photographer.

"Come on. Maggie. Don't keep me in suspense."

She was checking Alex's clothes, making sure he was perfect. He was devastating. "I can't talk about this now," she whispered. She was deliberately side-stepping the issue. "We're working. And we need to hurry."

The image she had in mind was one of her typical mash-ups. She'd styled the brothers in leather biker jackets with slicked-back hair *à la* fifties. The goal was to combine their retro look with an ethereal quality in her girls. She had two lovely models: one brunette, one blonde. With Alex being dark and Nick fair, they complemented the brothers beautifully. She and Hannah had high hopes for the outcome. To complete the look they'd borrowed a super sexy Harley-Davidson.

Natalie was working on Nick's make-up. "How's it going?" she asked.

"Nearly done. Do you like it? I'm thinking echo-of-vampire-alter-egos. The-living-dead-go-to-the-beach – not so much …"

Maggie giggled. "Love it!"

She was on edge. There was no shelter at the beach. If it rained and the clothes got drenched, she'd be responsible. She had four big umbrellas on stand-by just in case.

She needn't have worried. The morning rolled along like a dream, even though the tension in the air between Alex and Nick was tangible. They were barely on grunting terms with each other, but since the vibe they were aiming for was mean and moody, it didn't matter. And since the rain stayed off long enough for Hannah to get the photos she wanted, it was all good. She was a happy pixie again.

A seagull swooped and shrieked above their heads. "Thanks guys and girls, you were all awesome," she said. She directed a conspiring wink at Maggie. "Let's get back to the cottage before the heavens open." The sky had darkened some more and foaming surf was crashing onto the shore.

In some of the last shots taken Maggie had used a long, hand-painted silk scarf for one of the models. A diaphanous swirl of rainbow colors, Hannah loved the effect against the stormy back-drop. As the team prepared to head for the cottage, Maggie looked around for the scarf. To her horror it was rolling across the sand, carried on the wind like colorful tumble-weed. Each gust of wind off the sea blew it further up the beach.

"Oh …!"

"Quick." Alex cut her off in mid-expletive. He threw a leg over the Harley and jerked his head, indicating that she should get on behind. "Hop on."

Maggie's brows knitted. "Is this okay?"

Alex shot a glance at Hannah. He was already revving the engine, tweaking the throttle so that it let out a tiger growl. "Go for it …" Alex sped off across the sand with Maggie clinging on limpet-like behind. "Only, if you write off the bike don't come running to me about health and safety and insurance and … stuff," she shouted after them. "On your own heads be it."

"Don't worry, he won't trash the bike." Nick slung a friendly arm around Hannah's shoulders. "He's good for a Harley – or two."

The wind and salt on her face, the revs of the bike's engine, her arms banded around Alex's rock-hard muscular body, his scent of new leather and spiced man, sent a whoosh of joy rushing through her senses. Alex stopped the bike and Maggie jumped off. She ran across the sand, feeling a sense of exhilaration as the wind whipped at her hair. Laughing, she grabbed the runaway scarf, amazed that they'd got to it before it took a dip in the sea. When she turned around Alex's eyes were trained on hers. "Thanks. If it had gone in the sea the salt water would have ruined it."

"Let me see." Alex took the bunched-up scarf from her hands. She couldn't hide her tremble when his fingers touched hers. He shook out the long swathe of rainbow fabric. A little sand gathered in the folds fell away. "No harm done."

He reached out his leather-clad arms and pushed her hair behind her ears with his thumbs. The brush of his skin on her temples hypnotized her senses. Sweet sensation swirled at her core. She stepped away from him, hugging her arms across her body, instantly super-aware of her breasts, nipples hard beneath her shirt. "Brrr," she said crisply. "I need a sweater."

He stretched out, drew her back to him, and draped the soft silk over her head, looping the ends around her neck. "Turn." Maggie did as she was told. With her back to him, a frisson shimmied up and down her spine as he tied the scarf firmly behind her head.

Disguised like an incognito movie star, all she needed was the dark glasses. She turned to face Alex. "That suits you," he said. "You should keep it. It matches your nails. Blue one day. Yellow the next. Today?" He lifted her hand and looked at her fingers. "Purple! Tomorrow … who knows?"

Maggie laughed. He'd be so easy to be with, if he wasn't so flipping sexy. "It's my perfect accessory," she agreed. A split second later she shrugged the idea off. "Except I don't really do color. Just the nails."

"And the …" Alex stopped abruptly. His jaw clenched. A cheek muscle flickered. They looked at each other for a long, hesitant moment, neither of them capable of movement. Maggie broke eye contact and Alex stared out to sea. Whatever he'd been thinking, he'd thought better of it and said nothing.

He broke the silence. "Let's go for a burn."

"We ought to get back."

"It's just you, me, a bike and a beach," he coaxed. "What's not to like?"

Maggie's heart skipped a beat. Hannah had said something earlier about arranging a special one-off over-sand permit for the bike, so she guessed it would be okay. It was hard to say no to a dose of Alex; muscled, lean, in leather, on a motorbike. She climbed on and wrapped her arms around his middle. He felt warm beneath the smooth biker jacket, his firm abs divine. She'd heard that Cape Cod was a little piece of heaven. Speeding across the sand, wrapped in designer silk, clinging on to Alex like she'd never have to let go – it truly was.

Holding on to him, like he'd always be there, realization as transparent as a sheet of glass hit her. She'd told Alex that she didn't believe in The One. Not because she didn't think she could love one man forever. What she didn't believe was that one man could love her forever. It felt good that she'd got the AI off her chest, although his reaction had been weirdly nitpicky. Why should he care? She pressed in tighter to his body and flattened her face against his back. He felt sensational and she was going to relax and enjoy the moment.

Far along the beach, and far from the curious eyes of Nick and their colleagues, Alex pulled up and cut the engine.

He sat astride the bike looking at the ocean in silence. Maggie hopped off, bent down and picked up a shell. She held it in the palm of one hand and dusted the grains of sand away with the purple nail of her index finger. Amongst clumps of dry seaweed and mermaid's purses, she spotted a flash of green sea glass tumbled opaque in the waves. She went to pick it up and suddenly Alex was right there. He reached out and pulled her into his arms. She inhaled sea salt and sexy man.

"I'm going to have to kiss you. You know that, don't you?"

*Um – no. Where did that come from?* "I'm not your leading lady," she joked.

"Oh yes you are." Now that the photos were done he was smiling his big relaxed smile as if he'd reserved it for her and her alone. "Thanks for your message."

*What message?* "Oh, I see." She got where he was coming from. He'd put the clock back. He was talking about the message she'd left with Nick ten years ago wishing him luck and love. "You can't turn back time."

"I wish I could."

"That's crazy."

He tightened his arms around her and her bones dissolved. There was no way they could close the gap, but she went with the flow. Her hands flew up and linked about his neck pulling his head down until his lips met hers in a perfect kiss. Awed by the strength of his body holding hers and the sweet magic of his mouth, Maggie's heart soared and a flame of longing uncurled inside her. She tangled her fingers in his hair, loving the soft warmth of his clean-shaven jaw against her skin, exploring his soft mouth, craving with each moment just a little bit more heat. Tasting, touching, taking their time, they lost themselves in each other's spell.

Slowly, oh so languorously, they broke from the kiss.

Still reeling from Alex's heat, Maggie shivered incongruously. He took off his jacket and wrapped it around her. "Here," he said. "You wear this." She shrugged her arms into the sleeves, luxuriating in the leather, imbued with Alex's warmth.

*Kisses like that are all in a day's work for Alex!* He was an actor, for heaven's sake. He could produce kisses to order like he could weep buckets on cue, or do his own stunt work.

Back inside the temporary base at the cottage, after their blast across the beach, a reality check kicked in. He was a temporary fixture in her work life. Still, she couldn't wait to see Layla's face when she told her all about Hot Vampire Guy on a Harley. On second thoughts, maybe she'd keep it to herself. It had been a moment when she'd taken leave of her senses. Why in the world had she kissed him? So much for figuring that she and Alex could be just friends again. That was a giant fail. What was she playing at? One thing was certain. He might be too sexy to resist but she'd fallen for him once before and she wouldn't be doing it again anytime soon. Scratch that. She wouldn't be falling in love again – ever.

No matter how great the chemistry, what they'd had before was gone. They had new lives.

Maggie busied herself checking all the clothes. They were mainly press samples and she wanted to return them in good condition. She ignored Alex, tried to appear absorbed in her work, but it was obvious that he could tell she was avoiding him.

His eyes burned the back of her neck. Uncomfortable. They'd agreed to wipe the slate clean. It should be easy. Only he'd gone and kissed her, and she'd kissed him back, and now she was all over the place.

The atmosphere was dynamite. It was crystal clear to everyone that Alex and Nick weren't speaking. They had cooperated with each other during the shoot, just about. As soon it was over, a car had come to collect Nick and he'd left after a luvvy-fest of team hugs, but without a word of goodbye to Alex.

Maggie sighed. Since she'd kissed Alex on the beach she'd been like a cat on a hot tin roof. He was a distraction she didn't need right now. She wanted to know if her AI procedure had worked. A baby would make her life complete. The perfect man she could live without. A family of her own she could not.

The day her mum ran off, she collected Maggie from school, gave her a big hug and a fancy art kit full of paints and pencils in every color under the sun, and left. Maggie drew pictures until it was time for tea, designing clothes that she thought her mum would like. Only teatime came and went and she didn't come back. From age eight Maggie had lived with her grandmother. When she'd died the only strong branch on the family tree had gone.

She hadn't been able to bring herself to do the pregnancy test. She lacked the courage. Something was wrong here. She couldn't face making this very personal discovery so far from home, and in the midst of a bunch of strangers.

And Alex.

This was a one-woman project. Maybe she should have kept it that way. The best thing would be to wait until she got back to London to do the test. Or better still, go to her cottage in Cornwall and do the test with Layla there for moral support. She'd prefer not to find out alone in a faceless hotel room.

She was desperate to know, but she wasn't ready to find out. It didn't make any sense. She needed to relax. There'd be no harm in waiting a couple of days. She'd go on her whale-watch, then she'd fly home and find out if she was pregnant. She still had a feeling it was going to be a yes. Only the doctor at the clinic had advised her not to get her hopes up. She'd said it might take more than one attempt. It was something to do with sperm motility.

"Frozen sperm get lazy." Like a madwoman she whispered the words aloud to herself as she carefully folded a butter-soft leather biker jacket around some tissue paper.

"Pardon?"

"Oh my giddy aunt. Did I say that out loud?"

"Yes. You did." Alex's eyes glittered. They reminded her of sun on snow under a blue sky. They had a charm all of their own. "It's alright." His tone was husky and mockingly conspiratorial. "I think I'm the only one that heard."

"Sorry. I was just thinking." The clothes that the models had worn for the shoot were piled up around the place. Maggie folded and hung and organized methodically, ticking each item off on her check-list as she did so.

"Does this mean you're not?"

"Good grief." Maggie made no effort to hide the fact that she was rattled. Alex had made his feelings about her trying for a donor-sperm baby clear, but she'd thought they'd got past that. "It doesn't mean anything of the sort. If you must know, I didn't do the pregnancy test."

"Maggie? Don't tell me you're procrastinating!"

"Of course not," she lied, laughing as if it was some tiny insignificant detail, rather than the heart-swelling course of her future. "I'm just putting it off."

"Very funny."

She was out of sorts. Alex had no right to pry. Anybody would think it was his baby the way he kept going on about it.

"Have dinner with me tonight? We can celebrate or commiserate – whichever."

"I'm not doing the test. I'm waiting until I get back to London."

"Have dinner with me." His deep drawl gave her tingles and wore down her resistance. They could go back to Boston right now and never see each other again. She didn't want that. On all sane levels she knew that kissing Alex had been a mistake. In theory. In reality? *Oh. My. Gosh!* That kiss was dreamy.

She needed to focus. She wanted to say goodbye to Alex properly this time, and having dinner with him seemed like a good way to do that. Anyway, she didn't fancy another meal on a tray in her room with one eye on her laptop.

"Okay." Heart-stopping kisses aside, styling the Wells twins had been amazing; and it wasn't going to do her CV any harm.

The more time she spent with Alex, the more Hot Vampire Guy and the friend she'd been close to merged into the same man. Her heart told her not to let that happen. Too late. It had happened. For years he'd vanished into thin air, replaced by an impostor who inhabited television screens and newspapers. She'd begun to see through that, and she liked what she saw. Dinner couldn't hurt, but it was high time they stopped messing about. "We'd better lay down some ground rules."

"It's dinner. Not a space mission."

She was determined to nail this friends thing. That's where they'd started out a decade ago and that's where she wanted them to finish. "I need to make something clear," she insisted.

"Shoot." A lazy smile curved across his lips. *Darn it.* There'd been a sticking plaster on the crack in her heart from his half a seduction and desertion, but she'd been over him for a very long time. She'd flirted with him, and it had been lovely. She might be star-struck and hormonal, but her heart was rock solid. She needed to set out some conditions, because so far her resolve to Alex-proof herself hadn't really worked.

"No cheesy lines and no dodgy vampire moves." Alex laughed and his smile grew impossibly wider. "It's not like it's a date. Just friends?"

"Cheese is off the menu," he promised. "But I can't make any promises on the vampire moves." He quirked an eyebrow. "After ten years of Jago they're part of my DNA."

*Chapter Seven*

"I'm a cheap date, huh?"

They were sitting in a wharf diner. Reflected light glowed on the dark water. Headlamps from planes landing at the airport punctuated the night sky.

Ketchup, mustard, and a napkin dispenser sat neatly at the ready on the formica table.

"You're not a date. You're … just Maggie."

"I'm not sure how to take that." Her eyes were full of challenge.

"Take it as a compliment."

He'd kissed her because he wanted to. He shouldn't have. He thought he could find something he'd lost, recapture a feeling he couldn't name. He wouldn't let it happen again.

"Right. Okay. I'll do that." She lifted the laminated menu card.

"Were you expecting a swish restaurant?" He watched her face for a reaction. He'd been working on it, but it was impossible to forget that they'd very nearly been lovers. Their failed night together had left him wondering what if? He'd overstepped the mark. That kiss had smashed his no-action plan to smithereens.

"Well, yes, I suppose I was." She paused. "Only because of who you are now. Actually, I like this place. It's very 'old Alex.'" She smiled. Kissing her on the beach had fired up a chain reaction of attraction and temptation, flickering in his heart like the frames

85

of an old celluloid cine film.

"Whatever that means? There isn't an 'old' me, or a 'new' me." They only existed in her head, two versions of the same person. "Not unlike yourself."

"Meaning?" Her greeny-brown eyes glimmered.

"The new Maggie's very stylish." Alex was treading on eggshells. "The old Maggie wore more color."

"I went off color," she said sharply. "Neutral colors suit my work. They give me a professional look. I blend into the background and all my fashion focus goes on my clients."

"I get that it's all about Brand Magenta, the only color is in the name. Surely you can relax on the dress code in your downtime?"

"I could; I just choose not to." Actually she had eased up a little, he realized. She'd put on a graphite t-shirt with an asymmetric neckline and a swirly butterfly print etched on it in a lighter shade of grey. "I stopped liking myself in color."

"I like you in color."

He lifted his hand to his chin. He'd been clean-shaven for the photo shoot earlier. Now his skin was rough with a day's growth of stubble. He wanted to reach out to her, only he didn't know how. Something about her was closed off, a guardedness she'd let go of at the beach. Was this image thing more about hiding than looking professional?

"Hannah recommended this place," he said, changing the subject. His fingers brushed her soft hands as he took the plastic menu from her and put it back in its holder. "Her uncle owns it. It's a breakfast joint. But it happens to have a spectacular view. She said if I asked nicely …" He lowered his voice to a whisper. *And paid handsomely.* "…Uncle Marvin would open up and cook lobster."

Maggie's eyes sparkled with surprise. "Just for us?"

"Uh-huh."

"Is lobster *à la* Uncle Marvin any good?" There was a cheeky glow in her not-exactly-green-not-exactly-brown-eyed gaze.

"Apparently so. Let's find out." Not being on a date felt quite good. No reading between the lines. No expectations. Just Maggie. With her freckles. And her lips. And that sparkle in her eyes.

Over the last two days her curves had been infinitely distracting. A necklace with a bright amber stone dangled in the dip of her top, tempting his gaze into the out-of-bounds zone. He'd resigned himself to not doing inappropriate stuff like thinking about the color of her underwear. He needed to work on the "just friends" thing, although kissing her at the beach had been a knock-out detour.

Not in the habit of having to resist temptation, trying not to want to seduce her had turned things upside down, inside out, and every which way but straightforward. What's more, he was interested in her. Too interested. He didn't need to know why she was using a sperm bank to have a baby, but he wanted to understand.

The waitress came and stood at Maggie's shoulder, notebook in hand and pen poised. Alex looked up. He recognized her gawp. He'd seen that look on so many faces. He knew what was coming next.

"It is you, isn't it?"

*Just a second, I'll check.* He shot an apologetic glance at Maggie. She smiled back. Her eyes twinkled. "Yes, it is," he told the waitress.

"I knew it!" On the verge of an incomprehensible prattle, the woman physically wobbled, as if standing on the edge of a cliff. He'd been here before – numerous times. "I said to Marvin, it's him. It's got to be. It's that vampire guy – Jago," she trilled, delighted. "Some of the customers said you were in town, taking press photos, or something, so I knew it could only be you." She drew breath. Alex waited for her rush of enthusiasm to die. "Marvin's not a fan of *Mercy of the Vampires*. He's clueless. But as soon as he said Hannah sent you and that he was opening up specially, I put two and two together and sure enough …" She stared at Maggie, apparently displeased that she wasn't another celebrity. "Where's your brother? Is Jarvis not with you tonight?"

*We're not joined at the hip.* Maggie must have read his mind. She was stifling a giggle. He opened his mouth to reply but the waitress was not to be interrupted. "So, what do you say? Can I get an autograph?"

This had happened on countless occasions and he knew exactly what to expect. "Where would you like it?"

The waitress pouted flirtatiously and looked down at her cleavage. *Oh dear.* These moments used to amuse him – not any more. He was jaded from too many tussles with girls and marker pens. Fortunately, she opted to hand him her notepad. "To Lynette," she dictated. "Two e's, two t's."

He scribbled his name as legibly as he could, and risked adding an x, although experience had taught him that Lynette might be inclined to ask for it in kind. The marker-pen-ladies of this world weren't backwards in coming forwards.

Thankfully, no kiss was required. Lynette brought Alex a beer and an orange juice for Maggie. Marvin cooked the lobster, and for the rest of the evening they were left in peace.

"What are you doing tomorrow?" He pushed his paper plate away. It wasn't easy eating lobster with plastic cutlery. "Flying back to London?"

"Going on a whale-watch," Maggie was still doing battle with the lobster. "Why? D'you want to come with me?"

"I'd love to." There was a siren call in the invitation. He'd said yes without thinking. He'd been planning to hole himself up at the hotel and work on *Hamlet*. The lines wouldn't learn themselves. And he needed to work on his received pronunciation. The critics would be baying for his blood when he took on the iconic role in London next month. They'd shoot him down in flames if he murdered Hamlet with a mid-Atlantic twang. The last thing he needed was to spend a day at sea, but he couldn't remember when he'd actually taken a day off and done something different, just for the hell of it. His diary had been crammed with agent meetings, promo and rehearsals for months. Doubt flickered on her face.

"Was that the wrong answer?"

*Since* he'd be in London for a while, and *since* she'd like to be friends again, he was trying to be chivalrous. Only their latent electricity was definitely still there, and bad as that was it was the main reason he'd said yes please to the whale-watch.

She narrowed her eyes and scrunched her freckled nose. "Don't you have somewhere to be?"

"Not until Friday, then I have to be in New York for a movie premiere." He looked at his watch to check what day it said. Sometimes living out of a suitcase, doing PR, he forgot. "It's only Wednesday."

"Flipping Nora. Your plans make mine sound like watching paint dry."

"Come to New York with me." He locked eyes with her. Confusion clouded her features. "You can be my date." Her eyebrows shot up. "My not-a-date?" The idea had popped into his head out of nowhere. It was good getting to know her again. It would be a chance to make it up to her for treating her so shabbily in the past. He could do this "friends" thing. He *could*.

He'd have to keep his libido on lockdown.

"That's impossible. I'm flying home on Friday." She looked away, staring transfixed at the streaks of light on the water around the harbor.

"Change your plans. I'll do you a deal – your whale-watch for my movie premiere." He paused and threw in, "And a makeover when we get back to the UK."

"How does that work?" She turned back to him. A mischievous smile had replaced the puzzled look on her face.

"Easy. We change your flights and you come to New York for the weekend."

"In return for you coming with me to watch whales?" She folded her arms across her chest, unselfconsciously tightening her cleavage.

"Correct. Plus a re-style. I need you to fix my image."

"I can't drop everything and go to New York."

"What's to drop? Have you got plans for the weekend?"

"Sleep." Under any other circumstances, he'd have assumed she meant with someone.

"That's a lame excuse. Postpone it. You can sleep next week. Besides, you're my free single friend and I need a plus one for the red carpet."

"What happened? Did somebody stand you up?" She tilted her chin challengingly.

He overlooked the dig. His gaze dipped unintentionally to the distracting amber pendant.

"I have a cameo in this movie. Along with Nick and Ella Swift. I don't need a date. But I'd like it if you came along. It'll be like tonight. Just friends." Her hand rested on the table. He closed his fingers over hers. "I've only just found you again. I'm not ready to let you go." A shiver ran down his spine.

She laughed off his comment. "I'd stick out like a sore thumb on the red carpet."

"Rubbish. You'll be superb." He turned her hand over in his and traced a figure of eight on the palm. "Besides," he continued, "With you around, Nick won't be able to strangle me with the garlic."

"I haven't said yes yet."

"Say you'll think about it. I've got to go to a charity event at the Empire State Building on Saturday night. It's very glam. You'll love it."

Maggie's eyes shone. She pulled him to his feet. "Come on." Her sexy smile worked on him like a spell, and he began to wonder, not for the first time, if he'd actually be able to keep to the just-friends bargain. "I want to dance." She dragged him across the empty diner to an old jukebox in a corner. He stifled a groan, knowing he'd set himself a heck of a challenge.

He peered at the song titles. "There are some seriously old 45s in there."

"All 45s are seriously old. Got a quarter?"

Alex dug in his pocket and handed her a coin. He watched the concentration on her face as she chose a record and posted his quarter in the slot. The music started slow, his arms closed around her and he pulled her close, looked down into her upturned face and placed a feather-light kiss on her forehead. She smiled and spun out of his hold as the tempo picked up, dancing and singing along like she used to do when they were students.

When the music stopped he planted himself between her and the jukebox, refusing to let her avoid his gaze.

"It's just a weekend. Come to New York."

"I don't know." She bit her lip. "It's a bit spur of the moment."

Not used to having to work too hard to get a yes out of someone, and equally unused to hearing no, he wasn't about to give up.

"Spur of the moment's what you do. Spontaneity's your specialty. Or – it used to be before you decided to try for a donor baby at twenty-nine …"

That was the wrong thing to say. Momentarily she froze.

"Look, I'd like to come, but I can't." A shimmer of awareness zapped between them. *Bad timing.* "I'd love to go to New York with you. It sounds fantastic. But I have to focus on the future. I'm going home to find out if I'm pregnant."

"One. Week. End." He said the words slowly as if that would mesmerize her into saying yes. "When the baby comes you'll have someone else to think about for the next eighteen years."

"A baby's a lifetime commitment, not a life sentence."

"Sure." He applauded her positivity, her determination to make her dreams happen. "That's why, this one time, it's not going to hurt to live for the moment."

His father acted like a wife and kids were a prison he had to escape from. *Doesn't Count On Location* was Drake Wells' mantra. His conquests might have been disposable, but each new rumor, every tabloid photo, put Cassandra through hell. Alex had mostly blocked it out. Trying to figure out Drake was a waste of effort. Alex sometimes wondered if he'd resented being their non-biological dad so badly that he'd deliberately tortured their mother with his endless affairs. Maggie's baby plan forced him to remember things he'd rather forget. It got under his skin.

Drake moved out when Nick and Alex were six. The night he left was one of Alex's clearest childhood memories. He and Nick had been watching TV when it all kicked off – the shouting and Cassandra's choking sobs. He'd turned the volume way up. It didn't block out the door slamming, the rev of a car's engine, and the angry screech of wheels on gravel as Drake drove away. Afterwards, his mother, white as a ghost, came in and switched off the television. She'd read them a story – *The Little Engine That Could* – and put them to bed. The empty silence after their father had gone seemed louder than any of the noise that preceded his leaving.

He could have stuck around stoically in the wings of their life, but he chose not to; with the exception of fleeting visits to their boarding school when they were teens, occasions that were more about Drake being seen than about connecting with his sons. He might have won acting awards, but he wouldn't get one for playing the dutiful father.

"What are we waiting for? Let's go back to the hotel and do this pregnancy test. What'll it take? Five minutes?"

Maggie looked unconvinced. "About that."

"At least you'll know where you stand. If it's a yes, you can come to New York and party."

"And if it's a no?"

"Then we can really party! I'll take you to a high-style cocktail lounge and buy you the most expensive cocktail on the menu. No gummy bears allowed." Her brows knitted. "To commiserate, naturally."

# Chapter Eight

Any minute now she'd have her answer.

Three different pregnancy tests sat in a row on the marble counter top in the en-suite bathroom of Maggie's hotel room. She'd used a pink one, a blue one, and one that gave the result in words – "Pregnant" or "Not Pregnant".

Which would it be? Maggie was desperate to know. She'd been a little bit afraid to find out until Alex persuaded her to go for it. He was too funny offering to trade her a whale-watch for an A-list weekend in New York. Was he serious? Who wouldn't want to be his date? Or, in her case, not-a-date.

He'd been sweet tonight. They were getting into the swing of this just-good-friends thing, like they were going back to square one. It felt good, really good. Except the kiss had been a blip. It wasn't just the Jago factor, she fancied the pants off him, and if she went to New York, she might not be able to help herself, she might end up tearing his clothes off.

*Awkward.*

She'd buried her feelings for him years ago, but she and Alex had an unfinished fling between them, and she couldn't be sure of sticking to her own rules. What if she actually wanted him to try out some of those dodgy vampire moves after all?

Impossible to avoid her reflection in the vast bathroom mirror, she looked into it and gave herself a wicked little smile.

*Some rules are made to be broken.*

She checked her watch. Two minutes to go. She lowered the lid on the toilet and plonked herself there, picking at the purple varnish on her thumbnail as the seconds counted down. When the time was up she carried on picking.

There was a lump in her throat as if she'd swallowed a bar of hotel soap. Why was she doing this?

She wanted a baby because she wanted to put everything right that had been wrong in her own childhood. As a little girl she'd learned to fade into the background, being good, keeping quiet, trying not to be a nuisance. She didn't ask too many questions. The answers hurt too much. Deep down she knew that she'd been rejected by her mother because she reminded her of her dad. She looked at Maggie and saw Sam, and if she couldn't have Sam, she didn't want Maggie. She'd overheard her mother say so just days before she left. Standing outside the kitchen door she'd watched through a crack while her mother ripped up photos, her face tear-blotched. "Why does she have to look just like him?" she'd spluttered at Maggie's grandmother. "I don't see any Plumtree in her at all. She's got his eyes, his hair, his smile." She'd sounded cross, exasperated that her daughter had failed to be a mini version of herself. "She's arty like he was – a useless, head-in-the-clouds, fly-by-night … Why couldn't he stay alive? He didn't even do that much right!"

Maggie's sense of cold confusion was stamped on her memory. With a sperm-donor dad there was no danger that she'd ever end up so angry and disappointed with her own child. She was ready to be the mum she wished she'd had. For her it would be better without the mangled emotion of loving the baby's dad.

A wave of nauseous panic hit Maggie. She couldn't bring herself to look at the test results. She needed a friend to look for her and tell her yes or no.

There was nothing else for it. She grabbed all three of the tests.

Looking away and keeping her hand firmly over the result windows, she opened the bathroom door and marched into the bedroom.

Alex was standing by the window, staring out into the night. He turned to look at her, six foot plus of awesome man with the bluest eyes she'd ever seen.

"So?" Silence. "And?" Silence. "Please, Maggie. Don't keep me in suspense."

Silence. Maggie closed her eyes and stretched her arm out to him, fingers still wrapped around the test windows. Silence.

"I can't look."

Alex took her hand gently in his and unwound her fingers. "Would you like me to look for you?" His deep voice made her nerves jangle all the more.

"Yes please." Face unattractively contorted, she opened one eye, and kept the other scrunched closed.

"Ready?" He was still holding her hands in his, balancing the clutch of tests in their joined fingers as if they were as delicate as eggs.

"Uh-huh." She opened the other eye. "Ready."

Silence.

"Well?"

"You're having a baby!" He rumbled out the gravelly words on a breath.

"I am? Are you sure?"

"Look for yourself."

She clutched the sticks and stared. Sure enough: blue lines, pink lines and the word "Pregnant" in clear black letters.

"Should I do another one just to make sure? I've got one that shows up a plus or a negative sign. It might be more scientific."

"You don't need a control test. You've done three already. There's no doubt about it. You're pregnant."

Maggie's emotions had gone from panic and fear to disbelief, and finally pure joy.

"Oh my stars. This is fantastic. I can hardly believe it's happening.

I'm pregnant." She beamed. "I'm having a baby."

"Yep. It says it right there. You're going to be a mom."

"Wow. It's all I've wanted for the longest time. A real family of my own."

"Cool." His voice had turned to a solemn rasp. "It's great. Well done, Maggie." It felt like he was going to pat her on the back, or shake her hand, or something. She wanted to hug him, but she held back.

"You can kiss goodbye to sleep. And sex. Oh no, wait a minute." He clapped a hand to his forehead theatrically, "Silly me. You already did that."

Why couldn't he say he was pleased for her?

"I'm not a nun," she retaliated. "I just knew The One wasn't going to happen for me. And I didn't want to have a baby with someone who might end up losing interest and walking away from his child. A dad who's not in the picture at the moment of conception can't walk away because he was never there in the first place."

She didn't add that she wouldn't have to look at her growing child and see the face of someone she'd loved and who didn't love her back, see someone whose very existence made her ache because she spoke, moved, laughed like him and made her cry because everything about her reminded her of someone she wanted to forget. That's how it had been for her mother. That's why she'd run away.

"Listen, about New York. I didn't mean to pressurize you. If you're not up for it, it's fine."

"I've thought it over." Maggie jumped in before he could get another word out. "I'll have to pass on the fancy cocktails." She made a sad face. "But, if the offer's still there, I'd love to come. I haven't taken time off to do something fun for months. And now that I know – for sure – I feel like celebrating. It'll be lovely. I haven't got the foggiest idea what to wear, but I can figure that one out – there's time. And fashion's what I do, right?"

"It certainly is." His lips curved into a super-sexy smile. "I can make a couple of calls. Between us we should be able to guarantee that you're red-carpet-ready."

"You know what this means?" Alex looked straight at her, his eyes unguarded, the black pupils reminded her of two dots under puzzled question marks. "You're still up for watching whales, aren't you? We had a deal."

"Sure," he croaked.

"I need to go to bed. I don't like to throw you out, but I really need to sleep." She stood on tiptoes in front of Alex, leant up and brushed her cheek against his hard jaw line. *Mmm.* "Goodnight," she breathed against his ear. "And thanks, Alex. I really appreciate that you were here tonight, for this." She pressed the palm of her hand against her flat stomach. A new life was forming inside her.

He walked to the door and looked back over his shoulder before turning the handle. He was the same gorgeous guy he'd been when he'd walked away without a backward glance. And she'd let him go, heavy-hearted that he hadn't phoned. Her emotions were all over the place. She had to say something.

"I'd no idea how badly I needed a friend."

Alex stopped, walked back to Maggie, pulled her into his arms and gave her the biggest, warmest, loveliest hug. "See you tomorrow."

"Can't wait." Suddenly he was gone. There was an empty space where he'd been. And a whole heap of happy in her heart. She was in the best mood ever. Excited, and a teeny bit scared. Experiencing both feelings together was bewildering – and wonderful. She'd done it. She'd created her designer baby.

She sat down heavily on the end of her bed. Alone. Until about a minute ago she'd been elated, so sure that this was what she wanted. And it was. She was going to be a mum. A single mum. Unlike tonight she'd have no one to share this with. She'd thought she was prepared but now that Alex had gone and reality was kicking in, a seed of trepidation at what she'd planned for her future sowed itself in her soul. She might turn out to be just like her mother, unable to hack being a single parent. She steeled herself. She'd made this choice and she was determined to make it work. She had something to prove.

The high speed catamaran flew along, heading out to sea. The waves were still choppy from the stormy weather. White-crested, every so often the boat would hit a big one, showering the deck. The perky guide, a marine biologist, filled the passengers in on pertinent cetacean facts until they reached the place where the whales usually hung out, and the skipper cut the engine.

Amused at having Jago from *Mercy of the Vampires* as her new best friend, Maggie was getting used to the interest Alex generated – and the curious looks people gave her. Normally, she didn't get noticed. It was her job to make other people stand out from the crowd. Clients appreciated her neutrality. Unobtrusive, all her creativity went into her projects.

The epitome of male beauty, Alex was amazing. And so were the whales. At first she didn't think they'd see one. They scoured the grey sea, watching, waiting, and suddenly, before the marine guide had even spotted it, Alex saw one off the port bow.

He pushed his dark glasses up onto his head. "Look!" He stood behind her and pointed, guiding her eyes with the direction of his arm. The other hand rested on her shoulder. A zing of pleasure zipped through her body. "Over there."

The whale's slick back was clearly visible.

"Wow!" she gasped.

"Amazing," Alex admitted.

"Now you know how it feels."

"Are you suggesting that when people recognize me it's like they're seeing a whale for the first time?"

She tilted her head to look him in the eyes teasingly. "Something along those lines."

He smiled in that breath-stealing way of his. Her heart did a somersault. The roll of the ocean, seeing whales in their natural environment, and sharing the whole experience with Alex was too cool.

The boat rolled on a big wave and she lolloped sideways. She automatically grabbed onto him to steady herself. "Easy does it." His arms closed around her from behind, holding her firmly. He drew her securely against his body. A column of masculine muscle, his gentle strength felt fantastic. She shivered, despite being wrapped in fleece and waterproofs. "Cold?" He lightly rubbed her arms and massaged her shoulders.

"Brrr. Yes, kind of." It wasn't exactly true, more a frisson of sweet, spine-tingling desire. It was hard not to be attracted to him. For flip's sake, Alex Wells had to be the hottest friend any girl ever had.

He'd been her ordinary friend before he'd been her famous friend. She struggled to hang onto that fact. It was great that they'd got past the embarrassing blip of their disastrous night in bed together. It had been struck from the record – any glimmers of attraction were hiccups, a bi-product of the celebrity thing. Except, who was she kidding? Even allowing for the Jago factor, that kiss on the beach had been hot heaven.

The whale surfaced and gave a blast from its blow-hole. The whiff turned Maggie's stomach. It was like sharing an elevator with an appallingly flatulent being who'd been overindulging in a bout of extreme dietary indiscretion involving seafood.

Alex took a picture on his phone. He caught Maggie, looking greenish, at the very moment when the whale went into a dive. Its body an arc, the dorsal fin stood out clearly in the background.

"Glad you came?" she asked, when they'd stopped laughing about the dodgy smell and how awful she looked in the picture.

"Very." His deep voice ignited little flames of heat. His strong arms closed around her again, keeping her steady on the shifting ocean. Leaning against all that muscle felt delicious. The friends thing was becoming more of a conundrum every minute. She was a smidge out of control – all those overactive pregnancy hormones whizzing around her system. "How are you feeling?" he asked. "Has it sunk in yet?" Close against him, her limbs brushing his, he felt like a very sexy bodyguard.

"It's starting to." The mention of her pregnancy brought her back down to earth. "It'll take a bit of getting used to."

They'd been having a chilled-out day – apart from the hot fire that crackled through her when his body connected with hers, that is. All of a sudden his mood darkened. His jaw clenched and the blue glimmer in his eyes clouded, greyed like the sea and the sky all around them.

"You've made a brave decision." A muscle flickered in his cheek. He'd turned into an iceberg. "Choosing to become a single parent can't have been easy."

Over the tannoy the guide enlightened passengers with some stuff about whale tail markings. Maggie's head swam. Was she missing something? What was she not getting? He'd gone all serious.

"It's complicated," she admitted. "I know my grandma could be a bit of a dragon at times, but it was only because she loved me to bits. She was my substitute mum and dad, rolled into one all-purpose package."

Alex shrugged. "She didn't think you should trust men. I guess she had her reasons."

"It turned out she was right."

Alex drew in a deep breath, then exhaled, long and slow. His arms released her and she grabbed onto the handrail to keep her balance on the choppy sea. He looked down, glowering at the water. "I didn't exactly help. Leaving like I did. Not calling you."

The boat rolled, lifted and dropped by the movement of the ocean. Maggie felt as if she'd been slapped in the face with a cold clump of wet seaweed. Did Alex think he was the reason she was going it alone?

"We let each other go. If we'd talked, we might have made things harder for each other."

Alex reached out and squeezed her shoulders. She'd have had

to tell him she was in love with him, and he'd have had to tell her that he wasn't coming back. They might have started putting the kind of pressure on each other that ends up with people hating each other. Leaving a good-luck message and fading away was easy. She distanced herself from people because she didn't believe that she was worth sticking around for. Her mother hadn't thought she was worth staying for. Why should anyone else?

"Back then I needed to put Nick first."

"There wasn't a part for an extra," she joked. "It's okay. I understood." Alex running off to join the metaphorical circus in LA hadn't been the clincher. She didn't need to be an astrologer to predict that he'd have left her eventually. Still she'd remained cautiously optimistic on the boyfriend front. She had a tendency to cut guys loose before they got close enough to dump her first, but generally speaking she'd hoped to find The One someday. Until Marcus.

"I wouldn't have gone for the part of Jago if Nick – and our mother – hadn't begged me to. They made it impossible to say no."

"I know." Maggie stared at Alex's granite face. Shoulders hunched, head hanging, he didn't look up. Tabloid fodder, rumors abounded that Cassandra Wells had used shameless nepotism to guarantee that her sons landed the parts of the vampire twins. That must have been hell for Alex, but it was years ago. They'd more than proved themselves in the decade since.

"I couldn't let Nick down. He wanted it badly. And I went along for the ride. Now that it's all over, he thinks I regret the last ten years."

Alex's hands grasped the guardrail. Relieved that they'd strayed onto safer ground than why she was having a baby on her own, Maggie placed one hand over his taut knuckles.

"I want to explore the things I might have done if *Mercy of the Vampires* hadn't happened. Nick resents that. According to him, there's no going back, only forward. He thinks I should use the popularity of the show as a springboard. That's what he plans to do."

"Seems like six of one and half a dozen of the other, if you ask me." Maggie squeezed his hand. "If you want to retrace your steps in order to move on, why shouldn't you?"

"Nick doesn't believe I can go back to zero."

"Maybe he's got a point." She nudged him with her elbow, attempting to lighten the mood. "I mean, look at me. What am I if not a scene in your rear-view mirror? Right?"

He raked his gaze over her. "I wouldn't put it quite like that."

They both laughed. "You shouldn't be ashamed of *Mercy*. It's been an amazing success. You should be proud."

"It's hard to be proud when my own father called it the 'naffest thing on the goggle box'. He hates it."

Maggie breathed out a long, shrill whistle. "Harsh!" She whooshed her chipped purple nails through the air. "It's sour grapes. Didn't I read somewhere that he's starring as a sci-fi villain? That's not exactly Richard III!"

Maggie didn't get Alex and his family. He was devoted to Nick, even though they were behaving more like their on-screen characters than real-life brothers. Why couldn't he agree to disagree with Nick about there not being any more mileage in *Vampires*? And why was he so eager to please a father who did nothing but put down his work? As families went the Wells made her "one parent, one baby" plan look positively idyllic.

"Nick and I have been at each other's throats since *Mercy* ended."

"Maybe you're being unfair on him. The show might have started out more his thing than yours, but if you hadn't been into it, it would have shown. There's no way it would have lasted ten years."

"Yeah, you're right," he admitted, his tone mock-grudging, "Without Jago, I'd have been lucky to get a walk-on in *Hamlet*."

"Or Rosencrantz. Or Guildenstern. If you were *really* lucky," Maggie teased.

"And that's only maybe, on a good day, with the wind in the

right direction, and all the stars in my horoscope perfectly aligned and shining down on me."

Maggie giggled. "I read the horoscope on the plane."

"What did mine say? That I'm not destined to play a vampire forever?"

"I think it said something cryptic about Saturn's life-changing energy."

"Thank you, Mystic Maggie. What about yours?"

"Mine said I should prepare for an encounter with my destiny."

A deep chuckle erupted from Alex's throat. "Well, you encountered me. Only I'm not your destiny. It's not in my stars to play a part in anyone's destiny but my own."

Her heart plummeted. Inappropriately gutted, she couldn't for the life of her figure out why. She wasn't expecting anything from Alex. A quirk of fate had brought them together, but they'd be going back to their real lives soon enough. She'd return to the world outside his celebrity bubble, resume her place as a plankton speck he'd hung out with before he'd landed the top spot on a gazillion hottest bachelor lists.

The spark she'd felt from his kiss on the beach was all about the feelings she'd once had for him. He'd left her floating on air like a party balloon. None of it meant a thing. Acting was his job description. Friends would be fine for him because there'd never been any danger of him seeing her as anything more. For a few whimsical minutes at Cape Cod they'd slipped back like a couple of characters from a time-travel drama. In reality, there'd be no going back. Only forward.

"Anyway," he said, breaking the sudden silence. "You don't need to know what's in the stars. You know what you want and you're making it happen."

Wasn't that what he was doing? It bothered her that he was so sure he'd never find The One. She had Marcus to thank for that, but she only had to open her eyes and look around to see that Alex could have lovely women queuing around the block to share his life. She didn't really want to know, but deep down she couldn't help herself.

"Haven't you ever come close to meeting Miss Right?" she quizzed.

"A soul mate?" He gave a bitter laugh. "You've got to be joking." As soon as it was out there she felt bad for asking. Just like her mother and her grandmother's imperfect love lives, Alex's parents' marriage hadn't been a match made in heaven. Still before Marcus had shattered her hopes, she'd remained optimistic about love, so why should Alex let Drake and Cassandra spoil his chances of happiness? "The One is a flawed concept. Isn't that what you said?"

"Well … yes … but," she stumbled over her words, not wanting to confess all about Marcus.

"Here's the thing." He swept a hand through his hair. "True love in Hollywood doesn't really exist. It's a fiction like practically everything else that happens there. Take Nick and Ella Swift, for example."

"That's not fake?"

"Sure it is. Nick's love life is a publicity stunt. And Ella's a willing accessory."

"Oh, I see."

"No, Maggie. I don't think you do see. Nick and Ella are a publicist's dream. Being seen out and about at the right places with the right people? Great. Everyone's happy. Get papped at the wrong place with the wrong person?" He hesitated, frowning. "Well, actually, that can be good publicity too. It depends."

"It's not an exact science?"

"Precisely. And it makes any kind of meaningful relationship impossible." He stared at the horizon. "It does for me, at any rate." He stood tall, dark and steadfast, sea spray flying in his face. Her heart lurched. She stumbled and grabbed tighter onto the handrail. Alex put a steadying arm around her. Their bodies swayed together with the heaving waves. "If you must know," he said quietly. "There was someone. Rachel. She was a hand model.

And a jewelry designer. And a cocktail waitress."

"I like the sound of Rachel."

"Yeah. You'd have liked Rachel. She was a bit like … Well, yeah."

"What happened?"

"We were together for about a year. She moved in with me. Her picture started to appear in the tabloids. It freaked her out. She didn't like it. The final straw came when I was on location in Europe filming a perfume ad. The press announced our engagement." He choked out a sarcastic laugh. "It was news to both of us. She went nuts. Said the papers knowing more about her life than she did was intolerable." Tension rippled through his shoulders. "By the time I got back to LA she'd moved out. She didn't want to talk about it. She ended it by text."

"Just like that?"

"Just like that." Alex smiled. "It turned out the only part of her she wanted to share with the world was her hands. And who could blame her?"

"You always did hate publicity. It must make things difficult."

"Not everyone hates it. There was the TV executive's daughter. She let me wine and dine her until she found a bigger fish to fry. She loved the spotlight so much she kept a scrapbook. Go figure! And then there was the voiceover artist who begged me to get her a role in *Mercy*."

"Did you?"

Alex nodded. "Uh-huh. She dumped me very loudly in her made-for-cartoons voice the day she walked on set …" He mimicked the actress squeakily as if he'd been messing about with helium. "And got several column inches to show for it."

Maggie clapped her hand to her mouth to stifle her giggles. "Oh Alex. I'm sorry."

"You're smirking behind that hand. Admit it."

"Only because you made the voice-over girl sound so funny."

"It's alright for you. You've never had your heart broken." He laughed, and it rang hollow. There was silence from Maggie. She looked away, her mood cool. Alex reached out and touched her chin, gently turning her head to face him. "I'm an idiot," he said, his eyes fixed on hers. "That's what this is all about. This 'having a baby by yourself'. Someone hurt you." The dawning of her reality shadowed his face. "What happened?"

"I met someone," she confessed. "His name was Marcus. He took me over and organized the life out of me. He had a five-year plan. It was all mapped out. He had a spreadsheet." Alex winced, but he didn't say anything. "I know." She nodded, acknowledging that it was kind of wrong, not her thing at all. "The thing is – I thought I was happy. We got engaged on schedule, we were going to get married, have kids. The whole package. It was going to be perfect. Note – going to be." She'd been blind to the fact that it actually wasn't. "One day I walked into our flat and found him in bed with someone. They had wine." She pictured the scene in her mind as she spoke. "And candles, and there were torn-off clothes all over the floor." She coughed. Her voice had gone hoarse because she was having difficulty getting the words out. "I was a twit. The first thing I did when I walked in the door was pick up a ripped-off button from the carpet, and I was thinking, "What's going on?"" She paused, wondering why she was telling him this, and unable to stop now it was out there. "It was as if the floor fell away from beneath me." Her world had disintegrated. Instead of swishing her hand through the air, she curled it into a fist so tight the nails dug into her palm. "Poof." She uncurled her fingers. "My future vanished in a puff of smoke."

"Just. Like. That." Alex appeared indignant on her behalf. "When did this happen?"

"About three years ago. A month or so before my grandma died," she said sadly. "The irony of it! She'd been happy for me. She thought I was going to break the Plumtree women's run of bad luck with men with Marcus. I didn't have the heart to tell her she'd been right all along."

"Oh, Maggie. I'm sorry."

She pushed a strand of hair behind her ear. "I didn't tell anyone at the time. Not even Layla."

She'd kept it in – pretended everything was fine. When Marcus was a no-show at the funeral, she'd had to say something, so she'd crossed her fingers against the white lie and told everyone that they'd had a mutual parting of the ways.

Alex steered her into the shelter of the cabin. They sat close together in silence, huddled on a wooden bench. On the way back to Boston, going into the wind, the boat thrashed against the waves. The real storm was in Maggie's heart. If she'd kept her distance, she could have done the styling job and left. She'd been captivated by Alex. She'd reacted to him like they'd been apart ten days, not ten years. Now he'd rumbled her. She'd fessed up about Marcus and she felt certifiably stupid. Again. Just like the day she'd walked in on him and his lover.

"I know you saw something in him you loved." He spoke softly, his jaw hard set, every facial muscle tight. "You'll have to forgive me, Maggie, but I think he was a tosser. He wasn't right for you. He was the wrong one." He stared at the grey sea. "The guy for you is still out there."

"If he is," she laughed, "he's keeping himself well hidden." *Concealed below the surface, like a whale.* She smiled brightly up at him. What she'd liked most about Marcus was his sense of certainty, right down to the spreadsheet with their future on it. Only, as it happened, he wasn't certain about the one thing that mattered – love. He'd pleaded for a second chance, called the affair a hiccup. For Maggie his hiccup was non-negotiable. She'd rather have no love than a watered-down, unfaithful version. "Anyway, I don't need a man. He'd just get in the way. I've made plans."

If she played her cards right she could make the most of the opportunity that had landed in her lap when Alex had invited her to New York. It was high time she got noticed. She'd do her utmost to sparkle on the red carpet – in a little black dress, naturally. She loved being a behind-the-scenes person, but Alex gave her the confidence to believe that she could be more. She wasn't a rejected child any longer. Or a cheated-on fiancée. She could dare to come out from the shadows where she'd learned to hide.

# Chapter Nine

"Two people can't get together after a decade and expect things to start over as if they'd pressed an invisible pause button."

Alex and Nick were jogging in Central Park. In shorts, tees, dark shades and baseball caps nobody paid them any attention. They were just two guys – running. Balmy September sunshine dappled the trees with light and shade. Only a few paint-box spatters of yellow and red amongst the green hinted at the fall colors to come. Nick was in an upbeat mood. He'd tied up his movie deal. Finally, he and Alex were on the same page. He'd conceded that Alex's leaving *Mercy* had pulled the plug on the show at precisely the right time.

"Correct me if I'm wrong. She's based in London. So are you. And you used to have the hots for each other."

"Promise me that if the movie roles dry up you won't take up professional match-making."

"Why not?"

"She's having a donor-sperm baby."

Nick's mouth gaped. "Man. What are the chances? Why's she done that?"

"Because she wants to."

Alex didn't add because she doesn't believe in The One. He'd already said too much. His stride lengthened. He ran as if he was trying to get away from something. Nick matched his pace. Somewhere through the trees he heard the shrieks of happy children coming from the adventure playground. They got closer and he could see that kids were splashing about in a water feature. They jogged on, only to find themselves circumnavigating the tots' playground, where cute babies dangled in bucket swings and tiny kids toddled about in the sandbox. He didn't usually notice kids unless they were going feral in a restaurant or screaming on a plane. Suddenly, they were everywhere – being cute.

"You used to be pretty into her."

Alex drained the bottle of mineral water he was carrying and tossed the empty into a trash can. Nick seemed contrite, but he knew his brother well. If he could use a piece of information to his advantage, he probably would.

"The past is a no-go zone."

"You're not hooking up, then?"

"There's no going back to zero."

"That's too bad. She's awesome. And she's good at what she does. She was in her element in Boston." Alex ran faster, so Nick shouted after him, "Since honesty is the order of the day, if I'm not mistaken, she's still into you."

Alex suppressed his smile. He looked back over his shoulder. "Don't go there."

Nick ignored the warning.

"Let me see if I've got this right. You and Maggie are on separate paths."

Alex nodded, showing Nick nothing but the back of his head. "Uh-huh."

"If you and Maggie have moved on too far in life for there to be any chance of getting together, what exactly is she doing here with you in New York?"

Alex laughed. *Good question.* "We're just friends."

Back on a path through trees, the brothers jogged in silence until Nick stopped suddenly. He pulled off his baseball cap and pushed his shades up onto his blonde head. Running on the spot, Alex caught a glint in his brown eyes. It wasn't the usual mischief.

"What if 'just friends' just isn't enough?"

"I've no intention of wrestling with the 'what if' factor. Just friends will have to be enough. We're networking."

"If you say so," Nick called after him as he ran on, leaving his brother in his dust. Alex didn't see the disbelieving smile on his twin's face, but he sensed it. Right now Maggie was in his hotel suite getting red-carpet-ready. So what if the attraction was still there? He could control it, even if he didn't want to.

He still wanted to ask her for some style advice, get her to make him over. He could trust her not to dream up anything too bizarre. She'd be a reliable person to have on his side.

He shouldn't have kissed her on the beach. He'd been selfish. He'd done what he felt like in the moment, exactly as he had the last time he'd been with Maggie. Reality had kicked in. She'd been hurt. She was having a baby. She deserved to find the man of her dreams – a guy who'd be in it for the long haul. Apparently she didn't want to. Whatever. The last thing she needed was a fling with him.

He'd locked down how he used to feel about her. He was in no danger there. Since the whale-watch trip his concern for her had deepened. Her ex had erased the color from her life – quite literally. And the memories that started creeping in when she did the pregnancy test, reminding him of how his mother hadn't coped with being a single mother, were alarming. Darn it. He didn't want to have to worry about her.

Alex's suite in the exclusive Manhattan hotel was bigger than Maggie's London apartment. She felt out of place in the splendid luxury. From the huge beds and the rich-mahogany dining table, to the furnishings, upholstered in sumptuous shades of gold, the overdose of showy comfort made her uncomfortable. The view was awesome; she had to give it that. It looked out over the treetops of

Central Park. There was a telescope in one of the windows. She'd tried it out when they arrived. Meant for looking at the view, she'd used it to spy on people in the park.

Self-consciousness prickled through her, as if she was the one being inspected with a powerful telephoto lens. When she'd realized just how little time she'd have to get into tip-top style shape for the premiere she'd agreed to Alex calling in reinforcements.

Edwina Charles, uber-confident New York stylist was the result and she had Maggie quaking in her boots. She came with her own hair and make-up people. And they made a formidable team, all three looking as if they'd just stepped out from between the pages of a glossy magazine. They were totally look-at-me types, the antithesis of Maggie's personal blend-into-the-background ethos.

When Edwina had arrived at Alex's hotel suite with a bellhop in tow carrying four meticulously packaged designer dresses to choose from she'd been excited. When the wrappings were off and she'd taken in the fact that her request for an LBD had been ignored? Not so much. All four were red! Wearing red to a red-carpet event was notoriously difficult. There was a risk of clashing. Her confidence in her own styling beliefs whizzed right out the window. It was Alex's choice. Maggie's heart skittered and then her stomach churned as the fear of forcing herself out of her shell hit home.

"Oh. My. Giddy. Aunt. It's red, red, red. Or red!" She didn't try to hide her dismay. "I don't do color."

"You do now." Edwina, herself an artful combination of geometric-print trousers, an orange and purple top, and a bang-on-trend jacket, complete with platform shoes, dangly earrings, bangles, and a big, blingy ring, held two of the stunning dresses up close to the window and examined them in the daylight. "The question is … which shade of red will work best for you?"

She hung one of the dresses back on the rail. "I'm thinking not the tomato."

Maggie resisted the urge to debate the pronunciation of the

word tomato and break into song. But *"Let's call the whole thing off"* was on the tip of her tongue.

It was fine for Alex. He'd come jogging in, jump in the shower, and throw on a penguin suit. Done. The upside to this experience – if there was one – was that *now* she could identify with her clients, *now* she appreciated how much trust they put in her when they allowed her to plan their image, choose their clothes.

Instead of screaming "I hate me in red" and taking off on a jog around the park, she opted – albeit reluctantly – to go with the flow. She'd choose which dress she liked best and steer Edwina towards that. It would be a bit like doing her job in reverse.

"What do you think of this?" She pointed to the one she liked least.

"Hmmm." Edwina devoted her consideration to the short, sexy, diamante-encrusted red- velvet confection. It reminded Maggie of an upscale version of the Santa Girl outfit that Alex and Nick had teased her about in Boston. She didn't want to wind up wearing that.

"I like it." She crossed her fingers behind her back that Edwina would go for one of the other two.

Edwina narrowed her eyes and looked her up and down. Maggie crumpled inside. She felt like a worn-out cotton frock in the bottom of the laundry hamper.

"For a Christmas party – maybe, but it's September, so we're not there yet. Tonight's premiere requires something subtle, sophisticated. I want to get this right."

Maggie relaxed. She'd been scared of Edwina at first, but she was starting to feel intrigued about letting go of her style control. She could live with it – just this once.

"Which will it be?" Edwina eyed the dresses. The bangles on her wrist jingled as she ran her hand gently over the fabric and fluffed out the skirts, sizing up the two different shapes.

"They're both much too long." Maggie pointed out unhelpfully.

Edwina smiled sympathetically. "These gowns were designed for a six-foot model, not a five-foot-something stylist. Not to worry. We'll get around that."

Noticing the label of a designer she loved, Maggie's heart hammered. She'd used Amandine Kendal occasionally for her own clients; never ever dreaming that a day would actually come when she'd be wearing her herself. She held her breath. Both the dresses were gorgeous, but she really hoped Edwina would agree with her on this one.

"I wish I was in your shoes, Maggie. Which one do you prefer?"

"They're both lovely. But if it's up to me to choose, I'd pick the Amandine Kendal."

"Bravo." Edwina clapped her hands together. Her bangles jangled. "Good choice. My work here is done."

Maggie hugged her. "You're a twenty-first-century fairy godmother. I feel like Cinderella."

Edwina swept a jingle-jangle arm through the air grandly. "You shall go to the ball, my dear. There's just a little matter of a make-over to do before I send for a pumpkin and turn it into a carriage. By the time Alex gets back to the suite we'll have transformed you into a paparazzo's dream."

Hours later Maggie's usual trendy nail color had been replaced by a classic red. According to Edwina, it complemented her gorgeous designer gown magnificently. Her make-up was fabulous too. She'd insisted on keeping the lipstick as understated as a red could be. But since the words "red" and "understated" didn't really work well together, she'd drawn a deep breath and was going with the girly theme and praying that she didn't look like a man-eater. She couldn't believe what they'd done with her hair. She felt like a completely different person. The hair stylist had scattered a few sun-bleached highlights through her mop to terrific effect. Then she'd piled it up on her head, all soft and wispy, as if one breath of a breeze would send it tumbling, only it was so skillfully done and secure that nothing would shift it.

Finally it was time for the dress. She adored it. From the

intricately detailed embroidered lace of the sculpted bodice to the contrasting floaty silk skirt, it was the dress of Maggie's dreams. Only normally, she'd never have dreamed of actually wearing it – for real, outside of her imagination. It was enough to know that she could make that happen for other people.

Edwina had thought of everything. She'd located wispily brief red-lace undies and brought a size up and a size down in everything to be sure of getting the perfect fit. Maggie stepped into the dress. It was magical going from stylist to styled. Edwina zipped the impossible-to-reach zip and presented her with an outrageous pair of skyscrapers to finish off the look.

"I can't wear those."

"You've no choice on this one, honey. There's about a foot and a half too much dress as it is. Without those heels you'll be trailing too much fabric."

Maggie slid her feet into the shoes, feeling like Cinderella again. When she walked into the grand living room and saw Alex waiting for her, her heart missed a beat. Way more Prince Charming than penguin, she had to admit that he carried off a tux to perfection.

"Will I do?" she asked. "Safe to say, I'd never have styled myself this way in a million years."

He looked at her with a lazy smile, as if Edwina and her girls weren't there. "Wow." He rumbled the word out on a long breath, adding with a cough, as if he'd suddenly realized they had company, "You scrub up well." There was no disguising the flicker of get-a-room heat in his gaze.

*We've got a room.*

# *Chapter Ten*

Maggie stood on the red carpet under the lighted canopy of the New York movie theater and breathed in. Flashes exploded all around. She felt for all the world like a princess. It was practically an out-of-body experience.

In her incredible skyscraper heels her head reached above Alex's shoulder for once. Even so, when they paused to pose for the cameras, several inches of scarlet silk made a puddle at her feet.

Alex looked as unreal as she felt. At home on the red carpet, he sizzled – every inch a star. Presenters and journalists vied for the celebrities' attention. Maggie fired off smiles in all directions, as if she'd been born to it. Inside, her heart was beating like crazy. The phrase "deer in the headlights" sprang to mind. It didn't come close to covering how she felt behind the paparazzi-ready smile. What she lacked in *savoir faire*, Alex made up for. He had enough confidence for them both.

"Alex Wells, over here!"

Alex, Alex, Alex. His name rang in her ears. Devoted fans and vaguely interested passersby leaned across the barriers holding up phones, capturing him for their social media pages.

"Alex, Kerry Sheldon – *Manhattan Tonight Show* – can I have a word?"

Alex took Maggie's hand and stopped in front of a television camera. His fingers touching hers sent waves of heat pulsing through her. She smiled affably as Alex chatted away, charming the pants off the presenter. Maggie's fixed smile had started to make her feel like a Barbie doll, when all of a sudden the focus turned to her.

The presenter shoved a microphone in her face and shot a question at her. "Magenta Plumtree – who are you wearing tonight?"

"Me? Ohhh …" She glanced around in a daze. *Oh my.* "This is Amandine Kendal." She struggled to hide the tremble in her voice.

"And tell me, Magenta, did you style yourself for this evening's premiere?" A supercilious note in the presenter's voice made her suspicious. "Red on the red carpet. That's a brave look to pull off for a lady who's never walked the red carpet before!" Maggie gulped. Was she being got at by this pushy woman? She'd smarmed the words out making her insult sound as if it had been intended as a compliment. Normally so far behind the scenes, Maggie had never had to deal with any of this mad palaver before. She hesitated, her mouth opening and closing like a goldfish.

That instant she felt Alex's strong arm slide protectively around her waist. Feeling him close, helping keep her nerves steady, she floated on air. "I styled Magenta tonight," he cut in, rescuing her just in time. "She's here as my guest." He glared directly into the camera with the full potency of his blue irises. "She looks fabulous." He turned and moved away, his arm tightly banded around Maggie. "If you'll excuse us, please, we've got a movie to see."

As he swept her away from the cameras into the lobby, Maggie caught a glimpse of the presenter's face. Stunned, she was now the one doing the goldfish impression. Alex dipped his head, his mouth so whisperingly close to her ear that she sensed the heat of his breath on her neck. "You look amazing."

Inside, the place was a huge movie palace with chandeliers, gold trimmings, red walls, and plush red carpets. Who knew she'd blend so easily in red?

A waiter approached with a tray of champagne. Alex took two flutes and went to hand one to Maggie. She shook her head, shrugging apologetically.

"Oh, yeah. I almost forgot." He put both glasses back and lifted two sparkling-water-filled flutes from another passing tray."

"Good old fizzy water."

"Cheers." He clinked Maggie's glass with his and smiled at her in a way that made her already wobbly stomach slosh like a washing machine on the delicates cycle. "Listen. We don't have to stay, you know. We can do the rounds and slip off before the movie starts."

"We can't do that."

"Yes we can. The stars will be doing it. They'll do a little spiel at the beginning and by the time it's over they'll be happily downing cocktails in some hip bar, or halfway to LA, or London, or wherever they're doing their next promo. Believe me, they don't always stay to watch the movie."

A weird, flat feeling befuddled Maggie. "Do you mean to say that I've spent virtually the entire day getting dolled up like a dog's dinner just to step onto the red carpet and leave? I don't even get to see the film?" Alex gave her a very sexy grin. "What?"

She could have sworn she heard him mutter "lucky dog". She felt her skin start to glow in a shade that almost certainly matched her outfit perfectly.

"Fine," he said. "We'll stay and watch the movie. I haven't seen it yet. We made it about a year and a half ago. For all I know, the bit with me in ended up on the cutting-room floor."

"Hardly," she pointed out, "If you and Nick weren't in it, they wouldn't expect you to be here all bright-eyed and bushy-tailed, now would they?"

"All what?" Alex laughed. "It's not an animation, Maggie. I'm not some woodland creature."

"Well, okay then, let me rephrase that – looking all sultry and sexy – the way you do. Better?"

He quirked an eyebrow. "It might be if I thought you meant it."

"Well, I do mean it. Just not in a proactive, I want to go to bed with you, kind of way." *Liar!* "More in a helping out an old mate who happened to need a plus one for a film premiere kind of a way – and he happens to be looking pretty flipping ..." She couldn't find an appropriate, non-committal, not-interested-in-that-way word. "Dapper."

"Dapper!" Alex scoffed, over-doing the British accent. He glanced about the room furtively. "I say, old bean. Look at all these dapper chaps. Are we in a period drama? Spiffing!"

If it wouldn't have put her in danger of toppling off her high heels, Maggie would have aimed a kick at one of his designer-clad shins. Fortunately an announcement distracted her.

"Ladies and gentlemen." The disembodied voice was very grand. "Please take your seats for the New York Premiere of *The Magician of Arden.*"

Exactly as Alex predicted, the stars of the movie introduced the film and promptly vanished. Maggie had styled many important clients, but being a guest at the same event as these one-hundred-per-cent million-dollar Hollywood people took her breath away – even if they did disappear in a puff of smoke the minute the lights went down.

When the film began Alex shifted uncomfortably in his seat. He and Maggie had been placed next to Nick and their co-star Ella from *Mercy of the Vampires.* Nick and Ella made an appearance towards the end of the movie, but Alex's cameo came right at the beginning and he was dreading seeing himself on the big screen. The thought of having to view his performance under the scrutiny of a cinema fit to burst with celebrities and media people was excruciating. He totally got why the leading actors preferred to duck out early – quite apart from the brain freeze of having to watch their own movie far too many times than was good for you.

Stunning, Maggie looked the part – the perfect mystery hot date. He was glad she'd come to New York. She was easy to be with. She didn't play games, manipulate. He could get to like this friends thing – if it wasn't such a challenge to his libido. This weekend was about closing an unfinished chapter, not starting something new.

He wanted to be cool with her donor-baby decision. His own feelings, not knowing who his biological father was, colored his view. She didn't believe in one man forever, but what if that changed? What if Maggie found The One? Would he love her child? Or would he be the baby's dad on sufferance? He'd assured her that Mr. Right was out there. But what if he came along for a while, only to give up and abandon them like Drake had done. His mother had lost the plot, an emotional wreck, unable to haul herself back from a broken heart, incapable of being responsible for two small children.

He'd been watching the screen, taking in nothing that was happening up there as the whirlpool of concerns for Maggie spun in his head, when he twigged that this was his moment.

He leant close and whispered in her ear. "Okay, get ready, this is my bit." Her hair looked different up. It brushed his face, as soft as the silken threads in the fabric of her way-too-sexy dress. Her signature perfume, wild flowers, stirred him.

She touched his forearm, reassuringly. "Brace yourself!" Typical. There was no hiding anything from her. She'd picked up on his lack of interest in watching himself. She'd always been good at reading him.

He was looming like a human elephant on the big screen when Maggie clutched tightly at his sleeve. A sideways glance in the darkness confirmed that all was not well. While one hand tugged at his arm, she clasped the other firmly over her mouth.

"Maggie? Are you going to throw up? I didn't think my performance was that bad."

Maggie nodded frantically and dragged him to his feet. They squeezed out of the row of seats past Nick and Ella and headed for the exit as fast as Maggie's feet in her stilettos would allow them.

As she made a dash for the restroom one high heel caught in

a hot-air heating grid in the floor and snapped. Disastrously, as she stumbled to keep her balance, the other heel tangled in her excessively long dress. There was a horrendous rip and a tear wrenched up the seam, exposing one shapely leg.

She ploughed on in her state of disarray. When she burst through the door of the Ladies he followed right along, watching in dismay as she leant over a washbasin and vomited.

*Great!*

She remained doubled over the sink and ran the water. Less than useless, he stepped forward and touched her soft, bare shoulders lightly. He massaged the nape of her neck while she washed her face. He passed her a paper towel.

Maggie stood up straight. She was pale and wide-eyed and her fancy up-styled hair resembled a disheveled bird's nest. "Sorry."

"I'd have thought if anyone was going to throw up it would be me. I'm the one who should be sick with nerves."

"As if!" Her eyes glinted. A faint smile played on her lips. "Morning sickness, I'm afraid."

"It's half past nine at night."

"It's a figure of speech. I read up about it. First-trimester nausea can happen any time of the day. I guess I'm a night-sickness person." She shrugged.

"Okay now?" He stopped rubbing her neck, wrapped his arms round her and pulled her close. She rested her head on his shoulder. He rested his chin on the top of her head. She felt more like a waif than the glamorous woman he'd walked into the cinema with earlier that evening.

"Uh-huh," she said. "Shall we go back in? I'm fine now."

"Nah." There was a lightness about being with Maggie. He felt like a student bunking off from a lecture. "Let's not bother."

"I want to see what happens."

Her eye make-up had smudged, making her eyes bigger than ever. Bare-shouldered, she looked pale and vulnerable, and he didn't want to stop holding her. A loose wisp of hair fell across her face. He pushed it behind her ear. His fingers brushed her cheek as he did so. A tiny diamond earring glimmered in her earlobe. "I'll send you the DVD when it comes out." He'd been selfish expecting her to be his plus one at this event. He'd been thinking about himself when he'd struck this bargain with her. Some friend. He released her from his arms. Reluctantly.

"Come on. Let's get out of here. The hotel's only a couple of blocks. And you could use some fresh air. We can walk."

Maggie gathered two fistfuls of scarlet fabric and lifted the hem of her dress, revealing two slender ankles and feet with toes painted in the same shade as her fingernails, in shoes that, even with one broken heel, made his pulse race. He was quite sure this wasn't the effect she'd intended.

She slipped out of the shoes and picked them up. "I can't walk anywhere in these." Without the help of the heels, the ripped dress created an even bigger pool of fabric on the floor. "The designer will be apoplectic when she finds out what I've done to his dress." She gave a dismal sigh. "I'll never work again."

"There's no need to be so melodramatic." He held up a finger. "Wait right here."

Deflated, Maggie looked around the Ladies. There was nothing to sit on. In a place like this she'd have expected a velvet-covered chaise longue at the very least. She went into one of the cubicles, lowered the toilet lid and sat on it. This was a far cry from the way the evening had begun, arriving in a stretch limo to the adulation of the press.

She felt ropey, and out of her depth making a fool of herself in Alex's A-list world, but deep down she was certain of one thing. Starting a brand-new family was the right way to go. Her friends were holding out for the fairy tale. That was fine for them. She wished them luck. Maggie knew that there was no point. She'd given it a go; it hadn't worked out. Alex was wrong. There was no guy out there in the world just waiting for her to find him. That's why she was getting on with having a baby. With a dad who wasn't there when the baby was conceived. It was a top solution. She wouldn't have to deal with any more Marcus-style rubbish.

After a wait that felt like an eternity, a forthright knock on the restroom door made her jump, "Alex?"

He marched in. "Here." He handed her a plastic bag with the name of a souvenir store on it. "Change into these."

She pulled out an I Heart NY t-shirt and some leggings emblazoned with stars and stripes. "It's all they had," he said, completely unapologetic. "I'll wait outside."

"Wait. What about shoes?"

"You'll have to go barefoot."

She began to protest "How am I supposed to walk without …?"

He cut her off. "Hurry up. I've got us some transport."

The tee was extra extra-large. What was he thinking? She studied herself in a full-length mirror and pulled out the excess material, trying to imagine how she would look when she was nine months pregnant. Perhaps he'd been thinking ahead with the size choice. She eyed herself with displeasure.

Harrumphing with annoyance, she left the restroom and went to join Alex in the red and gold lobby. Barefoot, in stars and stripes leggings, she felt like such a letdown until she saw Alex and her heart cartwheeled. He was wearing a matching I Heart NY tee over his dress shirt. He cloaked his jacket around her shoulders, took her by the hand, laced his fingers into hers, and together they walked out of the movie theater to stand in the full glare of the canopy lighting.

A photographer appeared out of nowhere and pop, they'd been papped.

Maggie groaned. "See what you've done?" She splayed her arms in exasperation. Her balled-up designer dress dangled in the plastic souvenir store bag and the shoes that would make many women green with envy swung nonchalantly on the end of one of Alex's long fingers. Apart from the broken heel, they looked quite attractive there. "If anyone's crazy enough to publish that, it'll do wonders for my reputation."

Alex laughed.

*The cheek.* When she'd accepted Alex's invitation, she'd been hoping that any publicity that came out of this weekend might raise her profile, get her noticed, and help her land a TV styling job she had her eye on back in the UK. It was one of her new projects, something she hardly dared pin her hopes on. When she'd said yes to Alex she'd been counting on a side order of glamorous press photos.

"Where's the taxi?" There was a noticeable absence of yellow cabs, but a Central Park horse and carriage stood at the curb. Alex scooped her up into his arms. Caught by surprise, she had no alternative but to twist her arms around his neck. Held against his chest, his strong biceps tensed, she felt as light as a bag of popcorn.

"Your carriage awaits." He carried her to the curbside and hoisted her into the horse-drawn carriage. Her eyes must have looked like they'd popped out on stalks. Dressed like a twenty-first century Cinderella after midnight, she ruefully imagined that any minute the carriage would revert to being a pumpkin, the driver would become a frog and the white horse would turn into a rat. She shivered.

A flash popped relentlessly. The rogue paparazzo was still lurking somewhere in the vicinity.

"Where's security when you need them?" Alex grumbled ironically.

"Gone to call the police department, I shouldn't wonder. What possessed you? You'll get us arrested."

Alex chuckled. Maggie's mind churned. So much for her trademark fashion-conscious, but unremarkable, image.

"Magenta Plumtree – who styled you this evening?" She mimicked the voice of the presenter who'd interviewed them earlier. "Who designed your tacky leggings and the fabulous outsize t-shirt?"

"It'll probably be on the internet by the time we get back to the hotel."

"That's not helping."

"Don't worry about it. It's no big deal."

The carriage driver made a clicking noise with his tongue, snapped the reins and the horse clip-clopped forward. The sudden movement unbalanced her. She wobbled. Alex's arm slipped around her. The electric sensation of his warm body next to hers was enough to make her delirious. She ignored the pool of sweet heat at her core. She opted to argue with him. It was safer ground than facing how hot all that hard muscle and handsomeness was. And how overwhelmingly attractive she found him.

"That's easy for you to say. I'm a stylist, for flip's sake. Fashion's what I do. Why do you think I work so hard to stick with a neutral image? It's not an accident, you know. It's to keep my image low-profile. That way I can concentrate on giving clients my full fashion focus."

"Relax. There's nothing wrong with your fashion focus. Everyone loves what you do." His eyes glittered. "We're having an I Heart New York moment."

"You don't get it. I've just been photographed on a red carpet with a big-name celebrity looking like a tourist who just happened to be passing by and fancied getting a photo souvenir. And as if that wasn't bad enough, now, for the icing on the cake, you've got us trotting around Manhattan in a horse and carriage making a spectacle of ourselves. I'm going to look ridiculous if this goes up on the net. Is hi-jacking a horse and carriage from Central Park even legal? We'll more than likely end up spending the night locked in a police cell. You'll not be splitting your sides laughing then."

"I thought you could use some air and I wanted you to feel comfortable. That's not exactly a crime." Her heart fluttered. He'd done the best he could to be considerate – even if the I Heart NY t-shirt and hallucinogenic leggings did fall well short of the mark. "It didn't occur to me that anyone would notice. Let alone a pap. I thought they'd all gone."

She'd made a complete shambles of the night. An uncontrollable urge to giggle bubbled up inside her. She squashed it. "I guess I'm not cut out for this red-carpet stuff."

Maggie shut Alex out. Had saying yes to this New York extravaganza been a huge mistake? The sounds, the lights, the non-stop pace of the city viewed from a hi-jacked horse-drawn carriage felt exciting and lovely – and bizarre. Never mind I Heart New York. She was having a Cinderella-gone-horribly-wrong moment.

# Chapter Eleven

*Prince Charming does not exist.*

Maggie's grandmother had drummed into her that no matter how scintillatingly wonderful the Mr. Perfects of this world might seem, she should make no mistake – The One was a myth. Like aliens, unicorns, vampires, and every other fantasy out there. In the end, it turned out that she'd have loved to have been proved wrong. The thought made Maggie smile.

Safe in the cossetted luxury of Alex's hotel suite, she went directly to the bathroom to brush her teeth and freshen up, sorry that she'd ruined the evening, the dress, the mood. She should stick to creating images for other people. She'd stepped out of her comfort zone and things had gone pear-shaped.

She joined Alex in the living room. Hands in pockets, he stood at the window glowering at the dark treeline below, the planes of his face reflected in the glass, spookily distant. His broad shoulders and the long lines of his athletic body made her fizz.

This friends thing wasn't working.

When *Mercy of the Vampires* had taken off, she used to wonder if she'd ever meet Alex again. She'd imagined scenarios – bumping into him at a party or in a pub. And more fanciful ones like walking on an empty beach and finding him by the sea. He'd hurt her. She'd been falling in love with him and he hadn't bothered to say goodbye.

Her heart swelled, filling up her chest and tightening her throat. She wasn't over that will-we-won't-we thing they'd had. Why couldn't the attraction she felt for Alex in the here and now be the same shallow variety that made Jago fans the world over sigh wistfully and move right along to the next thing on their real-life agenda?

Maybe a fling with Alex would be mind-blowingly amazing. She'd love to know.

Okay, so in the Plumtree world there'd been a distinct lack of Prince Charmings. She couldn't have Alex forever, but more than anything she didn't want to go through life wondering what if? It was time to stop hanging on to the fact that once upon a time they'd been friends and let him be her fantasy man.

Alex unknotted his bow tie and sank onto a squashy sofa.

"Let's order room service."

She didn't need to think about it. The empty space in her stomach reminded her of the hole in the middle of a donut.

"Oh yes puh-leeese. I'm ravenous."

He passed her the menu and she pretended to think about it, but she knew exactly what she wanted. Needed, even.

"I'll have a cheeseburger with fries and ketchup and those little green things. What d'you call them?"

"Pickles?" Alex prompted.

"No, not pickles. Whatd'youmacallits? Like the London skyscraper? She snapped the menu closed. "Gherkins!"

"Really?" He sent her a questioning look.

"Yes, really." She bit her bottom lip.

"You hate pic … gherkins. You always used to pick them out and leave them."

"Well tonight I want gherkins."

"Gherkins it is!" There was a big, super-sexy grin on Alex's face. A flame of deep heat uncurled inside her. She wished she could put it down to dodgy pregnancy hormones. His smile and her fizz all but killed off her hunger pangs.

There were three big comfy sofas in the room. She could have had one all to herself. Instead, she plonked herself next to Alex. Their eyes locked and held in almost telepathic stillness.

Alex coughed. He got up, walked to the polished wood desk and switched on the lamp. The light cast shadows through the fine petals of three giant hydrangea blooms arranged in a glass vase. The flowers with their green leaves were three times the size of the ones that grew in her cottage garden in Cornwall. Alex, distancing himself, triggered a pang of uncertainty that shivered through Maggie.

"I don't eat burgers much – normally." She started to babble. "Hardly ever – actually. I can't even remember when I last had one. But tonight, for some reason …" She twisted a wave of hair around one finger. "I think I'll die if I don't get a burger."

"With gherkins." Alex lifted the phone. "Get me the emergency services." His lovely deep voice rumbled theatrically into the receiver. "We need a burger and we need it fast."

He dialed room service for real and placed the order. "Oh, and don't forget the gherkins," he reminded the person on the other end of the line. There was a pause. "Sorry … pickles. It's a matter of life and death."

Maggie curled up on the plush gold sofa island. Emptiness that wasn't hunger struck her. Her baby plan lacked a vital ingredient. Someone to share stuff. The highs. The lows. By default, Alex had taken on the role. He'd been there when she did the pregnancy test. He'd held her when she was sick. He'd made fun of her craving. It felt good. Too good.

He had hired the adjoining room to his suite for her. A communicating door linked the two. A knot of jealously clenched her gut. With other women – the ones that were lovers not friends – a second bedroom would not be necessary. She tortured herself a little wondering how many nights of passion he'd spent in hotel suites like this one.

A practically mute, robotic waiter arrived. He went quick-smart into the separate dining room and placed a bowl of delicate cream roses in the center of the solid mahogany dining table. Polished to such a shine, Maggie caught him admiring his reflection in the wood as he set down the burgers, which sat grandly under silver domes waiting for them to tuck in. She stopped worrying about being out of her comfort zone. Sitting opposite Alex on a posh dining chair she gazed across the expanse of shiny wood. "I think we've just invented the most upmarket burger joint in Manhattan."

She lifted the silver dome and realized that she didn't fancy the pickled green things after all. She picked them out of her roll.

"I thought your life wouldn't be worth living if you didn't get whatd'youmacallits."

"I changed my mind." Her voice wobbled ruefully.

"You always were a bit contrary." His dark hair had fallen across his eyes. He tossed his head, supremely masculine.

"Alex?" she blurted. What she was about to say was totally contrary, but there was more in the air between them than the celebrity crush factor. "Can I get an upgrade?"

Alex glanced around the room with a puzzled expression. "I don't think so, Maggie. This is the best suite they've got."

She held back a giggle. "Not the room. Us." She looked down at her red nails. Resisting the urge to pick at the color, she looked up again. This wasn't about what-might-have-been. He could leave his barriers intact, hide behind Jago if he liked. "I want to upgrade from friends to fling."

Alex stiffened as if his spine had turned to solid steel. His eyes glinted, the blue irises practically turning storm grey in the half-light. "That's out of the question."

He pushed his plate away and stood up, made a move to walk off, changed direction, jerkily ploughed a hand into his thick hair. He frowned, his dark brows knitted. "Not every woman I'm photographed with finds her way into my bed." He shot her a scornful look. "Believe it or not, the playboy image isn't everything it's cracked up to be."

He rounded the table, pulled out the chair next to her and sat on it. "Look." His voice softened to a husky murmur. Something she couldn't read flickered on his face. "We should stick to friends. A fling would be a bad idea."

*A ve-ry bad idea.* That was the point. She didn't say so. Clearly, she was a lousy seductress. Mortified, she forced out a syrupy false giggle. "What was I thinking?" She rolled her eyes. "Me having a fling with TV's Hot Vampire Guy? I need my head examining."

"Hot? Vampire? Guy?" Alex fired her a condescending look. "Really?"

She bit her lip and nodded, squashed. So much for sizzling attraction. What was wrong with wanting a walk-away-with-no-regrets-when-it's-over fling? She could do utterly emotionless. She couldn't undo the fact that she'd been deluded. The chemistry had been one-way after all. Hey, the guy was a great actor.

After an awkwardly silent dinner, back in the softly lit sitting room, Alex paced. He had a copy of *Hamlet* in his hand and his nose buried in it, going over his lines. Out of the corner of his eye he saw Maggie, curled up on a sofa flicking through a magazine she patently wasn't reading. No longer a vision in red, she was still sexier than sexy, even in the goofy leggings and I Heart NY tee.

He'd said the wrong thing, handled it badly. He'd made her feel unattractive when the opposite was true. She was complicated. She was a mother-to-be and every time he thought about it the hot blood flowing in his veins turned to cold porridge. Beneath that monochrome image of hers she was vulnerable. And he was getting too involved – pregnancy tests, sickness, cravings. He was out of his depth.

On automatic he retreated behind his own stony mask.

He turned his back on her and glared out the window at the skyline. Muttering under his breath he reeled off some lines. His concentration was zero.

*Hot Vampire Guy. Damn it!*

He was desperate to let go of that image, show people the real Alex Wells. But he'd been living with the character for so long he wasn't sure who the "real" Alex was. He frowned at his script, read some more, straightening out the torment in his head. Playing Hamlet would be a dream come true and he was going to crash and burn. He couldn't shake off Jago. Every move, every look, every step across the stage, every word was Jago. He stared past his cold reflection in the glass. The moon was a couple of slivers short of a round cheese in the black sky. When he stepped onto the London stage the audience was going to see the cheesy vampire guy. He threw the script across the room. Maggie let out a yelp and caught it in midair before it took out the hydrangeas.

"Sorry, Maggie. I wasn't aiming at you."

"What's up?"

He'd spent meaningless nights with quite a few women for whom that question would have begged a suggestive quip. Not Maggie. The tension from his knock-back bristled between them.

"I'm murdering Hamlet. Every time I open my mouth, I hear Jago."

"You *are* a bit mid-Atlantic." Maggie shrugged. "But hey, you can fix that. It's what you trained to do."

An English education, followed by years based in LA had turned his accent into a hybrid. But he wasn't talking about received pronunciation, he had a voice coach for that. The problem with Jago lay deeper.

He folded himself onto the sofa next to her. "My accent is exceeeeedingly mid-Atlantic."

Maggie laughed at the extra dose of British oomph he added to his words, easing the atmosphere.

"It wasn't a hindrance in *Mercy*," he mused. "The reverse; it kinda helped."

"I don't see the problem."

"What if I walk on stage and all anyone sees is Jago?"

"Jago in a doublet and hose. Isn't that part of the appeal? The production's unique selling point?"

"You mean I just have to work with it."

"I doubt make-up will be up for giving Hamlet vampire fangs, but I don't think your audiences will complain if you bring a smidge of Jago to the role, do you?"

Alex laughed. He pulled Maggie into his arms and hugged her. "You're a genius."

Awkward, his arms sprang back, letting her go like a failed turn on an arcade candy grabber.

"I can help with your lines." She opened the script. "Okay. Let me see. It's Act One, Scene Two, and we're in the council chamber in the castle. There's a flourish of trumpets." She made a trumpety ta-da-da-da-da noise. "Enter blah, blah, blah and last of all you, *Prince HAMLET*. You're dressed in black, with downcast eyes."

Alex suppressed a chortle. Her am-dram approach was too funny.

He ran a hand over his newly stubbling jaw. "Just give me the cue, please, Maggie, or we'll be here from now until Christmas."

They rattled through Alex's scene, then moved on and did the bit where Hamlet sees his father's ghost. By the end of Act Two, Maggie was flagging and yawning. It was very late. She passed Alex the book. He paced, reading aloud, while she curled up on the sofa and plumped a cushion under her head. Concentrating on the play, he ploughed a hand into his hair. "I'm ready for Act Three. You're Ophelia." He held out the script to Maggie, but she was fast asleep.

The place where he was supposed to have a heart lurched. Maggie was right. Jago was a marketing ploy. He could see past it, thanks to her. Make it work. To get to Hamlet, he'd need to dig inside himself. He'd stored up a deep well of hurt. He should put it to use and channel the confusion he'd felt growing up in the drama of his parents' real-life soap, into Hamlet's angst. The stone in his chest knocked against his ribcage.

His mother's television career had sky-rocketed about a year after he and Nick were born. A highbrow British actor, Drake Wells, landed a couple of great roles in LA. He won a prestigious award and for a while he got to write his own ticket. He was frequently away on location, but when he came home every day was like Christmas. Smarting from having to deal with her husband's doesn't-count-on-location attitude to his marriage, their mother didn't share their euphoria. Much too little to know about the infidelities and the crushingly public humiliation that he inflicted on Cassandra, the twins lapped up his over-the-top attention, a hail of toys and trips to theme parks. When he left for good the fun stopped, and worse, she went completely off the rails. She'd been admitted to rehab and they'd been cared for by relatives. Rejected by their father and separated from their mother, Alex had felt it was his job to protect Nick. Later, when their mother was out of rehab and back in their life, every time things got tough in the media glare, he felt responsible.

Perhaps because she still craved Drake's approval, Cassandra had decided to send them to a British boarding school. Mostly, at sports days and rugby matches, there were gaps where the Wells parents should have been. When he graced the school plays with his presence, Drake would sit looking dour in the audience, and sneer disapprovingly afterwards, belittling his sons and pointing out everything about the production he considered wrong.

Cassandra's visits had always been scheduled to coincide with press tours in Europe. It was during an alcohol-fuelled outburst when they were thirteen that the truth about Drake had come out. She'd flown in from somewhere, having arranged for a taxi to pick them up from school and deliver them to the airport. While she'd been waiting she'd fallen off the wagon. That's how they'd learned that the man whose name was on their birth certificates did not share their genes – in an inebriated ramble in Departures at Heathrow. "Drake's not your real dad." Alex got chills thinking about that day. "He might claim that you're his sons, but he can go take a running jump off a high cliff." She cracked some lame joke about denim genes and spilled the contents of her handbag on the concourse floor. In the scramble to wrangle lipsticks, crumpled till receipts and small change, the revelation had been brushed aside, but it was out there. Everything slid out of perspective for Alex because suddenly his father's rejection made total sense.

He knelt down next to the sleeping Maggie and touched her shoulder. "Maggie," he whispered. Out for the count, she didn't stir. Deciding against leaving her to spend the night on the sofa, he got to his feet and carefully scooped her into his arms. She moaned softly and her scent hit his senses. He steeled himself against his attraction. Shouldering open the door to her room, he carried her in and placed her gently on the turned-back bed. He covered her with the marshmallow-light duvet and for a moment he ached to take back his rejection, drop the mask of indifference. Touching two fingers to his lips he blew Maggie a kiss and closed the door quietly.

Shut away from her, he let out a disgruntled breath. He had to admire her confidence in starting a family on her own. He didn't want kids. He wouldn't know how to be a dad, although surely he couldn't be as diabolical as Drake. His heart squeezed thinking about Maggie's pregnancy. He needn't worry about her. She wouldn't go to pieces the way his mother did. No matter what life threw at her, she'd stay strong.

Being at a red-carpet event had felt miles better with Maggie. Even before she got sick he'd cared more about her than he did about the paps and the outside world. She'd given him a fresh take on making Jago work alongside *Hamlet*. He'd have to be careful. Maggie helping him channel Hamlet's pain was one thing, but he couldn't let her into his heart. Turning her down had been hard, but he'd done the right thing. Alone in his own room, he stripped off his I Heart NY tee and threw it into a corner. It landed on a chair, the red heart glaring at him.

# *Chapter Twelve*

Alex knocked on the door of Maggie's bedroom carrying a tray laden with a breakfast: orange juice, coffee, and buttery croissants so flaky and delicious they could have been teleported in straight from a boulangerie in France.

"Wake up, Sleeping Beauty. I've got an action-packed day planned for you." Maggie sat up in the king-sized bed and plumped one of the fat pillows. He was wearing his solemn celebrity face, but by the sound of things her impetuous moment of madness had been forgotten. Her stomach churned. Embarrassment washed through her. She'd got carried away. Alex thought a fling was a terrible idea, but no one could blame a girl for trying.

"That sounds intriguing." She looked at him from beneath lowered lashes, pulled the corner off her croissant and popped it into her mouth, being careful not to drop crumbs on the bed linen.

"Have you ever taken time out to be a tourist in New York?"

"No." She met his eyes. "Never." She'd worked in the city lots, but her schedule had been too frenetic to take in the sights.

"Me neither." Alex grabbed a croissant and lolled on the end of her bed. Fresh from the shower, hair damp, his uber-masculine body made her pulse stutter. His spiced man smell knocked her sideways. *Mmm. Yum.* The hotel bathrobe gaped across his chest, revealing an expanse of bronze skin. "I've lost count how many times I've been in New York and not done the tourist stuff."

A coppery flake the size of a British two-pence coin fell onto the white duvet. Maggie picked it up between two red nails and put it back on the plate. She couldn't wait to change her nail color, start afresh.

"What's the plan?"

Alex suppressed a teasing half-smile. "It's a mystery tour. I'm not telling you what the plan is. You'll have to trust me."

First stop, the Statue of Liberty. They waited in line to take the ferry with the other tourists. With his dark glasses and upturned collar Alex remained incognito. Just before leaving the hotel, Maggie had stuffed *Hamlet* in her handbag and was flicking through the pages.

"So fill me in. Who's Polonius?" Maggie asked. She'd done *Hamlet* for A level, but that was a long time ago. "I've mostly forgotten it." She peered at the script. "And what's an arras?"

"It's a curtain and Polonius is Ophelia's father. He's eavesdropping behind the arras and Hamlet stabs him with his sword not knowing who it is."

"So Hamlet kills off his girlfriend's dad? That's not good."

"It's a tragedy."

Maggie nodded earnestly. "It certainly is."

They climbed the three hundred and fifty-four steps into Lady Liberty's crown, took photos of the Manhattan skyline, and talked more about *Hamlet* while they were up there.

In the afternoon they walked between the trees in Central Park, wandering aimlessly, along paths, over arches, and under bridges. Sometimes they stopped to run through a scene or two of the script. Maggie loved the splatters of color amongst the green where the leaves were just beginning to turn. By the Conservatory Water her heart twinged watching a little girl launch a sailboat with her dad. At the Alice in Wonderland sculpture, she let out a gasp of delight as kids clambered over the toadstools and clung to the White Rabbit's ears. A proud father hoisted his tiny tot onto the big toadstool. Maggie sucked in a breath. She couldn't miss what she'd never had. Her heart squeezed. Was she wrong to deprive her child of a father's love, right from the off? Because she'd grown up knowing she'd never meet her dad she hadn't had any qualms about it – until now.

Alex picked up on her preoccupation. "Is something wrong?" he asked. "Are you tired? Would you like to go back to the hotel?"

"It's not that." She shook her head. Suddenly dads were every-where. "Dadless is all I've ever known. I guess that's why I'm okay with the idea of a family that's a dad-free zone. Mine's not on my birth certificate. He might as well have been a sperm donor."

"You've taken a negative and turned it into a positive. I wish I could have half your optimism. The San Andreas fault would be hard-pushed to do more damage than my father."

Maggie's heart went out to him. When she'd known him before he wouldn't talk about his dad. Still, he had to be exaggerating. The name Drake Wells was revered. "I know you hated the things that got written in the tabloids, but he can't have been all bad. Surely?"

A muscle flickered in his face. "It's a waste of breath discussing my father. I don't measure up. I never have. I never will."

"My mum's the one I couldn't measure up for," she admitted. "If I'd been more like her, I don't think she'd have left. When she went to work in Spain my grandma overcompensated. She filled my days with fun stuff, like she was on a mission to make sure that I didn't feel unloved."

It had sort of worked. Despite her mum's rejection, she'd had no sense of being unwanted. There'd been postcards and presents, and although her mother refused to come home to Cornwall, her grandma had saved up for budget flights and taken her to Spain for holidays. But did she feel loved? What she'd felt in bucketfuls was gratitude, so she'd returned her grandmother's care by behaving impeccably, helping around the house, never being a nuisance. It wasn't until uni that she'd been free to be her real self. She'd stopped trying to match the wallpaper for a while. She'd started blending again since Marcus. At the heart of things she'd lost a vital part of her self-worth.

Maggie let go of Alex's hand. She loved the warmth of his touch, but she couldn't process being this close without wanting more. "Basically," she blurted, "What you call my optimism is nothing more than a refusal to be beaten by rejection."

"You don't have to do this solo, you know." He reached out with both hands and gently pushed her hair behind her ears. "You can count on me. When we get back to London, if you need anything, anything at all, promise me you'll call. I'm going to be in the UK for a while. I'll do whatever I can."

"That's very sweet." She sounded like she was accepting an invitation to coffee. "Thanks."

"You shouldn't have to be on your own."

"I don't have to be. I chose this," she insisted, a touch too vehemently. She took a step back, reluctantly moving out of range of the hands that had been smooth heat against her skin. She didn't want to push Alex away. Nothing tempted her more than the urge to kiss the sincerity right off his lovely lips. Instead she tested his offer to do anything at all for her. "Is my every wish your command?" she asked.

"Within reason." A hint of a smile flitted across his serious face.

"In that case. I'd like to go to the zoo."

Alex's electric laughter cracked through the tension. "Then the zoo it is."

Alex and Maggie were like a couple of big kids on their whirlwind tour of Central Park Zoo. They ate hot-dogs and cotton candy, and saw penguins and polar bears. In the gift shop Alex spotted a three-foot-high penguin. Part of the display for a range of books stuffed with animal facts, it wasn't for sale, but Alex turned on the charm, signed autographs, and negotiated with the sales assistants to acquire it in exchange for a donation to wildlife conservation.

"What do you want that for?"

Alex held the penguin at arm's length next to Maggie, comparing the two of them. "It's your perfect accessory. Black and white with just a hint of yellow." He handed it to her. "It's for you. For the baby."

"Don't be daft. I can't take this back to London. It's huge. It'll need its own seat on the plane."

"He'll have to make do with being stuffed into the overhead locker."

Holding a flipper each, they were admiring a beautiful snow leopard when a woman tapped Alex on the shoulder. She held out a camera and said something incomprehensible in French or Spanish. Alex did a double-take.

"You want *me* to take a picture of *you*?"

Maggie stifled a giggle. "It's usually the other way around," she explained unhelpfully to the woman and her blank-faced entourage. "They're obviously not fans."

Alex organized the photo and butterflies skittered in Maggie's stomach. They were the full-package family – yummy mummy, baby in a ditsy flower dress, too-cute toddler in a dinosaur t-shirt, a grumpy older kid with sneakers and a kid-sized back-pack. And a dad to complete their picture.

Maggie hugged the penguin and watched as Alex took charge of the first photo shoot in a week that wasn't of him.

"Say cheese," he coaxed smiles out of the family. "Fromage? Queso?"

"Cheese," they chorused, with the exception of the sullen boy in sneakers, who could give Jago a run for his money, and the baby, who blew dribble bubbles winsomely.

The photo shoot done, Alex surprised Maggie, and everyone else for that matter, when he transformed from temporary photographer into impromptu magician. With sleight of hand he produced first one quarter, then another, out of thin air, and two more from behind Sneaker Boy's ears, finally eliciting a reluctant smile.

"Where did you learn to do that?" Maggie asked, delighted.

"My dad taught me." Alex frowned. "Right before he left. It

took me two years to master it. I practiced on Nick." He looked abashed. He laughed. "I never got the chance to show him that I'd got the hang of it."

Maggie smiled. "Well, it's coming in handy now."

Recognition suddenly dawned on the faces of the parents.

"Are you?"

"Is he?"

"Alex Wells? Yes – he is," Maggie confirmed.

The woman clapped her hands excitedly and together the couple exclaimed, "Jago!"

By the time they all parted, after another quick photo call to include the yummy mummy's favorite vampire, everyone was smiling – even Alex.

Towards the end of the afternoon Alex hailed a yellow taxi and took Maggie and the giant penguin to Bloomingdales.

"What are we doing here?"

"We've got shopping to do."

"Shopping's what I do best. It's practically my career." She frowned, puzzled. "Frankly, it's a bit of a busman's holiday in my time off."

"It's my mother's charity gala tonight. You need something to wear to the ball, Cinderella."

Maggie stopped in her tracks. New York's pedestrians diverted around her, as if she, Alex, and the penguin were rocks in a stream.

"After last night's fiasco I think I'd prefer to stay holed up at the hotel in front of the TV with my friend here." She jabbed a finger at the penguin. "I don't think I'm cut out for all this red-carpet palaver."

"I'd like you to come." He pulled off his sunglasses and spiked a hand through his dark hair. "The event's being held at the Empire State Building. It's an excellent place to end our day in New York. The dinner guests get access to the observatory." Maggie didn't budge. "Come on, Maggie. Work with me here. What can I say to tempt you?"

Despite her reservations, Maggie was tempted. Ve-ry tempted.

"On your own head be it. Don't blame me if I jinx another high-profile occasion."

"Excuse me for thinking that you'd like to come. That you might actually – heaven forbid – enjoy it."

"There's no need to be snarky." Truthfully, it sounded like a lovely evening. She'd get a second chance to prove to herself that she could be the perfect date, and to the world in general that she could do that front-of-camera stuff as well as the next person. After last night's mishaps it was a wonder he hadn't stuck her on the first flight out of here already. But Alex styling her for the second night in a row was a step too far. She couldn't risk appearing in red again. Or pink.

"I'll come with you on one condition."

"Name it."

"I style myself."

He put his shades back on. "It's a deal. Lead on, Macduff." Maggie smiled at the much- misquoted line from Macbeth. Alex was going to make an awesome Hamlet. In a few weeks' time the London theater reviews would be raving about him. Alex Wells would be the hottest ticket in town. And not just for his versatility as an actor. "Just one thing, though … I think I should mention … It's a kind of tradition … A little matter of a color coordination thing that Cassandra insists on …"

Maggie was off. She wasn't even listening. She waved a dismissive hand. She'd had all the color coordination she could take. She couldn't face another red-on-the-red-carpet situation.

"I'm wearing black. It's what I do."

Inside the store Maggie shopped like a fashion missile. She targeted a shimmering black sequined sheath dress with a demure neckline and a back scooped seductively low. It came from the collection of a stylist turned designer. It was exactly right with a shadowy graphite and black zebra print that she loved. Both sexy and subtle. She'd no idea if she could pull it off, but she was flipping well going to try.

Next she went in search of shoes. She found a gorgeous pair of black-satin stilettos that she could actually walk in. They were fab, with a lovely ribbon detail at the ankles.

Last thing, she headed to the lingerie department. Not convinced by the adhesive options for backless dresses, she opted for braless. She was done inside of an hour and most of that was spent waiting for one sales assistant to meticulously pack the dress while another one provided a chair for the penguin and made a production of processing Alex's credit card. Judging by the moony looks on their faces Maggie suspected that they were taking their time just to keep him from leaving.

She mentally pinched herself. All day Alex had been doing a convincingly good impression of the perfect man. She'd do well to remember that perfect men didn't exist. He wasn't into her. He wanted a stylist. Not that he needed one. For tonight, she'd be concentrating her efforts on her own style. There would be no more Cinderella-gone-wrong scenes on the streets of New York, not if she could help it. She couldn't make any more of a fool of herself than she already had. Was there a chance that this time she could actually get it right? There was only one way to find out.

# *Chapter Thirteen*

What on earth was she doing in there? At this rate getting ready for the gala event was going to take Maggie even longer than it had the previous night with stylist Edwina and her hair and make-up team on hand to string the palaver out.

Alex glared at the laptop screen while he waited for her to emerge from her half of the hotel suite. Who knew Maggie would be such a stickler for her "I-only-wear-black" thing? He'd thought she'd enjoy being styled for once. Not a bit of it. She hadn't liked being taken over. And with good reason, as it turned out. He was staring at the result. On the internet, the red-carpet pictures were great, but in the ones of the two of them leaving the premiere he looked more like a comic turn than a serious actor. As for Maggie – she wasn't going to thank him when she saw herself all over the celebrity news pages looking like a fashion disaster. And she'd be shocked for her pregnancy to be announced to the world this way. Seeing her personal news on the laptop he felt as if he'd been punched in the gut. He wished he'd taken better care to protect her privacy. He'd no idea how word of Maggie's pregnancy had got out. That press favorite "the source" was mentioned. That was probably a chambermaid who'd found the packaging from the umpteen pregnancy tests in the hotel bin. He should have been more discreet.

He held his head in his hands and closed his eyes. The night had gone into a nosedive and the photographic evidence was out there. The media wreckage amounted to a "pregnant former flame". The headlines were ridiculous. "Baby Surprise for Glamorous Grandma Cassandra Wells" made him smile, though. She wouldn't cope well with being labeled "grandma". He took out his phone and quickly sent Cassandra a text – damage limitation. Amazingly their publicist hadn't contacted him. Perhaps she hadn't clocked the gossip pages yet. She'd be after his blood when she did. So much for media training.

It could be worse. The story had turned out to be a hit with the no-publicity-is-bad-publicity charity organizer. She'd already texted her congratulations. Both on the great PR – and the news of the happy event. He'd have to take her aside later and put her straight.

Maggie had walked back into his life and he'd taken leave of his senses. He felt surprisingly calm, given his hatred of shambolic publicity. Growing up in the Wells' spotlight was nothing to the full-on multi-media madness that periodically accompanied the on- and off-screen brothers. If anything, his parents had prepared them for things to come.

After the scene at the airport, one parent or the other frequently threatened to make the fact that Drake wasn't the biological father of Cassandra's sons public. All these years later and still neither of them had actually done it. He wondered how Drake would react to the false reporting that he was a soon-to-be grandpa. He hoped he wouldn't do anything rash, like follow through on his currently dormant threat to disown his sons. His mother was on an even keel, and he didn't want her upset.

He clicked haphazardly through the internet images. He didn't give a toss about damaging his efforts to be taken seriously as an actor. What he cared about, above all else, was Maggie. Showing her off as his mystery date on the red carpet had backfired. He'd dragged her into a three-ring circus.

To top it all, it was getting harder by the hour to resist her. Last night she couldn't have been clearer about wanting a fling, although frankly he figured rampant pregnancy hormones had skewed her judgment. It's not that he wasn't tempted. In different circumstances they'd have been tearing each other's clothes off since the middle of last week, but right now no woman could be more complicated than Maggie. The desire to say yes burned inside him. Could he risk getting into something he mightn't want to stop?

He glared at the time in the bottom right corner of the computer screen. He'd give her five more minutes – then he was going in. He jagged a finger at the touchpad, scanning photos. Maggie looked as lovely as any of the A-listers and every bit as gorgeous as the Manhattan elite who'd wangled invitations to the movie screening. His mouth was dry. A rock had taken up residence in his throat. He swallowed. It refused to be shifted. He should have snuck her out a side door and into a cab. What was he thinking when he pulled the stunt with the horse and carriage? It galled him to admit it, but having her here was rapidly turning into one hell of a media muddle.

Weirdly he quite liked reading that he was going to be a father. He must be going crazy. He'd be starting to believe what he read in the tabloids next.

He had a really strong sense of déjà vu. Five years ago, he'd read the report that he'd got engaged to Rachel. He'd cared about her, but he hadn't had any intention of asking her to marry him. She'd gone ballistic. The fallout from press intrusion had been disastrous, and this could get messy too.

He clicked onto another screen and he couldn't help the grin that broke out across his face.

*Cute!*

There was another picture of Maggie in her I Heart NY tee and stars-and-stripes leggings. All he could do was hope she'd see the funny side of this. The headline read "Cinderella of New York City", and the horse and carriage was hilarious. Looking on the bright side, the not-so-perfect Cinderella moment had harnessed some great impromptu publicity; the fairy-tale angle worked brilliantly for the children's charity the Wells family supported.

He heard Maggie coming. He closed the laptop and stood up, hands in pockets. He'd have to break the media intrusion to her … *Wow!!!*

She walked into the room, elegant, sophisticated. And in black. He wished he'd been more insistent about the dress code. He hoped his mother wouldn't be abhorrently rude, but he wasn't counting on it, especially in the light of the grandma allegations. Volatility was her default setting.

As far as he was concerned Maggie looked great. He was getting used to her monochrome tendencies. He couldn't care less if she was wearing multi-colored polka dots instead of the customary Wells Wish Foundation colors, but she looked truly stunning, shimmering in shades of black. He should at least warn her about Cassandra's pink and blue theme, and give her the heads-up on the press speculation.

Press photos? Or dress code? Given the choice he'd ignore both topics and stay right here addressing his impulse to finish what they'd almost started much too much time ago already.

He needed to get her out of his system, move on. He wanted to believe that he could be her friend. He really did. But every time he made a stab at it, he ended up more confused. It was a non-starter. Did she want a fling? Did she want someone to hold her hand at her first baby scan? Did she want someone to pick out a buggy and adorable dinky clothes? What did she want exactly? The more he thought about it, the more he figured that what she required was a gay best friend. He was much too attracted to her to be a good friend, no matter how badly he wanted to try.

Once upon a time he'd imagined that if there was anyone on the planet it might be worth trying to be more for it would be

Maggie. Angry at being at the center of his parents' latest public spat, hurt by harsh criticism from Drake, he'd been a mess that December when he'd quit university. Maggie had snuck past his defenses and gone straight to his heart. He shouldn't have gone there. When he realized that he'd let her get too close, he'd frozen her out, and if he'd felt guilty about it then, what he felt now was worse; deep and strong and unquantifiable.

He squashed it. Blocked-out feelings were an improvement on messy ones. He'd watched the love bleed out of his mother when her marriage had failed. Seeing someone he loved self-destruct because he couldn't love them enough, give them all that they needed from him, would be worse than any other personal failure he could imagine. He couldn't risk doing that to Maggie – and her child. The stakes were much too high. He wasn't a one-woman-forever guy. Falling in love and making commitments wasn't for him.

Maggie looked achingly seducible. She didn't want a forever guy, and he couldn't be one, so why not get this thing between the two of them out of the way and let her go?

"You look a million dollars." The cliché was inadequate. Gorgeous didn't cover it. Chic, understated, beautiful, her hair was piled up with diamantes sparkling enticingly here, there and everywhere. He wanted to pull her into his arms and remove each jeweled hairpin slowly until her soft curls unfurled into his fingers. She'd left an artful strand falling in a corkscrew tendril at the pulse point in her neck. He stepped forward, reached out and cupped her face. Her make-up was flawless. She'd matched smoky eyes to the dark shades of graphite, black and grey in her figure-hugging dress. He stifled a groan and curled one finger in the frond of loose hair on her neck.

Her eyes flashed confident challenge. "No vampire moves. We made a rule."

"Uh-huh," he said in a husky tone he barely recognized as his own. "Rules are made to be broken." He dipped his head slowly and placed his lips against her neck. Her scent rocketed through his senses. He hardened. He raised his head. He shouldn't kiss her, but he ached with temptation.

"If you kiss me, you'll ruin my make-up and if I have to go back in the bathroom to fix it, I may never come out."

A deep chuckle rose up from his diaphragm. Kiss her was exactly what he wanted to do.

"Is that a threat?"

"It's a fact," she whispered, her eyes never leaving his. She was doing a very good job of appearing not to feel the attraction between them. She felt it, all the same. It shimmered in her dilated pupils.

"It's just as well we have an important event to attend. Otherwise I'd be tempted to risk it."

She wasn't taking any chances. She turned and started to walk to the door. He took in the expanse of bare skin and the way her dress dipped below the small of her back to the curve of her bum. He needed a bucket of ice to cool him down. The way it clung to her curves there could only be an infinitesimal wisp of thong beneath.

Fabulous, she oozed confidence. Forget friends. He'd frazzle if he didn't make Maggie his lover. When he'd kissed her at Cape Cod, he'd made time stand still, pretended it didn't mean anything. He'd have to let her go. She was having a baby and he wasn't the right guy for her. His fight with want had run out. They could be right for each other, right now. He couldn't be her one, and that was okay because she didn't want a permanent man in her life. It was a no-brainer. They could be together for one night without hurting each other.

Heads turned as the couple walked through the hotel to the limo waiting at the curb. Alex took Maggie's hand and she slid in. He followed her onto the back seat. She'd been so pre-occupied with choosing the little-black-dress-to-die-for and the best-high-heels-in-Manhattan that she hadn't asked Alex a single thing about the charity.

"What's this gala in aid of? Fill me in. I need details."

"It funds small projects to help underprivileged kids, mostly here in the States. Tonight's one of their big fundraisers. A night like this attracts publicity to the work The Wells Wish Foundation does."

"You have a children's charity named after you?"

"It's nothing to do with me and Nick. It's our mother's pet project. She's a bit of a fanatic. We help out with the annual gala. But that's about it. I'm no good with kids."

*Methinks Alex doth protest too much!*

He acted like kids were an alien species. Yet he'd been sweet with the family at the zoo. And here he was putting his face to a children's charity.

"Listen," he started to explain, "My mother's a bit pernickety when it comes to her charity."

"Pernickety? What's that?"

Alex grunted out a fractured laugh. "Fussy. She gets hung up on minutiae. Her heart's in the right place and I know she's a total diva, but she's in a much better place than she was few years ago. She means well. I don't want you to think badly of her."

"I won't. I don't. Why would I?"

"There's been such a lot written about her over the years. After my dad left she stopped eating, got much too thin. She got by – just about – on a self-prescribed diet of over-the-counter drugs and herbal remedies. When that stopped working she got hooked on sleeping tablets and alcohol. Eventually things got so bad that she was admitted to rehab."

Maggie felt the urge to scrape at one of her nails. She'd covered them in a clear, shiny polish and if she did, she'd ruin them. She and Alex used to joke about their families. What they hadn't really done before today was tell the whole truth. He would barely talk about his father and she'd had next to nothing to say about hers. When he spoke about his mother, he made light of things, throwing out quips about how she outdid her soap character with her real-life scandals.

"Sometimes I think her obsession with the children's charity is her way of making up for not loving Nick and me enough when we were kids. It's not that she didn't care; she just couldn't show it."

Maggie admired his honesty. She'd seen through his comedic version of Cassandra. After all she'd done the same. Instead of talking about the woman who'd made the first, deep crack in her heart, she'd painted a clown of a mother to her friends. She was someone with a perma-tan and an unhealthy devotion to karaoke, who ran a bar in Spain.

"I guess she fell out of love with herself." She pictured the last article about Cassandra she'd happened upon in a magazine at the fertility clinic. It said she'd cleaned up her act and found "lurve" with a younger guy. She'd taken years to get over the blow of Drake leaving. She'd kept his name after the divorce and forced contact with him to continue the only way she knew how, sparring with him publically in the press. At long last she'd let it go, found equilibrium in new love and pride for her sons.

"It must be hard to love your children if you hate yourself," Alex agreed. "Look, there's a couple of things I need to warn you about."

"Too late. We're here." She touched his upper arm gently. Beneath smooth fabric, she felt rock-firm muscle. "It'll be fine," she assured him, "I'm excited to meet Cassandra."

The limo pulled up outside the Empire State Building. Glancing upwards into the twilight sky Maggie saw that the tower's lights were pink, white and blue for the night – magical. Out of the limo in an instant, Alex offered his hand to Maggie. As she stepped out his arm banded around her and flashes popped. Alex tensed, giving out the requisite Jago vibe. Under his breath he cursed the press presence. He dipped his head and whispered in her ear. "If they ask questions, say nothing. Leave any comments to me." The hairs on the back of her neck rose. His strong arm circled about her waist made sweet, honeyed heat swirl at her core.

She smiled easily. "Happy to." The words came out in a throaty whisper.

Compared to the movie premiere, the charity gala was low key. There were a few photographers on the street and just one reporter. Alex looked ahead purposefully, his face frozen, jaw clenched, walking her quickly towards the entrance in the protection of his arm, strangely less relaxed in this setting than he had been on the red carpet.

"Alex!" A beady-eyed reporter with tousled fair hair that made him look about fourteen and as though he just got out of bed beckoned. "Can you spare a moment for a couple of questions?"

"What do you need to know?"

"Tell me about the projects funded by Wells Wish?"

"There'll be a press release." He held Maggie close. "You'll get all the details you need there."

She'd pasted on a fixed smile. It was her second outing in the glare of publicity and she was wary, but she steeled herself, determined to nail the being-on-show thing as Alex continued. "The charity mainly funds play schemes, literacy programs, theater-in-education initiatives." His touch and his deep drawl swirled through her senses.

A sly smile contorted the reporter's ever-so-slightly lopsided features. "Any plans to fund a nursery? Baby-and-toddler groups? Breast-feeding awareness?"

Alex's jaw tightened. "Not that I'm aware of."

Maggie smiled like a waxwork of herself, panicky inside at the reporter's hints.

He turned his attention on her. "When's the happy event? I hear congratulations are in order."

She almost gawped. Sticking to Alex's advice, she said nothing.

Bedhead Boy honed in on Alex. "You must be excited," he probed. "Are you looking forward to becoming a dad?"

Maggie's jaw hit the floor. She wanted a hole in the ground to open up and swallow her whole. She pulled herself together. If she was going to snag TV work she'd have to be able to think on her feet. Before Alex could utter a word, her reply sliced through the night air.

"Alex is not the father." Her skin turned to goose flesh, but she persevered, "I'm having a donor-sperm baby."

Alex's hand gripped her waist tighter, hastening their move away. He turned back to the reporter and said with studied calm. "It's great news. I'm thrilled for Magenta."

Inside the building, milling amongst hundreds of guests, when the pressure of effusive greetings and social niceties settled down for a moment, Maggie cornered Alex. "How did that reporter know that I'm pregnant?"

"Your guess is as good as mine." He gave a big shrug. Harsh tension shadowed his features. "Someone told the press. It was on the net."

"You knew?" She couldn't control the wobble in her voice. "Why didn't you tell me?"

"I was going to. I got side-tracked trying to warn you about Cassandra and her color scheme."

Maggie's brain fogged up. How could he be fussing about a color scheme at a time like this?

"Pesky-reporter-of-the-year put two and two together and got it wrong. Ve. Ry. Wrong."

"I know. Awkward." A muscle twitched in his face.

"Extremely." Maggie simmered. "What are we going to do?"

"Nothing. You handled it fine. For the record, I'd have been happy to go with the flow and be your baby's father for the night."

"You would?" Maggie's nerves jangled and her heart skipped.

"Why not?" He gave a big, nonchalant shrug. "The press getting hold of a whiff of information and making a mountain of tittle-tattle out of it is my normal." He shrugged again. "What can you do? They need column inches and we have to make the best of it." He fiddled distractedly with a cufflink. It didn't help that he looked so devastating in a tux. "It's not ideal." He hesitated, clearing his throat with a gruff cough. "But people like baby news. It's a misunderstanding with a positive spin. If that increases donations to the charity, then I'm happy to run with it."

Maggie's heart sank. For a micro-second she'd thought Alex was saying that he didn't mind people thinking he was having a baby with her. That's not what he'd meant at all.

"I should have said nothing. Like you told me to do." She hadn't told anyone yet. Not her friends. Not her mother – although that might be difficult since her mobile phone had a semi-permanently flat battery. No one knew except Alex. And now the rest of the world.

She was contemplating hailing the first passing taxi and high-tailing it back to the hotel to hide, when Nick and Ella arrived.

"Is this your doing?" The tension ramped up a notch as Alex glared suspiciously at Nick.

"No way. I haven't said a thing." Nick held up his palms. "Actually," he added, looking contrite, "I may have mentioned that Maggie was an old flame."

"That's not exactly true, Nick," Maggie chided.

"The rest is anybody's guess. An indiscreet bellhop or something. By the way, Cassandra's on the warpath. That reporter called her 'grandma.'"

Maggie let out a long, panicky breath. "Your mother's going to kill me."

Ella, in hot pink, touched Maggie's arm reassuringly. "She'll get over it. She's used to dealing with PR problems. Congratulations, by the way."

Across the room, in the midst of a throng of guests, Cassandra, clad in shimmery blue sequins like a shiny mermaid, was graciously accepting everyone's good wishes. She was giving an award-winning performance as the delighted grandma-to-be.

"I sent her a text," Alex said. He pressed a finger into the furrow between his brows and shook his head. "What's she playing at?"

Practically in sync with his twin, Nick shook his head. "Evidently she didn't read it."

Ella's super-glossed-up lips set in an I'm-saying-nothing moue. She wrapped Maggie in a hug. "Don't worry. Alex will sort it out. Welcome to our world."

Her heart somersaulted. Who knew getting noticed could be so fraught with complications?

"Thanks." She smiled trustingly at Alex. "I think."

Nick and Ella melted into the room, leaving her alone looking into his eyes.

"I shouldn't have exposed you to any of this."

"It's PR pandemonium."

"It's my life, and I should have done more to protect you. I'm sorry."

The organizer stepped up on a raised platform at the far end of the room and banged an auctioneer's gavel. The room hushed. She thanked everyone for supporting the Wells Wish Foundation, encouraged them to give generously, and informed them that there'd be an after- dinner address from the inimitable Cassandra Wells followed by an auction of promises, including kisses from each of her dreamy sons.

The news sparked an unnecessary pang of jealousy in Maggie. It was bad enough that her body was operating on a different frequency from her head as far as Alex was concerned, but possessive emotions were completely uncalled for.

"Keep your credit cards at the ready, ladies," the organizer enthused with a diva-in-training sigh. "And now, without further ado, dinner is served."

Alex and Maggie took their places at the top table, alongside Nick and Ella, and Cassandra with her younger man.

She didn't have a clue who any of the other social elite at the table were. The men rose to shake her hand and their partners smiled warmly – all the while giving out extra-cool vibes. How come some women had a talent for that? She picked up on the curiosity behind their fake eyelashes and bright lipstick smiles. No doubt they were itching to know all the gossip.

At that point her brain-fog cleared. The penny dropped. There wasn't a single woman in the room who wasn't wearing either electric blue or shocking pink – the charity's signature colors.

"Why didn't you tell me there was a dress code?" Maggie hissed at Alex in a whisper.

His eyebrows shot up. "I tried. You didn't listen."

"I stick out like a sore thumb. You should have said something."

"Like what?"

"Don't wear black would have been a good start."

Alex raised his eyes to the roof. "Black's what you do," he reminded her. A sexy smile played on his lips.

"I look like I should be waiting tables."

"Dressed like that?" Very slowly Alex raked his gaze over her. How could his ice-blue eyes make her feel so hot?

Shadowy staff delivered the delicious meal with attentive precision. The courses came and went, glasses were filled and refilled. The event had been organized with attention to detail that verged on finicky. Like the dress code, the flower arrangements and the lighting echoed the charity's colors – every single thing pink, white and blue. Throughout the proceedings, Cassandra Wells' eyes fired daggers at Maggie. She clearly wasn't impressed.

So much for the neutral image she'd worked so hard to perfect. Her black dress might as well have been a gorilla suit. How could she have got it so wrong? Getting noticed was uncomfortable in the extreme, so much so that she was beginning to think this whole idea of landing a job on a television show was pie in the sky. She just wasn't up to it.

The conversation murmured around her. When the time came for the auction, Alex leant in and whispered close against her neck, "Nick and I always outbid the highest bidders."

Unwanted heat spiraled through her body, transmitting awareness impulses into every nerve cell.

"You bid to kiss each other? How does that work?"

Alex chuckled. The wide smile lit up his face.

"It's a bit of a tradition. I give Nick's kiss to his date – it's been Ella for the last few years. He gives my kiss to my date ..." He paused, a teasingly blasé and annoyingly seductive look stamped on his face. "... Whoever that might be."

Her heart skittered. "That's me." She fought the urge to know who'd been on the receiving end of Nick's generous gift last year and the year before that ... and ...

"You catch on quick."

After dinner the organizer introduced Cassandra. She gave her spiel, thanking people for their generous support. Gracious and humorous, she commanded the attention of the room. From what Alex had said earlier their relationship had been difficult when he and Nick were children, but clearly she was beyond delighted with her grown-up sons. Before dinner Alex had straightened things out about the surprise grandchild, so mercifully she stuck to her planned speech and didn't make any off-the-cuff remarks about Maggie's pregnancy.

She wondered how her own mother would take the news. At forty-five she'd be even less enchanted than Cassandra with being dubbed a granny. Contact had been pretty patchy since her grandma died. She still flew out to visit her from time to time. Usually, she didn't stay more than two or three days, although at the beginning of the summer they'd been short-staffed at the Green Flamingo Bar, so since her diary was clear she'd stuck around and helped out for couple of weeks. Still, they were a long way from close. She hadn't shared her pregnancy plan with her. Dedicated to celebrity gossip, her mother would be wowed when she found out her grandchild-to-be had a famous dad, and absolutely gutted when she learned that it wasn't true.

Ripples of polite applause filled the room.

The auctioneer's gavel knocked loudly and the gathering fell silent. Nick's kiss was the first promise to be auctioned off. Maggie watched it all, remaining attentively remote, like a spectator. The bids went steadily higher and when the hammer was about to fall Alex bettered the last bid by ten thousand dollars. The hammer fell and the kiss was Ella's. It was awarded right away. Nick and Ella both stood, playing to the crowd, and performed a very stagey smooch to the cheers of the well-wined-and-dined guests.

Various generous gifts and promises followed. The sums of money raised practically made Maggie's eyes water. She tuned out. Under the table she crossed her legs defensively and twirled one high-heeled foot in a circular motion. The image of the ribbon at her ankle and the thought of Alex slowly untying it swam in her head. She couldn't kiss him. She didn't have the necessary skills to perform a convincing stage kiss. There'd be no need to hold up a sign saying "She's going to fall in love if she's not careful!" like in a silent movie. It would be fairly obvious. She didn't want to push him away, but she had no choice. She was starting to want much too much. And he didn't want anything. He was doing his best to honor her friend request, but he'd been quick to decline her wanton no-strings fling proposition. She'd been all over the place since he'd arranged her upgrade. She didn't know what she wanted from him, but it wasn't a fake snog.

Finally, it was time. There was a hum of excitement in the room. Apparently kissing Alex was the evening's pièce de résistance.

Maggie's heart turned somersaults. Cassandra Wells watched her like a tigress about to pounce on its prey. She had the longest, reddest nails in the room. Lethal. She might have made a quick recovery from the pregnancy problem, but she wasn't going to forgive the dress-code blunder in a hurry. What would she make of Maggie winning Alex's kiss? Maybe it wouldn't happen. Nick might be outbid.

"How much am I bid for Alex? Don't be shy, ladies! This is Jago I'm talking about here. Dig deep. You won't be disappointed." Alex's face had taken on Jago's sexy-solemn quality, complete with the roguish promise of an almost imperceptible smile.

"You're the Mona Lisa of vampires." Maggie whispered. He wanted to laugh, she saw it in his eyes, but he held his stance, keeping his cool, ever the professional actor with only the faintest ghost of a smile on view.

The bids mounted high quickly. Maggie listened with bated breath. She so didn't want Nick to win the auction. She'd have to kiss Alex – right here, right now – in front of who-knew-how-many-hundreds of people. *Flipping Nora!* She surreptitiously looked him up and down. He was standing for the auction. Towering above her he was a stud of a man. He could have been made to model the tux. Aware of many-eyed scrutiny focusing in on them, it took immense effort to ignore the exchanges of silent glances that said "who in the world is *she*?" more clearly than any words.

"Gentlemen. Treat your date tonight. She won't regret it. But you might." There was a chortle of good-humored laughter.

A vampish-looking cougar lady called out a huge sum and Maggie's heart thumped. She bit back a gasp.

"Are we all done? Going once. Going twice." Maggie's heart rate soared.

At the last micro second Nick cut in with the winning bid.

"You took your time!" Alex jibed.

"I thought I'd let you sweat a little," Nick bantered.

"Sold to ..." The organizer squinted across at the top table.

Cassandra Wells picked up her glass of red wine as if it was a poison chalice she planned to force upon Maggie's lips. She sipped in silence. Maggie did a double-take. Clearly she'd got far too into running lines from *Hamlet* with Alex. She had to remind herself that Cassandra wasn't Queen Gertrude.

Nick stood and gestured in a grandiose manner towards Maggie.

"Magenta Plumtree."

# *Chapter Fourteen*

In the dim, atmospheric glow of the function room all faces turned on Maggie. Moody beams of deep-pink, blue and white light peppered the darkened room. The attention of hundreds of pairs of eyes hit her like a physical force as she was trapped in the glare of a movable spotlight. She blinked, startled. Alex reached out and drew her to her feet. Clasping her fingers and lifting them to his mouth in an act of old-fashioned gallantry he gently pressed his lips against the back of her hand. Time might as well have lapsed into slow motion. The warm pressure of Alex's mouth on her skin felt incredible. Sensual. Delicious.

*Phew!* He wasn't going kiss her for real in front of all these people after all.

Murmurs of disapproval emanated from the room. Someone booed and others followed suit. Desire and panic flooded her senses. Alex looked deep into her searching eyes. Before she had time to register what was happening he swept her into a Hollywood dip and while she was bent over backwards planted a kiss somewhere about her earlobe. She fizzed, even though she wasn't meant to. He was hamming it up for the crowd. They cheered. In an instant she was back on her feet, reeling with surprise and pleasure, and aching to be kissed – properly.

"Sorry about that," he almost growled.

"Please don't apologize," she replied, playing along.

"It won't happen again, I can assure you."

Her heart skittered. She hated to admit it, since he'd rejected her on the fling front, but she was disappointed. And yearning for more. Of Alex. Or Jago. Whichever.

Cassandra's eyes burned. They practically scorched Maggie's skin. A jazz band started up with the first lively bars of a can't-help-but-dance tune. Couples spontaneously headed to the dance floor. "May I borrow my son?" The words in the older woman's deep, actressy tones were more of an order than a request.

"Of course." A polite smile of resignation sat on Maggie's lips.

The strains of breezy jazz filled the room and a voluptuous singer's dulcet voice drew more people to their feet. Cassandra's partner led Ella onto the floor. Maggie looked up at Nick, hopefully. Tonight, he seemed quite different from the love rat she'd thought she met on the plane. It was hard to believe that he and Ella were faking it for the sake of convenience. Perhaps, since he was channeling his gentlemanly side, he'd ask her to dance. It was the least he could do to make up for his "old flame" remark to the press. Instead, he excused himself and disappeared, leaving her feeling like a wallflower left to wilt in a corner. Five minutes later she couldn't help smiling when she spotted him admiring the wildly out-of-sync disco moves of the cougar he'd saved his brother from in the auction.

"Magenta Plumtree? Sylvestro Salvadori." She recognized the Italian silver fox instantly. He was a big name in special effects, some sort of CGI wizard. His wife had hired her to style their family's Christmas photograph about a year ago. The woman had more money than sense. She'd been a very exacting employer.

It was a second marriage, a blended family, three children that were his, two hers, and a little cutie that was theirs. Styling the family to the second Mrs. Salvadori's taste had been quite a task. It was energetic chaos. She'd pitied the photographer. They were a handful to keep still long enough to get everyone looking gorgeous – no grimaces or eyes closed.

Sylvestro sat down next to Maggie, chatting charmingly about New York, the weather, the charity event. Maggie glanced around. "Is Mrs. Salvadori here tonight?"

He gave a low chortle. "Leonora and I are no longer together." Maggie was about to express some kind of sympathy, but he cut her short. "The divorce came through last week. Dance?"

He was on his feet, leading her to the dance floor by the hand. Before she knew it his snake arms were locked around her body pulling her close. *Oops.* How did that happen? Her technique for fending off the advances of Sylvestro types needed some work. He was very seductive. But she wasn't looking to be seduced. Not by an over-sexed Casanova type, at any rate.

Luckily the music stopped almost as soon as they began to dance. Maggie was about to seize the moment, free herself from Sylvestro's arms and flee the dance floor when he cut to the chase.

"Let's skip the dancing. No pun intended." A predatory leer spoiled his otherwise handsome features. "My hotel's a couple of blocks away. How about we take this back there?"

She cringed. Whatever "this" was, she had no intention of taking it anywhere.

As if on cue – thankfully – Alex butted in. He dwarfed Sylvestro, tall and imposing, with a look of grim skepticism on his face. "The next dance is mine."

Reluctantly the silver fox released her, muttering something smarmy about hoping to catch up with her later. The music struck up again and she melted willingly against Alex's chest.

"What the hell were you doing with him?"

Maggie made a stab at a withering look. "I beg your pardon? This isn't the eighteenth century. I can dance with whomever I choose." She wasn't about to admit how relieved she'd been that he'd stepped in and rescued her from the lascivious Italian. "Have you got a problem with that?"

"Sylvestro's the problem. He's a Lothario looking for wife

number three." Maggie rolled her eyes and a little smirk of disbelief twisted her lips. Was Alex jealous? "Or a temporary mistress before wife number three comes along." Her smile grew a bit wider. "Or a one-night stand until he finds a temporary mistress."

"You're very cynical all of a sudden." The truth was she'd sensed right away that the guy was looking for more than just a dance. "What's wrong with a one-night stand?" she challenged.

"Nothing as long as there are no feelings involved and everyone's on the same page."

Since when had Alex become her protector? Her guard might have been down when Sylvestro had whirled her onto the dance floor. But that didn't mean she wasn't perfectly capable of looking out for herself. No longer clear if this was about Sylvestro or Alex, she tipped her face up to his. "What page is that?"

"The page with The End written on it. A one-night stand is exactly that. One night. End of story."

His words catapulted her back to the night they'd spent together. What they'd had in London belonged to a place in time that they could never get back to, even if they wanted to.

"Guys like that are short on commitment. You don't need one of those."

"And you know what I need?" she countered, keeping her cool.

"Tonight," he drawled, so whisperingly quiet that she had to tilt her head closer to hear his words. "I want you to need me."

If no-strings sex was what she desired she could have it with any available commitment-phobe. What she was feeling for Alex was more than that. Like it or not, her emotions were tangled up in knots and that was dangerous territory.

The music started up again, conveniently cutting through the conversation. Alex swung Maggie out on one arm and then pulled her back in close, as they realized that in spite of the spirited intro it was actually the start of a rhythmic slow dance. Her body moving against his, Maggie had never felt so sultry in her life. The attraction she felt for him was devastating. Alex might be a celebrity crush to millions, but right now she was the only woman he was interested in and the heart-stealing feeling that gave her was incredible.

All around them couples moved in tandem. She loved every second of dancing with him, and even so she couldn't wait to break the contact, distance herself from him. These feelings would go away. They had before. For sure and certain they couldn't lead anywhere. She needed to get out of the heavenly circle of his arms.

Arrows of desire speared through her body. An untidy mess of contradiction, she recognized with frightening certainty that Alex's bone-melting powers meant only one thing. She didn't just want him in her life. She wanted this place locked in his hold to be hers. His heat. His strength. His sexy gorgeousness. All hers.

Her head and her heart told her she couldn't have those things. They'd spent a few great days together. It was nearly time to go back to their own lives.

When the music ended Alex and Maggie remained locked like two magnets. People noticed. Alex reluctantly relaxed his arms and let her go. "Come on." He took her by the hand and entwined her fingers in his.

"Where to?"

"You'll see."

Outside, away from the prying eyes of the other guests, he took something out of his pocket. He unfolded it. Maggie let out a gasp, suddenly recognizing the pretty multi-colored scarf from the fashion shoot at the beach. "What's that doing here?" Her heart sank. Had Alex begged, borrowed or stolen it? "I'm going to be in so much trouble."

"Relax. I acquired it." He paused and looked at her for a long moment, as if inspecting her for damage. "For you." He twisted the beautiful silk and stretched it between his hands. "Turn," he instructed. Automatically she did as she was bid. Facing away from him, the bare length of her back exposed to his view, a frisson of electricity crackled between them. He placed the soft silk over her eyes and gently blindfolded Maggie, tying the scarf in a tight knot at the back of her head.

"What the …? Alex, what are you doing?"

"Shh. No questions," he warned her. He turned her back to face him. The warmth of his hands scorched her skin like branding irons. "Do you trust me?"

"Implicitly." It was true. Her heart did a little leap. "Although it's not every day I get kidnapped by everybody's favorite vampire. Where are you taking me?"

He placed a firm finger on her lips. "Watch it. I might have to gag you if you're not careful." There was humor in his tone. The blackness of the blindfold should have made her uncomfortable, out of control. But trusting Alex to take charge didn't faze her.

He turned her again, put strong hands either side of her waist and moved her gently forward. Next thing she knew they were in an elevator. She had a weird sense of moving upwards, fast. Her stomach flipped, like a bubble in a lava lamp — only faster.

"We're going to the top, aren't we?" With fake petulance she made a deliberate attempt to spoil his surprise. He was way ahead of her on tactics. His arms were wrapped around her from behind, holding her against his statuesque body. He dipped his head and placed his mouth in the curve of her neck, feathering his lips sensuously across her skin. Sweet hot lust shot to her core. Not seeing him, but feeling Alex — hard against her — thrilled her.

Powerfully erotic, he feathered kisses across her shoulders, his scent of male spice making her high on hot man. When he traced his famous *Mercy of the Vampires* figure of eight symbol onto her bare back in big sensual curls, with his finger pressed on her skin, and his hardness pressed against the jut of her bum, she was undone, sensitized to the aching, soaring heat he'd triggered inside her. She'd never desired anyone like this before in all of her life. Only him.

When the elevator arrived at the eighty-sixth floor he walked her out onto the observation deck. The night air enveloped her, cooling, soothing – a welcome contrast to the boiling point she'd reached in the elevator. His hands at the back of her head as he started to untie the scarf made her quiver. Impatient for him to undo the knot she raised her hands and pushed the fabric up from her eyes.

"Wow." All the breath in her lungs escaped with that one word.

New York City was a magic carpet of light below. A gazillion twinkling pinpricks spread all around. A saxophone was playing a haunting melody, evocative, beautiful. The scarf unknotted, Alex placed the rainbow silk over her shoulders. He waited in silence while she took in the awesomeness of Manhattan by night from the top of the Empire State Building. She barely noticed the other people: dark figures, milling, chatting, laughing, looking.

Seemingly blasé about being seen, or worse, photographed, Alex turned Maggie to face him. Their eyes locked. He gave her tingles, hands gently hovering on the layer of silk between his skin and hers. A cool waft of air made the scarf flutter, rippling the kaleidoscope colors. His fingers tightened on her shoulders. She sucked in a breath. He brought her close and her heart beat faster. One arm slipped from her shoulders to circle her waist and gather her against his body. Instantly fragile, his hold turned her bones to jelly and filled her with contrary, demanding need at the same time. Alex's magnetism rocked her world. He mesmerized her.

Tortured, hesitant, she tensed as he lowered his head, his mouth so close. Right then she crumbled, spinning like a meteorite into blissful, wanton, urgent submission. Her lips parted, dead set on a collision course with his kiss. He angled his head and his mouth took possession of hers, gentle and determined, deepening the kiss, plundering, tasting, teasing her into flames of desire. Heavenly heat swirled at her core. She wanted him. Badly. Fiery pleasure swept through her. She luxuriated in the strength of his arms, his tight hold, the warmth of his breath on her neck. She practically inhaled him, craved his masculinity with fierce need.

His mouth was divine. It was a never-ending champagne

cocktail of a kiss. Long. Lovely. A moment suspended in time. He drew away slowly, leaving them both reeling, drugged on the inevitability of too-long ignored potential.

No two ways about it. Alex Wells had an intangible power over her. And she knew one certain thing. She wanted him more than anything she'd ever wanted. She needed to touch him, hold him, feel him inside her.

She searched the dark for something to fix on, picking out splashes of neon – green, red, blue and the Brooklyn Bridge – a string of light over the black East River. Sounds rose up out of the night, a foghorn, the wail of a police car's siren. Thousands of feet up in the sky butterflies turned somersaults in Maggie's stomach.

"Let's get out of here." Urgency had turned Alex's rumbling, voice hoarse.

Anticipation with the weight of pure lead hung in the air around them. Alex summoned his driver. They descended in the elevator, packed in with other people whose presence heightened their impatience to be alone together. They went straight to the waiting limo and slipped into its interior of soft, smooth leather.

In silent expectation, primed, as if on a pre-determined path, they sat apart from each other in the dark. There wasn't a whisper of a touch between them. Even so, they both knew exactly where they were headed.

Maggie trembled. Impatient desire for Alex held her in thrall. She couldn't regain control even if she wanted to. A tide of emotion crashed through her. The sexual energy that blazed between them amounted to unfinished business. An ending, not a beginning, for one night only; it had no future.

There was only one sure-fire way she could do this and survive. She wouldn't make love to Alex. She'd have sex with Jago. If she pretended that Alex was his vampire character, if she could fabricate the perfect fantasy in her mind, there was a chance that she could revel in her one-night stand and still walk away emotionally unscathed. Falling in love was out of the question. She'd been here before with this man. He didn't do "lasting". This time she needed to say goodbye without being doomed to be hooked on the "what if" factor of Alex Wells for the rest of her days.

The limo moved slowly along through the New York streets. Inside Maggie and Alex had slipped into a tinted-glass time warp. There was no need to speak.

He ached with desire. He imagined an invisible line between them – a force field that couldn't be crossed, preventing him from touching her. The snarl of traffic slowed their progress towards the hotel. The ache consumed him. He'd been suppressing the yearning, ignoring her allure. So much for sticking to the strategy he'd come up with on the plane. He'd blown it when, instead of wishing her luck and waving goodbye, he'd invited her to New York. It was a big fail.

And about to get bigger. He had a deep need to finish what they'd started all that time ago. His barriers were down. Could he be what she needed for longer than one night? Absolutely not. Would she want him to be? No. They'd reached boiling point. Hot love was better than the lasting kind.

He sat with his back pressed hard against the leather of the seat and told himself to cool it. Tempting as it was, he wouldn't jump her in the back of the limo like an adolescent on testosterone overload. Tonight would be his last chance with Maggie. He intended to savor every moment. Make it last.

He turned and looked at her profile. She was so pretty; the line of her nose, the tilt of her chin, silhouetted in the shadows of the night. No matter how badly he wanted to he couldn't let himself touch her again, not yet. There were things that needed to be said. He wanted to be sure that they were both on the same page. No strings. Whatever this was – this infuriating electric hell that crackled between them – it would be a one-off. One night in bed together and they'd both get this unfinished thing of theirs out of their systems.

Maggie turned and looked at him, her hazel irises glimmered, green-brown flecked with amber, around bright, dilated pupils, their beauty quixotic. A mischievous smile quirked her lips and suddenly she was in his lap. Her thighs straddling his, she pressed against his erection.

"I want you. Now."

He choked out a raucous half-laugh, half-groan as she tangled her fingers in his hair, sending delicious spirals of sensation echoing through him. She lowered her head to his, shaking loose her hair, letting it fall like a curtain around their faces. Her lips, plump and soft, found his, probing, teasing, until he kissed her back, deep and hard, sinking his tongue into her mouth. He slid his hands up and down her silken back.

Hell. So much for good intentions.

He twisted her in his arms pressing her down against the black leather. Outside the-city-that-never-sleeps was a muffled symphony of constant activity. The car wended steadily through the streets of Manhattan, its driver discreetly screened from the couple behind.

Alex broke the kiss and drew back. He placed one hand beneath the gossamer-light fabric of her dress and deftly moved upwards to the apex of her thighs. With gentle precision he pushed aside the scrap of lace and slipped his finger inside her.

"Like this?"

She moaned. Her reaction told him that she wanted more of him than he was prepared to give her, right here, right now – even though he burned to take her, enter her completely. She writhed, his rhythmic touch eliciting a response that was instant and potentially explosive. She was a whisper away from shattering. His fingertip circled, exciting her body's sensitivity, reading her expertly, decoding her responses, heightening her pleasure, until, with perfect timing, he applied precisely enough gentle pressure to make her come. Shudders rocked her body. Her orgasm tortured him with urgent want.

If he didn't have her tonight, he'd burn in hell.

The limo drew up in front of the hotel. Maggie smoothed her dress back down to its proper ankle-skimming length. Lips swollen from his kiss, face sexily flushed, she forked fingers through her hair, pushing flyaway wisps behind her ears.

Alex took on board a painful thought. If he did have her tonight, he'd burn in hell.

He had feelings for Maggie he couldn't quantify. She'd crashed through his defenses. When he'd seen her with that sleazebag Italian it was as if a switch had been flicked. What he felt was deep and strong and protective; and so much more than jealousy, or the need to prove that if anyone was going to seduce her it should be him.

Technically he'd left the "friend" zone. They wouldn't be able to re-enter the land of "just friends" after tonight.

# Chapter Fifteen

Privately ensconced behind the closed doors of his hotel suite Alex gathered Maggie into his arms and held her close. He lowered his face to hers and kissed her – softly, gently. He imbibed her – hot, feminine, fragrant. He ran the fingers of one hand to the back of her neck and caressed her nape.

She broke the kiss and tilted her face to look into his eyes. "Make love to me," she whispered.

He pulled back, releasing her from his arms, semi-paralyzed by her choice of words. Out of the corner of his eye he spotted the laptop. The shiny rectangle was a reminder of the cyber world that lay beyond the walls of his hotel room.

What new stories lurked out there?

What latest headline loomed?

He jabbed a hand into his hair, huffed out a breath and turned away from her. He should stop before they went any further. The best way to protect Maggie from the venom of any more press tittle-tattle would be to go to his room, close the door and stay there – alone.

He turned back and faced her looking for some kind of signal in her enticing eyes. "This can only be for one night. You know that, don't you?"

She gave a mysterious half-smile, tossed her head, tipped up her

chin and fired him an impatient look. Her hands played distractedly with her hair and she glanced away. Gathering it all into a
single swathe, she curled it around the back of her neck and let
it lie across one shoulder. Its sheen glinted. "Look at me, Maggie.
This is important."

She met his gaze with a sparkling, playful smile, put one fist
over her mouth and contorted her voice so that it sounded like
she was speaking through a loudhailer. "Roll up! Roll up! Ladies
and gentleman. For One Night Only. In a hotel suite near you …"

"Stop it." He grabbed her wrist, drew her close. "Don't play
the clown." He kissed her deeply. Suppressing a groan, he forced
himself to stop, pulled back from her. Did human beings ever really
spontaneously combust? On *Mercy of the Vampires* there'd been
an episode when his wicked half-werewolf, half-vampire cousin
had exploded into flames and melted into an unattractive pool
of putrid gloop. All he wanted to do was scoop Maggie into his
arms and carry her straight to bed. "I'm being serious."

Maggie reached up and touched his face, her palm smooth
against his jaw. "I'm not looking for a relationship. We both know
that."

He pressed his forehead to hers. "We're on the same page then?"

"Sure," she said, twisting away and heading towards her
bedroom. "One night. End of story." She turned back, met his
gaze, and since he hadn't budged, took his hand and laced her
fingers through his, tugging so that she could uproot him from
his spot and pull him after her. "We've already hit the headlines.
Might as well make the most of it."

"The newspapers are a law unto themselves."

"I get that."

One minute Maggie was leading Jago the merciless vampire to
her bedroom, and the next she was off her feet and in the arms of
Alex, as if she was lighter than air. She let out a squeal of delight
and anchored herself by circling her arms around his neck. He
was too gorgeous for words. And tonight the top-of-the-hotties

was all hers.

She trembled, remembering that she needed to hang on to the vampire fantasy and not risk letting her heart believe that she was finally spending a night with her fabulous lost-but-found-friend.

She gave a kind of internal shrug. Either way, it was unreal. He was taking her to bed.

*Result!*

She'd left her scarf draped on the back of a sofa. As Alex carried her to his room she reached out with one hand and grabbed it.

"What's that for?" His voice was gravelly hoarse.

"I want you to blindfold me."

"Oh no, lady. Your wish is my command. But not that. I want to see your face." Silent for a second, he added throatily, "Your eyes."

He tossed the scarf across the room. It unfurled, opening up into a rainbow parachute as it billowed in the air and floated to the floor. Alex shouldered open the door to his bedroom. Maggie tried to kick off her shoes. They were bound fast by the ribbons at her ankles. He sat on the bed with Maggie across his lap and slowly undid the ties. First one shoe, then the other, hit the deep-pile carpet with a muffled clunk.

He stood, lifting her with him, and setting her on her feet beside the ridiculously super-sized bed. Giddy, she steadied herself with one hand on the bulge of his biceps. She traced the line of his mouth with one finger.

"I want your lips to cover my body in figures of eight," she whispered huskily, adding stupidly. "Like you do with your conquests in *Mercy of the Vampires.*"

His jaw tensed. Hands balanced on his broad shoulders, beneath her fingers a shudder rippled across the muscles.

"I thought you weren't into the vampire stuff."

"I changed my mind. I've unbanned it."

"It's always a lady's prerogative to change her mind." His quiet words spelt it out clearly. She had the option to back out if she wanted to.

She shook her head slowly, knotting her arms around his neck, twisting her fingers into his hair and drawing his head down. "I haven't changed my mind about anything else." He'd put a spell on her. Magnetic desire had turned her spaced-out and rubbery-boned. Backing out now would be an impossibility.

He dwarfed her, a tower of rock-hard muscle. Smaller without her heels, she felt as if she'd swallowed a shrinking potion. Her confidence wobbled. Alex wasn't a passing fancy. But imagining that she could have any kind of life with him in it would be a fantasy.

*It's a fling. One night. Nothing more.*

She resolved to immerse herself in the pretense that she was being seduced by Hot Vampire Guy. If she admitted it to him, she'd risk losing the one night she craved with Alex – forever.

He clasped her tight against him. She melted into his muscles, lost in his hold. It felt so right, far beyond control.

She took a deep breath as if she was about to jump into the deep end of an infinity pool, somewhere hot and beautiful.

Holding her so close that she could feel his heartbeat, Alex's erection pressed hard and urgent against her middle. He slipped the fabric of her dress off her shoulders and it fell to her waist. Outside a moon, now only one sliver short of a full circle, hung high above the trees in Central Park. Her naked breasts stood out pale and rose-peaked, bathed in silvery light. With one swift move Alex found the zip and expertly freed the fabric covering the curve of her bum so that it dropped at her feet, leaving her standing in nothing but a wisp of lace with a shimmering pool of black silk and sparkly sequins at her feet. As he was about to kiss her, he let out a raw groan and stepped back, striding quickly across the room to close the curtains.

Along with the moonlight she shut out emotion, erasing her feelings like darkness stripping away color. Her body quivered as he picked her up and laid her on the bed, compelling her to acknowledge that he was no fantasy.

With impatient fingers she unknotted his bow tie and tossed it aside. She pushed his jacket off his shoulders, hurrying him to shuck it. Her hands fumbled for his buttons, her undoing of them awkward and inexpert. He breathed heavily as she pulled at his shirt, held fast by cufflinks at his wrists.

"Flip. Sorry," she whispered. He gave a low, seductive laugh, rolled onto his back, unfastened the cuffs of his shirt, and dropped them – somewhere. He rolled the shirt into a ball and launched it across the room. Maggie's eyes had adjusted to the dark. She straddled him. She smoothed her hands up his arms, feeling her way over his biceps to his shoulders, down across his broad chest. She paused on his rock-solid pecs, hard nipples under her palms, and continued her quest down across his perfect abs until her fingers made contact with the cool metal of his belt buckle.

He stopped her, gently clasping her wrists.

He rolled her over onto her back until he was astride her. His mouth grazed her neck. "Figures of eight, you say?"

*Oh yes!*

He cupped her breasts. Rapture lapped at her center. He kissed her deeply and broke from her mouth to work his way down her throat and across her collarbone, plotting an unrelenting course towards her breasts. Every inch of her zinged with heat. Her nipples jutted as his mouth pleasured first one, then the other, slowly running his tongue over the hardened tips.

Ever so slowly he went lower, tracing the loop-de-loop of a figure eight around her midriff.

Her body arched into him as his mouth feathered her abdomen, moving down with the velvet caress of butterfly wings. A lava flow of hot sweetness pooled at her center. Her desire grew greater by the second, her body crying out for him, screaming for more. He went lower, proving her lacey thong was insubstantial when he ripped through it with his teeth, first the strip at her left hip, then the right. He flicked the torn black lace onto the floor before parting her thighs and going down on her, pressing his mouth to the soft fold and plunging gently with his tongue. Pops of sensation ricocheted through her like the first bright rockets of a firework display shooting into a night sky. She vocalized the ecstasy at her core with a guttural cry. The room spun. He teased her clitoris with skilled strokes, bringing her in waves to the pinnacle of desire until, with a final deft strike of his tongue, he drove her over the edge. The pleasure rush thrummed at her center, spreading out through her body like ripples from a pebble dropped in a pond.

She touched his shoulders, drew him back to her until his mouth met hers and she tasted her essence on his lips. "I want you. I need you. In me. Now." The rasping command spelt out her want.

He palmed one breast. His mouth lowered and opened over the other, warm and wet. Half a day's stubble growth grated against her skin, pushing her desperation to feel him inside her off the scale. She craved him like a drug. He persisted in keeping the jigsaw fit of hard meeting soft just outside her reach. His hand went between her legs. He played with her body, resisting her hot, moist sex, until she was so turned-on that she let out a cry of wanton need.

"I don't want to hurt you. Or the baby." He rasped out the words like a solemn vow.

"You won't. You can't."

Urgently his hands undid his belt buckle. He littered his clothes on the floor and sheathed himself.

Finally – finally – he braced his body over hers, parted her thighs with his, and entered her, filling her up completely. He moved inside her with gentle strokes – strong, graceful. A living, breathing statue of muscular male beauty he yielded himself to her – purposeful, determined.

Totally in control.

She pulled him close against her, letting herself be absorbed by him, legs and arms entwined.

Sex with Alex, until now unimaginable, unattainable, and better than any craving she could dream up.

"You're better than strawberries in champagne."

"That's good to know," he groaned against her ear, breath hot. His mouth on hers silenced her before she could make any more food and alcohol-based comparisons. She wanted to tell him he was a magic potion, an elixir of love. Someone should bottle him.

His heavenly physique, holding her, moving inside her, fabulously in tune with the rhythm of her very being stopped her wandering mind in its tracks.

In that instant, perfectly joined, so that where he ended she began, and where he began she ended, their limbs locked in visceral harmony, she finally twigged that she'd been conning herself with the idea that she could pretend she had a super-crush on Jago to satisfy. She wasn't having sex with a vampire. She'd surrendered herself body and soul to the only man she'd ever come close to falling in love with.

*What if he's The One?*

The thought was much too heavy to bear. Feverishly her lips found his and she fought to lose herself in his kiss.

A fusion of sensation rocked both their bodies. Together, in perfect sync, they tipped each other into a dynamite orgasm. Locked together in release, despite her determination to hold on to nothing but the moment, an overwhelming tide of emotion engulfed her.

Afterwards, she lay on her back and stared up into the dark space, where she knew somewhere there was a ceiling. *Pah.* She aimed a cynical snarl at herself. *So we came together with intuitively good timing. So what?*

That didn't make Alex The One. There was no such thing.

She rolled onto one side, her back to him. He ran the pads of his fingers lazily over her skin, drawing large loopy eights. She turned back to face him. He drew her close. And they made love again.

Much later Alex's voice was the first to break the sated silence.

"Magenta," he drawled. Her heart fluttered. "It's official. I'm beaten. You've worn me out." She laughed, licked her finger and marked up a point scored in the air. "What is it with you?"

"I'll add you as a notch on my bedpost when I get home." Her bravado was completely fake, but convincing enough for him to raise an eyebrow and quiz her.

"Are there many of those notches on your bedpost, Magenta?" The way he rumbled out her name made her heart quiver.

"No," she answered truthfully. "Not really." If there were, she thought ruefully, she wouldn't have needed to go to the trouble of making a baby on her own. Admittedly, she'd been avoiding rejection. In any case, there'd been no one who'd made love to her like Alex just had. Certainly not Marcus. He'd been low on passion – at least where she was concerned. She'd been duped into believing that she was loved and safe and cared for when she'd been none of those things.

He gathered her onto his chest and she lay for a long time, one cheek flat against his skin, listening to the thud of his beating heart. She traced a lazy figure of eight on one smooth pec. "Don't get big-headed. I mean it was great and all, but I think it's more down to loopy pregnancy hormones than anything else."

His face dropped in mock displeasure. "Ouch. And there was me thinking my technique might have improved over the years."

She placed a kiss just below his collarbone and raised herself on one elbow to look him in the eyes. Their blue depths remained ever-cool. "It has," she confirmed. "It so-o has." She lowered her head and tracked her way over his body, softly moving her lips across his abdomen, following the line of dusky hair that arrowed downwards. "And so has mine," she murmured as she sensed his officially done-in erection surge back into life.

She acknowledged with pure delight the low, deep groan of pleasure that escaped from his throat in that moment.

Much later, when the grey dawn light intruded through a chink in the curtains, Alex lay propped on one elbow, wide awake, watching Maggie sleep, and listening to her breathe. Earlier, when he'd held her close, joined so inextricably that his body had melded with hers, he'd felt her heart beating and been consumed by a sense of rightness.

And wrongness – for there wasn't just one beating heart in her body. There were two. A mire of emotion, from which he couldn't begin to extricate himself, swamped him. He admired her determination to have a family of her own. But could he get past the fact that he'd been gutted when he'd seen the positive test result? That was everything to do with how he felt about himself, and nothing to do with his feelings for Maggie.

She'd been a spectacular lover; fiery, sexy, responsive. Lying beside him she looked pale and beautiful in the dawn light. What if he could stay in her life and take care of her? There was no point in asking that question. It couldn't happen. She'd misunderstood when he said that he didn't want to hurt her or the baby. He knew enough biology to be certain that sex couldn't physically harm them. What he'd meant was that he didn't want to risk being with her long enough to let her down. It would be a mistake to wonder if they could make it last. She'd been categorically clear that she wasn't expecting any more than one night. And she didn't have room in her life for a permanent man. Even if they were to give it a go, it wouldn't be long before the flipside of his fame dragged them down. The pressure of being in the public eye would get in the way. It had already started. Every which way he wrestled with his feelings, it boiled down to the same thing – great sex might keep them together, but everything else would drive them apart.

He'd had a second chance with her and he would be rock-solid. He'd love her for one weekend and leave her to get on with her life.

# *Chapter Sixteen*

Maggie slept and slept and woke to find that, instead of being on a flight to London Heathrow, she was still in bed with Alex. *Oops.* They spent a languorous hour or two of Sunday making love, pausing to punctuate their love-fest with a delicious brunch courtesy of room service. For reasons of Britishness, Alex ordered scones with strawberry jam and cream especially for her.

"Afternoon tea for brunch?"

Alex picked up his watch from the bedside table and checked the time. "It *is* afternoon."

"You need to keep your strength up." With a smirk on her face she spooned a dollop of cream onto a halved, jam-spread scone and passed it to him. She'd taken up residence in the middle of Alex's big bed and, wrapped in a bed-sheet toga, she sat cross-legged, scoffing scones and feeling no inclination whatsoever to budge. She didn't care that they were making crumbs.

"You did put out the do-not-disturb sign, didn't you?" she asked for the umpteenth time.

"Check." he replied, without impatience.

He downed his last scone half, and gulped from a teacup in a not-so-genteel manner. "I'm going to take a shower. Care to join me?"

She shook her head. She watched his smooth brown back

disappear into the bathroom without her. She took in his height and the breadth of his shoulders with a touch of awe.

Abandoning her sheet toga she ventured off her bed island and snatched up Alex's discarded I Heart NY tee from the night of the premiere. She put it on. It swamped her. She gathered a fistful of fabric, pressed it to her nose and inhaled the manly-spiced scent he'd left behind.

She wandered barefoot into the sitting room. In spite of the scone feast, she was ravenous. She chose a green apple from a fruit bowl on the coffee table and plonked herself on the sofa, legs tucked up under her on the cushions. She bit into the apple. It hit her taste buds with a fusion of sweetness and tang. She set it on the coffee table and picked up the laptop.

Quickly she typed Alex Wells and New York. The search brought up a stack of hits.

"Oh. My. Gosh." She uttered the words between hyperventilating breaths as she clicked on the first one, then the second, and the third. It was the biggest shock seeing herself on a celebrity lifestyle page described as "Cinderella of New York City".

Fresh from the bathroom Alex walked into the room. A towel wrapped tantalizingly around his waist, he rubbed at his wet hair with another one, pushing dark strands that had fallen across one eye out of his face.

She made to close the screen. Too quick for her, he peered over her shoulder, halting her action by reaching over and closing his hand over hers. "Catching up on celebrity gossip?"

She picked up the apple, took another bite, and gulped. "Uh-huh." She ate the last mouthfuls of her apple and tossed the core into a bin.

"Anything interesting?" The rumble of his voice and his half-naked body ignited new sparks of desire in her.

"Not really." She tried to keep the tremble out of her voice as she added lightly, "Just some guy who plays a TV vampire, or something."

Alex massaged her neck. "What about him?"

"He's been bonking his stylist." He rounded the sofa and sat next to her. She passed him the computer. "Allegedly."

He scrolled through the photos. "That takes the biscuit." Color drained from his freshly shaven face.

Maggie gawped at the screen. "Is Jago the Daddy?" She'd only just found out that she was pregnant and there was a picture of her going into the charity event at the Empire State Building with a baby bump the size of a beach ball.

"What the …?"

"They've altered the photo. It's the press's current favorite trick." He closed the laptop. "It's best not to look. Try not to let it bother you."

She was out of her depth. "That's easy for you to say."

"This isn't rhino hide." He pinched the skin on the back of his hand. "Sometimes it's best to ignore stuff. Wait for it to go away."

Maggie gently touched his hand with the pad of her thumb, moving it in circles over the spot that he'd pinched. "That's why I told the reporter you're not the dad. I thought the story would go away if they knew I'd had donor insemination."

Alex pulled his hand away abruptly. "Evidently that's not the story they wanted to run."

Unsettled by his abrasive reaction, she jumped up and hurried to the bathroom. In the shower she closed her eyes and turned her face up into the comforting warmth of the water. The streams trickled over her. Sadness clouded her mind like a storm spoiling a perfect day. Some crazy, stupid, mixed-up part of her wanted Alex to be her baby's dad. It was a bigger fantasy than trying to convince herself that last night she'd been making love to a vampire. Who was she kidding? That notion had been a non-starter from the micro-second after the moment she'd dreamt it up, and so was this. She and Alex had both accepted that no matter how good this was, it had no future.

She lathered her hair with an excessive dollop of the hotel's freebie shampoo. The citrus aroma filled the shower cubicle. She tipped back her head and ran her fingers into her hair, rinsing out the sudsy froth with grim determination. She'd given in to one night with Alex. She remained in control of her life. She felt more for him than she'd wanted to believe at first. A lot more. He could turn her beliefs about the non-existence of The One upside down with just one word – if he wanted to. She was in love with him. But she couldn't make him love her. And she couldn't make him feel something he didn't. She was okay with that. She had to be. She'd always known she'd never have him. There was something about him. Something isolated, remote. He was hers for now. She'd given herself totally to him and in doing so her heart hadn't shattered into a zillion tiny pieces.

She wasn't like one of those airhead girls his character seduced on the show. She was still standing. In charge of her world. Mistress of her own destiny. And undeterred by an intrusive story on the internet.

Suddenly she felt his body. Strong. Smooth. Hard. Like hot marble.

Incongruous. And tempting.

His arms closed round her, drawing her close against him so that his erection jutted against the curve at the base of her spine. Hot, wet and naked in the shower with Alex she was powerless; unable to resist his potent sex appeal, the deep sensuality of his lips on the back of her neck. She turned into his arms and kissed his solid chest, moving her mouth gently over his sun-golden skin. Water showered over them.

Her body responded to his magnetism. On automatic.

"Get a condom," she urged. He did as she bid.

Clear. Decisive. She knew her own mind. She'd make love to him one last time. And leave.

His mouth, softer than before, slippery, deeply sensual, closed over hers. He cupped his hands under her bum and lifted her. She entwined him with her legs. Water pooled in her cleavage and trickled over her breasts. The contact of her nipples with his skin pushed her desire off the charts. He entered her. The concoction of wet, hot bodies was more than she could bear. A moan of pleasure formed low in her throat. Their bodies powered up in unison, driving each other higher. Towards climax. Locked in ecstasy. She came first. His release followed seconds after.

"Alex!" The cry that had been building inside her escaped in a groan of supplication and satisfaction. "I have to leave."

They relaxed their hold on each other. Shadows darkened his eyes where blue light had danced moments before. He stepped out of the shower. She watched him from beneath lowered lashes, admiring his physical perfection.

For the last time.

He held out a plush bathrobe. She stepped dripping onto the tiles, slipped her arms into it and tied the belt. She grabbed a towel and made a turban. He undid it again, dried the ends of her hair, and threw the towel on the floor. He ploughed his hands into the long, damp strands and massaged her scalp, moving his fingers in sensuous circles. He touched her chin, his fingers firm, forcing her not to avoid his eyes. "Look at me." His deep voice sent tingles rippling down her spine. He pressed a soft kiss to her mouth, lingered, and she ached to let it deepen. Except he broke away. "There's no 'have to' about it." His tone was direct, his mood electric. She opened her mouth to insist. He cut her off. "We're going out."

"I'm not going anywhere but the airport. I need to rebook my flight."

He put a finger on her lips and replaced it with a light kiss. His mouth moved upwards, feathering first her nose then her forehead. Thrown by the tender gesture Maggie froze.

"Stay," he insisted huskily. "You've missed one flight today already. What's the hurry? Besides, there's somewhere I'd like to take you."

"Wh-Where?" All too ready to cave, she knew that staying

would be like putting skates on her heart and allowing it to take off across the thinnest ice.

"Broadway," he announced. "I called in a favor. I've got us comps for a show."

His big break-your-heart-smile spread across his face so that creases hollowed his cheeks, like brackets. "You're not leaving New York without taking in a show on the Great White Way. I won't allow it."

She was topsy-turvy with doubt and desire. She'd had her one-night stand. She really didn't want to leave, but she didn't know if she could stay without blathering about her feelings all over the place. And that would make a terrible mess.

The temptation was too much. Alex wasn't going to happen to her again in this lifetime.

"Oh, you won't?" She rose to the challenge. "We'll have to see about that." She ran her hands over his broad, golden chest, skimming tauntingly downwards to where he'd tucked a towel around his waist. He groaned and halted the downward progress of her hands, circling her wrists with the gentle force of his big hands. His erection stood proud under the white towel.

"You'll pay for that later." He spoke raspingly. The effect she had on his gorgeous body delighted her.

"I'll settle up now if it's all the same to you."

With that she jumped into his arms, and wrapped her body in a tight tangle around his. Leaving wet towels scattered on the floor, he carried her back to bed. Living in the moment, she squealed with delight and gave herself over to a bout of delicious Alex-style pleasure.

Resigned to the fact that she was about to set off for *JFK*, Maggie swooned a little as Alex shoved the big, stupid penguin with the silly fixed grin on its beak into the back of a yellow taxi outside the hotel where they'd spent another blissful night. The show had been great, but rather than risk any more run-ins with photographers, or worse still, would-be paps with their phone cameras, instead of heading for an upscale restaurant where New Yorkers go to see and be seen, they'd gone back to their suite and ordered room service.

It was fine by Maggie. She was much happier alone with Alex than being seen out and about with him. After a night of passion and intensity, things had been left unsaid. What would have been the point in telling Alex how she felt about him? He couldn't say he loved her back if he didn't.

Alex swept Maggie into his arms in a strong hug. It felt as if she'd melt there and then on the New York street and trickle down a drain, never to be seen again. She inhaled the freshly showered scent of his warm skin as his cheek brushed hers. It was over. She was clinging on to her self-control by a thread. If he asked her to stay any longer, she'd fall so hard for him that she'd never recover. She needn't have worried. It was over for him too. He had a full day of press stuff scheduled and his taxi was waiting, engine running, an impatient driver drumming his fingers on the steering wheel.

"Bye, Alex. It was nice …"

"Nice?" Both eyebrows shot up.

"Better than nice." She climbed into the cab. "It was …" She searched for a word. Why did this have to be awkward? She sounded so prim. He watched her closely, mesmerizing her with his eyes.

"… Wicked?" he supplied. His Jago hint of an almost-smile slotted into place.

Maggie didn't reply. She quivered inside, suppressing a bubble of emotion. She wanted to do this goodbye thing with the poise of an actress in a black and white movie.

An irritable blast on the horn came from the taxi behind. "Time to go." Alex closed the door of Maggie's taxi and slammed his hand down on the roof, signaling to the driver that he could set off. "See you in London."

The words stung. She couldn't bear to go down the road of imagining him in her life, loving him, relying on him being there. Through the open window she heard his voice boom theatrically. "I want you at my first night. And, don't forget, I'm counting on you for a makeover." As the taxi drove away he signaled with a thumb to his ear and his little finger to his mouth that he would call.

# Chapter Seventeen

London had been grey since she'd flown back from New York. Grey sky. Grey river. Grey buildings. There hadn't been a blink of sunshine in a whole week. And to make things more glum, the crazy stories about Maggie and Alex in the gossip mags and on the internet had had the opposite of the desired effect on her work. Instead of being more in demand, a television presenter who'd booked her for style advice prior to a big awards ceremony had cancelled. Maggie refused to let the greyness get her down.

In the galley kitchen of her Battersea studio apartment she located her big jar of duty-free jelly beans. She took it down off a shelf crowded with assorted, pretty, mismatched crockery and shook it. She'd already picked out all the peachy-pie flavor. She started hunting out kiwi, extracting them carefully between an orange-tipped thumb and forefinger.

She was steadfastly ignoring her mobile phone. Every time she picked it up it reminded her that she had three missed calls from Alex – deliberately missed.

She cursed herself for failing dismally to separate emotion from sex in New York. She'd been a thrill-seeker to the hold his body had over hers, and entranced by the effect she seemed to have on him. She'd been a complete idiot. She'd allowed herself to become so wrapped up in him it hurt.

She could delete his calls, go on avoiding him, but it wouldn't make her feel any better. Facing up to Alex would be better than hiding from him, so after popping a small selection of jelly beans to fortify her she picked up her phone and pressed call.

"Hey. How've you been?" Alex's deep, smooth tone gave her butterflies.

"Fine," she said, trying to sound casual. "Doing this and that."

There was a moment of lead silence.

"Any baby news?" He sounded like something was stuck in his throat, as if he too was scoffing jelly beans and had swallowed a handful in one go. "Have you had a scan? Or anything?"

"Nope. Not yet." She had an appointment in her diary for the following week. It was on the tip of her tongue to say so, but she held back. Alex wasn't part of her baby plan. It would be a mistake to share any more details than she already had.

"I've got a favor to ask." Alex got straight to the point. "I want you to give me that makeover."

Maggie laughed. "You don't need one."

"I need to make some changes. I want to lose the Jago look." Now Maggie had a lump in her throat. She thought he'd got past stressing that he wouldn't be taken seriously as an actor as long as he was associated with having played a vampire. "Please, Maggie." Her heart flipped. "Say you'll help me out. I need to change my image – fast. Frankly yesterday wouldn't be too soon."

The misgivings in her head counted for nothing when an hour later she found herself sitting with Alex in a café, discussing ways he could tweak his appearance, and sketching out ideas on napkins in pencil; not because that was in any way necessary, simply to keep her fingers busy. She'd got a surprise when she first saw him. He was wearing a beanie and when he pulled it off she saw that he'd had his hair cut short in preparation for playing Hamlet. It suited him, accentuating his chiseled bone structure.

"How have you got time for this?" she asked. Her pencil whisked deftly over a fresh paper napkin. When she looked down she'd doodled a wonky heart. She obliterated it with a criss-cross, coloring between the lines until it was an unrecognizable grey blob. "Shouldn't you be busy with theatrical luvvy stuff?"

"I'm not needed. They're ironing out technical glitches." He smiled a big, lazy smile. "I'm all yours." His smile was infectious. She'd love him to want her. What he wanted was her expertise in the style department.

Maggie stirred her hot chocolate. It smelt sweet and milky and soothing, and much better than coffee. She'd gone right off that. "You don't have to leave *Mercy of the Vampires* behind, you know. In fact, the sooner you accept that it will always be with you, the better."

"Are you saying I can't change?"

Maggie leant her elbow on the table and propped her chin on her hand. "That depends. You can change your image. You've already started." She flicked a glance at his haircut. "I like the hair, by the way." She wondered how it would feel beneath her fingers. *Aghhhh! Thoughts of that nature would be best avoided.* She picked up her pencil again and aimlessly doodled. "I think you need to trust people more. There's a world of difference between Alex Wells and Jago."

"He's a fictional character – obviously. But sometimes it feels like the distinction between him and me gets blurred."

It hadn't escaped her notice that a small gang of well-groomed ladies were giggling behind their coffee cups and sending furtive glances in his direction.

"What exactly is it you're trying to achieve? I can take you shopping. I can advise you about what's on trend. I can change your look. But I can't change you." She tried to rein her opinion in, but couldn't help herself. "And really truly," she added, "I wouldn't want to. In ten years' time Jago will be part of a whole range of work that you'll have done. You've got to stop wanting to pretend that *Mercy of the Vampires* didn't happen."

Alex ran a hand over his newly short hair. "Put like that it sounds like I'm ungrateful. I'm not. I've had ten amazing years."

"And here's to the next ten!" Maggie picked up her hot chocolate and clinked it against his coffee mug. "Be proud of Jago," she suggested gently. "And be grateful that he's led you to where you are now. You did the right thing when you went to LA."

They hit the shops and time flew. Revamping Alex was a dreamy assignment, and with New York fresh in her memory, it was even dreamier. It was hard to keep reminding herself that whatever craziness had happened between them in those few out-of-this-world days they'd spent together, it wasn't real, it had nowhere to go.

And if he asked her to have dinner? Or go back to his apartment? What would she do? She'd better get used to it. The fantasy had ended. What happened in New York stayed in New York.

While Alex was paying for his things, Maggie ducked into the nearest Ladies.

She couldn't walk past a toilet these days without needing to pee.

She avoided the mirror, unsettled by the empty-shell reflection she'd glimpsed looking back at her. Uncertainty hit her hard. A man to love forever hadn't happened for her. She'd like to love one. Could one love her back? Right now Alex was the only man on her radar and there was not a chance that he'd love her back. She was pretty sure that he was immune to twenty-four-seven love. Even her mother hadn't been up for loving her all day, every day. The odds weren't stacked in her favor. People weren't meant to stay together forever. They went their own ways and did the things they wanted to do. That's why she'd come up with her man-free family plan in the first place.

Alex would keep her around for a while. She'd go to his first night. He might invite her to kill a couple of hours over a hot chocolate between performances. But she wouldn't be his, and he wouldn't want her. In the end he'd let her go. Just like last time.

A peculiar thought niggled at her. Maybe – just maybe – the right guy would be like buses in her Cornish village. It was a standing joke in the local pub, where would-be passengers preferred to wait rather than spend an hour at the bus stop. Always jovial, the landlord would say "If you wait long enough one'll definitely be along." He'd qualify the statement with an aside, adding, "Some time." Baffled tourists would mutter about the lack of accurate timetables and he'd pour them a pint. Perhaps she just had to wait a bit longer and Another One would come along. Could there be more than one possible perfect fit for everyone? She and Alex were a really great fit. Really. Great. Perhaps somebody else – another great guy – would be along when the time was right.

Something about this theory wasn't working for her. For a micro-moment Alex had given her back her optimism about finding love, and taken it away again because she'd gone and fallen for him. As long as he was in her life he'd be in the way. He couldn't be The One, no matter how badly she wanted him to be. Nothing was clear any more. In New York he'd shown her how two people could be indescribably good together. Together their bodies had been on fire. She'd have to force herself to let that memory go. They'd been moseying around a London department store and she was giving him fashion tips. Alex had got to know her again, and all he wanted was a stylist friend. On those terms she wasn't cut out to be in his life long-term. What she felt wasn't infatuated crazy-4-U-type love. It was the real deal.

She'd given him a piece of her heart. She should have known better. Since she couldn't rely on love to always be there, it was better not to risk letting it in in the first place. Long-haul love was designed for other people. Not her. Not Alex. Not together. She clung on to her one certainty. Her love for her baby would be strong and unwavering and unconditional.

She'd forgotten how good it felt being with someone she cared about. That was the trouble. The biggest problem was no longer the onslaught of his sexiness; although she didn't know quite what to do about that. Right now she needed to unravel the Alex-shaped knot in her heart and say goodbye.

By the time she came out of the loos the knot in her heart had been banished by cold dread. She'd noticed a brownish-reddish spot in her knickers. Her heart froze. Was she going to lose the pregnancy? She stood, statue-still in the middle of men's fashion and panicked. A handful of customers browsed, picking things up and putting them back, studying colors, labels, prices. Oblivious, Maggie's head spun. She'd put her free-wheeling life on hold, made new plans, pinned all her dreams on repopulating the cottage her grandmother had left her with a new little Plumtree family member. She could have taken the donor insemination not working first time on the chin. Losing the baby now that she was pregnant? She couldn't bear it.

"Maggie?" Alex touched her arm and she jumped. "Are you okay? I've been looking for you everywhere?" He frowned. She'd gone as white as a sheet.

"Yeah. Yes," she said. "I'm fine. I've got to go. I'll call you."

She looked distracted. Something was definitely wrong. "Maggie?"

She clutched her handbag to her stomach, hazel eyes wide. "I'm not fine. I don't know what to do. I think I might be going to lose the baby."

She was trembling. Bleak fear spread through his chest. The intensity could have buckled his legs. He fought it. He needed to take care of Maggie. He found a shop assistant and took her down to the ground floor in an elevator normally reserved for merchandise. Leaving the store discreetly by a side door, he flagged down a taxi and gently bundled her in as if she'd been covered in the store's white sticky tape with "fragile" printed on it in big red letters. From the taxi he called the nearest hospital with an early-pregnancy unit and told them that he was bringing her in. Reeling at the sadness in her eyes, he realized grimly that he couldn't be more devastated for her.

At the hospital they seemed to wait forever. Finally she was taken away and interviewed by a nurse. He waited, stupidly, helplessly, and surrounded by carrier bags dumped on the grey linoleum. Maggie had been right. He could change his appearance, get a cool new look, but it wouldn't change what mattered, who he was on the inside. His heart twisted. Choked-up emotion erupted inside him. He suppressed it. Maggie had come so far since he'd gone and become famous and dropped her like a hot potato. Unlike him she'd done it all on her own – not thanks to a famous name, the way he had. He admired her. She was proud of her life and excited to be having a baby. His heart cracked, hoping against hope that everything would be fine.

Pallid, she reappeared in the waiting room and sat gingerly in the chair next him. "Well?" He grated out the only word he could manage.

"They're going to do an ultrasound," she whispered. "Check for a heartbeat." She looked at the floor, drawing his eyes back to the jumble of bags.

Had he wanted a makeover? Really? Or had he just wanted to see her, be with her? He'd figured that if he could lose Jago and start again with a clean slate, he could become the actor he aspired to be, earn his father's approbation. Sitting next to Maggie, waiting, he didn't give a monkey's about Drake's approval. She was all he cared about. Drake wasn't his biological father, but that wasn't what made him a bad dad. He'd messed up. He hadn't taken care of Cassandra's heart, and he'd been careless with his sons' feelings. All through his teenage years, his father had sniped at his mother via the press, and been photographed with serial generically glamorous girlfriends. Some role model!

"Mrs. Plumtree?" The nurse's voice jolted through him. She eyed him sympathetically as Maggie stood up.

"Aren't you coming with us, Mr. Plumtree?" she asked.

"Oh, he's not the dad." Maggie swept a dismissive hand through the air. She shook her head. "He's just a friend."

Alex remained seated, feeling like an idiot. Smoldering under his TV front was an easy out when he didn't want to confront real feelings. He'd been so completely stuck in his belief that it was impossible to have a relationship – to get to know someone properly – without his fame intruding on some level, that he'd failed to recognize his superlative arrogance, imagining that just about everyone on the planet knew who he was.

The nurse, fortyish in navy scrubs, looked him over shrewdly. "Well, whoever you are, you're here now and I'm sure your friend would appreciate some moral support."

Her composure transparently fragile, Maggie frowned. "Hold my hand?" How could he refuse? Her uneasy suggestion sounded half-plaintive, half-hopeful. A deeply entrenched memory of his mother's isolation and dismay in the time after his father left them lanced him. Time splintered, and a powerful emotion burst through him. His heart ached to do something, anything, to make everything alright for Maggie.

"This way, please," the nurse instructed. "You can leave Ms. Plumtree's shopping with the receptionist. She'll keep an eye on it."

A bemused smile briefly wiped away Maggie's worried frown as Alex scrambled to round up the bags. He deposited them at the desk and the bespectacled receptionist, who'd been handing notes to a deceptively scatty-looking junior doctor, removed the pencil that was jammed between her teeth and murmured dreamily, "Is that who I think it is? I wouldn't object if he held my hand."

"It's all looking tickety-boo." The sonographer slid the ultra-sound thingy through the blue-tinted gel on Maggie's belly. "Nothing whatsoever to worry about."

"Wow." She stared at the screen, awed at the notion of seeing the new life beginning inside her. The close-to-retirement-age woman sent her a kind smile. Her reading glasses dangled on a chain around her neck. The specs must have had an accident because one arm was held on with a sticking plaster. She calmly went on clicking, measuring, and recording. "This is my first," Maggie said. She squinted at the grey image struggling to pick out a recognizable form. *What should I see? A peanut-sized baby?* "You must have seen hundreds of these."

"Indeed. But it's not every day I see two at once."

Disbelief gripped Maggie. "Two?"

"I believe so. You're expecting twins. If you'll excuse me a minute I'd like to see if the consultant's free to come in and take a look."

Reeling from the news that she was expecting two babies, Maggie didn't know if she was thrilled or terrified. Instant family. It was everything she'd dreamed of. But two?

"Oh. My. Giddy. Aunt."

"Twins!" Alex's hold on her hand tightened. "Awesome."

Everything whirred into a bit of a blur after that. The consultant arrived and explained that breakthrough bleeding was fairly common in early pregnancy, and that everything looked fine. She told Alex to bring Maggie back in if she experienced heavier bleeding or pain. Weary of explaining that he wasn't the father, and utterly relieved that nothing was wrong, she nodded and agreed. So did he.

Together on the pavement, outside the hospital, she pushed down the rising sense of panic that simmered beneath her upbeat surface. In silence, she zoned out to process the fact that she was having two babies. She'd gone into meltdown.

A London bus whooshed by with a mugshot of Ella Swift on its side. In the genes lottery she'd got eyes of two different colors. With one blue eye and one brown she was the poster girl for unique. She'd started out in modeling, done runway, been on the cover of countless glossy mags, and played the werewolf's sister in *Mercy of the Vampires*. She'd just made the jump from TV to movies, and on top of all that Maggie had heard in New York that she was the new face of a cosmetic brand. "Wow. Look at Ella! Now she's someone who got lucky with her genes."

Not caring what direction she was headed, Maggie started to walk.

"Sure," Alex agreed softly. Questioning concern shadowed his face. "Amazing looks are just a part of what makes her special, though. Right?"

"Absolutely. But people like to know who they get their family resemblances from. What if my children resent the fact that I can't tell them that stuff?

What if Donor Guy lied on his details form? Or worse," she gabbled. "What if there was a mix-up at the clinic and I didn't get the guy's sperm I chose? My babies could have got some other random donor's DNA by mistake."

"Maggie." He dropped his carrier bags on the wet pavement and gripped her upper arms gently, turning her to face him. "Look at me." She avoided his face. "It's too late for what-ifs. Genetics is a random business, whatever way it happens. You said so yourself. A genetic lottery? Isn't that what you called it?  The reason you were okay with this in the first place was because your own dad was pretty much a sperm donor. Remember?"

She locked eyes with him. "What if I was wrong?"

"Take it from me," he insisted. "It takes more than an ejaculation to make a real dad."

"I've been fixated on needing to be the perfect mother and now I'm having two babies, and I don't know who their dad is, and one day they're going ask me where they got their eyes and their nose and their smile from, and ..."

"And they'll be able to get that information when they're old enough." He pressed a finger into the furrow between his brows.

"I know," she admitted. "It's just that I hadn't thought about the baby – babies – wanting a dad. What if I'm not enough?"

Another red double-decker bus sailed past, full to almost bursting with passengers. Its wheels sloshed through an enormous puddle by a blocked drain and sent up a bow wave of filthy water. Alex laced his fingers through Maggie's, pulling her behind him, shielding her with his body, so that he got spattered and she didn't.

At that moment the heavens opened and his efforts to stop Maggie getting drenched were ruined.

"Right, that's it," he announced. "You're coming home with me. You've had a scare and you've found out you're having twins. You can't be alone tonight."

# *Chapter Eighteen*

Alex didn't take no for an answer and a taxi ride later he showed her into his penthouse apartment. He ran Maggie a warm bath and filled it to the brim with bubbles.

"This is kind, but there's no need for a fuss."

"I'll be the judge of that."

"It was just jitters." She straightened her shoulders, composing herself. "The scare threw me, but I'm fine now. Really. I don't need to stay, but I wouldn't say no to dinner."

"You'll not say no to breakfast either," he said firmly, "Because you're staying here tonight. I have to be sure that you're okay."

She lolled in luxury, letting the warmth seep into her bones, the twin news taking root in her mind. Calmly she told herself, "You can do this. You've thought it through from every angle." She trailed her hands through the bubbles, her nails a bright-orange contrast to the white froth. "Except the one where you get two babies for the price of one." With twins, being a single mum was certainly going to turn out tougher than she'd expected, but she didn't have any regrets.

Wrapped in a bathrobe she padded about barefoot on the soft carpet, a warm mug of tea cradled in her hands. Thanks to Alex's upmarket bath soak she smelt unusually spicy; grapefruit and bergamot top notes, the bottle said. Through floor-to-ceiling glass, lit-up London was spread out all around.

"The closest I've come to a view like this was on the London Eye," she said.

Alex stood next to her. "It's over there." She picked out the distant circle of lights and the Houses of Parliament beyond.

Stripped of his wet clothes, he'd changed into one of his new shirts.

"I'm modeling my new look for you. What do you think?"

She gave him the thumbs-up. She'd forgotten all about the makeover.

He tore off the shirt that she'd okayed and stood in the center of his minimalist living room, completely filling up the space with his fabulousness.

She'd fallen into the trap of wondering what it would be like to have Alex in her life as more than a friend once before. She didn't intend to make the mistake again.

Maggie rummaged in a bag. It was killing her trying not to think about touching that body, being touched back. Sun-golden skin. Taut muscle. Broad chest. Divine six-pack. The dark arrow that speared down from his navel. She pulled out a shirt.

"Here. Enough of the fashion parade, already. You're too fab for words. And I have complete faith that it all looks great on you." She threw it across the room and he caught it. His body was driving her to distraction. "Put that on. It's got dinner-cooking-shirt written all over it. I'm going out of my mind with hunger over here."

He grinned, shrugged his muscular arms into the shirt and quickly did up the buttons. In his hurry he'd done them up wrong. Her stylist's compulsion to fix it got the better of her. "Something's not right. You look a bit squiffy."

"I haven't touched a drop," he protested, mockery in his eyes.

Maggie's hands hovered over the fabric covering his chest as she undid and redid the offending buttons. For an electric moment she craved his kiss. Her head spun. An out-of-control compass point, she ached to lose herself in him. It wasn't going to happen.

"That's better," she said primly. She walked away, putting some space between herself and Alex, feeling all the while as if she was attached to a bungee and that if she dared to let go she'd ping straight back into his arms.

"Right. Dinner," he said decisively. He headed into the kitchen area of the amazing open- plan space and set to work, taking out pans and hunting out ingredients from the huge fridge. She couldn't help noticing that it contained a row of champagne bottles, just sitting, chilling, waiting for someone suitable to come along and pop the corks. A twinge of agony spiked through her, knowing that she wasn't that someone suitable. She hitched herself onto a stool, and Alex passed her a glass of iced water. As he cooked dinner the ice cubes slowly melted.

Twenty minutes later he'd magicked up tagliatelle with smoked ham and mushrooms in a red pesto and crème fraiche sauce. It was on the tip of her tongue to say "I could get used to this". She held back, biting down on her bottom lip. He sat on the stool next to her at the kitchen island. "Did I forget something?" he asked. "Black pepper? Parmesan?"

She shook her head. "No," she said. "It's perfect." *You're perfect.*

"Where's the spare bedroom?"

"There isn't one. I'll sleep on one of the sofas."

Like all things delicious, one more glass of wine or cracking into the second layer in a chocolate box, Alex was too much of a good thing, and Maggie knew she ought to go. She didn't want to, not if she didn't have to, so she stayed.

Alex produced some fresh linen and together they stripped and remade the bed. Until Alex she hadn't realized just how good having a man in her life to rely on could be. It threw her decision to become a single parent by choice into sharp focus. Was she being selfish? Was she even up to the task? She wouldn't get bored and make a shambles of being a parent like her mother. She'd tracked her down and filled her in via a video chat. She'd seemed quite enthusiastic about becoming a grandma. She'd also had some news of her own. She was selling the beach bar, returning to the UK, and getting married.

"My mother's leaving Spain." Maggie stuffed a pillow into a fresh white pillowcase. "She's met someone called Frank from Scotland. He's a builder. A widower. He has three grown-up kids, and a two-year-old grandson. They're planning a small wedding in a Scottish castle, no less, just as soon as she finds a buyer for the bar." Alex raised his eyebrows and together they straightened the duvet. "Anyway she's promised to be there for the birth, and to help out whenever she can."

"With the best will in the world, Scotland and Cornwall are at opposite ends of the country."

"She's genuinely making a new start. She's promised to try and be a cool granny."

"Isn't that an oxymoron?"

Maggie threw a pillow at him. "Not necessarily," she insisted. "Mind you, she was disappointed to find out that you're not the dad. She was pretty excited at the idea of having a celebrity in the family."

Looking at each other from opposite sides of the bed they both rolled their eyes.

When the bed was made, Alex took a blanket from his wardrobe and went off to sleep in the living room. Alone in his very big bed Maggie lay on her stomach, turned onto her side, flipped over on her back, turned onto her other side, and started the whole cycle again. Fifteen minutes later she was no closer to falling asleep. She got up and went to find Alex, dragging the king-size duvet behind her.

"Alex?" she whispered.

He sat bolt upright.

"What's wrong? Did something happen? Are you in pain?"

"No, no," she assured him. "It's nothing like that." She was sorry that she'd worried him, and added sheepishly, "I can't sleep."

Her eyes adjusted to the half-dark. Sprawled on a cream-leather sofa, propped on one elbow and naked to the waist, Alex's swoonworthy body took her breath away. Again.

She felt like a child who'd announced that she was scared of monsters under the bed as Alex got up and arranged her duvet on the enormous sofa opposite his. "You'd better stay here with me," he suggested.

"You did say I shouldn't be alone tonight." She sounded embarrassingly petulant.

She burrowed into the duvet and got comfy. Alex returned to his sofa, a safe distance away.

"Better now?"

"Yes, much." She hushed her voice, as though she might wake someone if she spoke normally. "I'm over my meltdown."

"You had me worried," Alex whispered back.

"There's no need to be concerned. I'm back on plan."

"I'm glad to hear it." He stayed silent a moment. "If you don't mind me asking, what is the plan? I mean you can't go directly to the maternity ward, do not pass go, do not collect two hundred pounds. You need to get organized."

"I'm getting organized," she protested, a little too testily. "I don't have anything concrete yet, but I've got new work plans, and when it's time for the baby … eeeees, I'm going home to Cornwall."

"That's great, Maggie, but who's going to be there – for you?"

She rolled over, turning her back to him. "I have friends," she said defensively, "There's Layla, and old friends from school, and neighbors of my grandmother's, and I told you, my mother said she'd help, and …" She stopped abruptly, suddenly hesitant. "My life's not as random as a board game. I'll manage."

Too wide awake, a childhood memory floated in her mind. A few months had gone by since her mum had gone and not come home. It was Layla's eighth birthday party. Her parents had hired a magician and he'd made a rabbit disappear. Lying in the dark with Alex so close, Maggie could still feel the sadness that had overwhelmed her when the rabbit vanished into thin air. Instead of being delighted, she'd been horrified. She'd cried and worked herself up into such a state that her grandmother had been called to collect her early. All cried-out, she'd waited by the door with her party bag and balloon, sucking in shivery, distressed breaths. Before her grandmother had arrived to take her away, the magic show had ended. The other children sat in a circle and took turns holding the white rabbit. Deceived, rejected, Maggie watched the party continue without her. So many times when she was growing up she'd ached for her mum to be there. After that day, even if it got her down, she never let it show. She'd like to think that her mum would stick to her promise. If she didn't, she'd survive.

It wasn't her mother's love that she wanted now. It was Alex's.

She couldn't protect her heart. He had it. She'd sneered when he said she needed a man to make her heart sing. How could she look him in the face and tell him that it was him? He was the one that did that. When she thought about not being alone, she couldn't imagine not being alone with anyone but him.

Alex lay still in the darkness, jaw clenched, holding back on making any kind of stab at articulating what was on his mind. He hoped her mum had meant it. The Maggie he knew ten years ago had a tendency to view life from the sunny side, even where her let-down of a mother was concerned. Nothing would make him angrier than to discover that her mother had been paying lip service to the notion of playing happy families. She hadn't exactly been reliable in the past. Maggie had come through thanks to her grandmother, but she wasn't there now. She needed someone she could count on.

A smile broke onto his face listening to her steady breathing that only just stopped short of qualifying as a snore. She was the only woman he'd risk his heart for, but she'd been crystal- clear. Her heart wasn't up for grabs. Her loving for one night meant more to him than he meant to her. He'd accepted that. She'd armor-plated herself against hurt. She wanted to be a single parent, and he respected her decision, although for days he'd been stamping down on the temptation to ask her if she'd change her mind. It was fortunate that he had *Hamlet* to absorb him, because when he wasn't throwing himself into the role, she was all he could think about. The way his heart sat in his mouth at the hospital, staring at the two heartbeats on the screen, he'd almost convinced himself that he could be a dad to Maggie's children, and then she'd gone into free-fall, freaking out about her babies' genes, and wretched fear had kicked in, opening up old wounds, reminding him of his family's chaos, his mother's irreparable unhappiness.

After he'd left his mother, his father had become emotionally cold. He couldn't be in a relationship with Maggie because if it didn't work out, he'd be ruining her carefully thought-out plan. He couldn't risk hurting her, repeating the past, walking away from his family. With Maggie, he'd stopped caring that he didn't know where half his DNA came from. Biological or not, Drake was the man he called his father, and he'd abandoned his mother, played a heartless game of reject-you-reject-you-not with him and Nick, and set up expectations where the bar was so high that neither of them could ever measure up.

The feelings he had for Maggie were so strong they hurt. He couldn't do anything about that. He'd left Maggie behind once before. He owed it to her not to take a chance on failing. Second time around, the best thing he could do was guarantee to be there for her if the going got tough. He'd always care about her, he wanted to support her, but beyond that anything more would be an almighty mistake.

# Chapter Nineteen

On the day of Alex's first night Maggie decided it was time for a re-style.

She called a snazzy West End hair salon. Hooray. One of the stylists had a cancellation. She booked herself in and went straight over. She had a couple of inches cut off her hair, plus a sweepy fringe and highlights.

It had been ages since she'd done a shop-till-you-drop session for herself. She knew exactly what she wanted. Color. Out with the grey and black. In with the colors of the season. First off she bought herself a fab pair of boots in dark-green suede. With those dreamy little numbers in a carrier bag, the rest had been a piece of cake. Alex's first night was an excellent excuse to splash out. No more blending into the background. She spent her life putting the glamor and color into other people's wardrobes. It was high time for some va-va-voom of her own. She'd been using monochrome as her personal style-mask. Alex had given her the confidence to be happy with herself again, to trust her instincts. From now on she planned to dress how she liked, express her personality through color, be her authentic self, with no need to hide behind black, white and grey every day. After her shopping spree Maggie headed home to her tiny apartment in Battersea. She had so much to think about and plan for. Just for tonight, she decided to put it all on hold.

Tonight would be everything Alex had dreamt of. Nick and he had got over their bust-up over *Mercy of the Vampires* ending. He'd stopped wanting to disown Jago, accepted that if he hadn't spent the last ten years playing the character, he'd never in a month of Sundays have landed this theater role.

It had been over a week since the night she'd spent at his apartment, and her best efforts had gone into sorting out her feelings about him. He'd been busy. He'd sent texts and a couple of heart-stoppingly funny photos. There'd been a technical run and a dress rehearsal. He'd be in his element – apart from the promo. Her heart flipped. Her head was struggling with the fact that she was in the "friend" zone, and her emotions were in the danger zone.

When the time came to get ready, she had a bad case of butterflies. She lined up a row of nail-varnish bottles. What would be the perfect color? She couldn't decide on one, so she chose five that coordinated with the shades in her not-like-any-animal-known-to-zoologists pink and green leopard-ish-print skirt. She carefully painted each fingernail, a different color on each one matched to its counterpart on the other hand.

Alex would be on a high after the show. They'd probably both say polite things about not losing touch. She doubted that friends could work. It had been a slippery slope. Once she'd allowed Alex to steal like warm sunshine through the chinks in her emotional mask there'd been no way of going back. Re-finding her friend, finishing their long-overdue fling and going back to square one of their friendship had turned out to be more difficult than she'd thought.

She'd enjoyed the ride. But the longer she stuck around the more likely she was to end up saying something she'd regret. Like *I love you*. The worst thing she could possibly do would be to ask for something she couldn't have. Something he wasn't able to give her. He would never love her back.

She slicked on a layer of confidence-boosting lip gloss, gave herself a squirt of her new zingy perfume, grabbed her handbag and the keys to her apartment and set off for the theater. She needed to lose Alex again. And she planned to tell him soon. Would the *Hamlet* after-party be too soon? He'd probably be relieved. He'd be off the hook. No more scares and no more talking her down from the ceiling. Not that she'd be freaking out again. She'd got her act together.

Alex was fantastic as Hamlet. After the performance she almost got cold feet. She was tempted to slink off home and send him a polite excuse and congrats by text. He was a magnet. She couldn't just skulk away and de-friend him. She needed to be strong and tell him face to face.

The first-night party was a far cry from the New York movie premiere and Cassandra's gala dinner. It was a chilled-out do in the understated theater bar. Most people hadn't even bothered to dress up, least of all the actors, and the director was wearing a moth-eaten old sweater and faded jeans with rips that definitely hadn't been put there by a designer.

Maggie strutted in to the after-party wearing her brand-new green-suede boots, circulated, made small talk with complete strangers, and held her head high until Nick spotted her.

"Maggie. Looking good, darling." They air-kissed. "You've had something done. Did you get a boob job?"

"I changed my hair." She shrugged. "Highlights."

"You're different, though." He put a hand to his chin and gave her his undivided consideration. "I know what it is. You got color."

"I'm not Monochrome Magenta anymore."

"Monochrome Magenta? Really?" He gave her a hug. "I've no idea who she is, but you were never that to me."

Maggie smiled. "London's so grey. I had to do something," she joked. She was doing a good job of covering up the jittery feeling she had waiting to see Alex. "I took it upon myself to brighten the place up."

"Go Maggie!"

Nick drained the contents of his champagne flute and plucked another from a passing tray. "What are you drinking?"

Maggie pulled a face. "Organic elderflower and melon cocktail."

"Yum. Get you a refill?" Maggie shook her head. Nick lowered his voice to a conspiratorial whisper. "You and Alex caused quite a stir in New York. What's the story? Are you and he …?"

Maggie blushed. "We're friends."

"What's with you two and this 'friends' thing? You're single. He's single. You've obviously still got the hots for each other. "

Maggie couldn't believe her ears. "Nick? Are you matchmaking?"

He laughed. "You've sussed me. That's why I persuaded the people at the magazine to book you for the Boston shoot. Not that they needed persuading. They were happy to oblige."

"What are you talking about?" She'd had masses of compliments on the photos they'd done, but she felt like the rug had been pulled out from under her. "What am I not getting?"

Nick forked a hand into his blonde hair. His brown eyes pinned her with intensity. "Alex missed his moment with you once before. I thought I'd give you guys a helping hand – a shot at another chance." He knocked back his champagne. "You two are avoiding each other like the plague. That's the thanks I get!"

Her heart felt too big for her chest cavity. She knew the way she got that job at the last minute was odd. "Hang on a minute. Let's rewind this conversation. Are you telling me that I didn't get hired for those shoots by accident? You arranged it?"

The horror in her rising tone wasn't lost on Nick. "If I was wide of the mark, I apologize," he said solemnly. "I promise you. It was well meant."

Maggie shook her head and sighed. "What were you thinking?" Clearly he wouldn't have done it if he'd had a crystal ball. "How could you? I mean, I get that you wanted to do something nice for Alex, but having me turn up like the Ghost of Christmas Past is a bit of risk compared to a basket of muffins." Nick looked repentant. She should be furious. Quite apart from anything else, her pregnancy hadn't been factored into his scheming. Thanks to his meddling, her heart was in a mess. Somehow she couldn't bring herself to be angry. "Your timing's awful!" Her jokey tone masked sadness that sluiced through her veins. "I'm having twins."

"Twins?" Nick gawped. He lowered his eyes to her belly. "Are you sure?"

She nodded.

"Who's having twins?" Cassandra's interjection made Maggie jump.

"Maggie is."

"With donor sperm, I hear. Congratulations, dear. I can't recommend donor insemination highly enough. And twins! Look at the two dreamboats I got." She clinked glasses with Nick and winked at Maggie.

Confusion swirled in the air and tied her tongue in a knot. Alex's family was too much. They'd hit her with a double whammy. As if Nick's admission that he'd plotted to throw her and Alex together wasn't bad enough, she was struggling to decipher what their mother had just come out with.

"By the way, I'm sorry I was rude to you in New York," Cassandra gushed. "That grandma business was quite a shock."

"My fault, I'm afraid." Although, strictly speaking, Nick was to blame for turning them all into press fodder, Maggie graciously accepted culpability. "Sorry." She was still trying to get her head around Cassandra's revelation. Was Alex donor-conceived?

"Don't apologize. Actually, I'd gotten to quite like the idea when Alex told me he's not the dad. Go figure."

Nick, contrition still stamped on his face, spotted someone he wanted to speak to and darted off, leaving her stranded with Cassandra. She'd been at the party for the best part of an hour and she hadn't even said hello to Alex yet. Desperation set in. The minute she got a chance, she'd say hi and congratulations, then she'd leave. After everything she'd just heard she was ready to put her plan to distance herself straight into action.

Cassandra unnerved Maggie. "One word of warning." She held up a ruby-taloned index finger. "Advice, really." Her tone softened and she tapped the nail against her glass. "Make sure you tell your kids the truth. Right from the start. Don't keep anything from them. I made that mistake. I kept my boys in the dark, used the fact that Drake wasn't their real dad to get at him. I …" She corrected herself. "We hurt them." There was real remorse beneath her air of superficiality. "Now they're hung up on not knowing who they really are."

Maggie's heart thudded. Misery seeped through the cracks in her outwardly cheerful appearance. Alex knew exactly who he was — a no-commitment, no-strings guy.

Cassandra twiddled her champagne flute distractedly. "Wasn't Alex a marvel? It's like Shakespeare could have written the *Hamlet* role especially for him." Maggie stifled a hysterical guffaw. She didn't want to snort organic elderflower and melon. "He always wanted to be just like Drake, despite his genes. I think he can safely say that tonight he's proved himself."

Maggie was intrigued by the woman Cassandra had been — attention-seeking, broken-hearted, needy, hooked on drugs and alcohol. Her heart went out to the little boys at the center of that mess. Was that chaos behind Alex's determination to be the perfect son, the reliable brother? He never talked much about his dad. Now she understood why. No wonder he'd been thrown by her wanting a donor-sperm baby. He must despise her choice. She wished he hadn't kept it from her. Apparently his mother assumed he trusted her enough to have told her. Her confidence sank, realizing that he didn't.

Cassandra's partner descended like a bird of prey, "Darling, there's someone I'd like you to meet." He whisked her away.

Maggie looked for a place to set her glass. She found a table crammed with glassware and rejected canapés. She put it there. Right above the table was an enormous poster of Alex in Elizabethan costume, angst-ridden, and still sexy as hell. Sexier maybe. Who'd have thought he'd carry off the doublet-and-hose look so well? No doubt she'd soon be seeing his face plastered all over digital advertising screens on the escalators in the Underground, a weird memento of their New York fling.

Tonight Alex was a rare species, glimpsed across a vast, crowded space.

Isolated from the chat and laughter, alone in the crowd, her head throbbed. Emptiness crashed through her like a wave pounding a Cornish beach out of a wintry sea. Suddenly she knew where she wanted to be. She had to get out of London. She turned to go and walked smack into the barrier of Alex's rock-face chest.

"Woah!" His arms shot out as if to catch her, banded strongly around her and drew her into a hug. "How did you like the play?" The deep timbre of his voice speaking just to her made her wobbly. She did her best not to look in his electric-blue eyes.

"Fantastic. I kind of nearly nodded off once, during that bit with Rosencrantz and Guildenstern in Act Two. I never get what they're about. Spies, or students, or something, right? Otherwise, it was great."

Alex laughed. "I'm glad you came." He tore his eyes away from her face. "Guildenstern is over there with Cassandra. I'll introduce you to him if you like. I'm sure he'd be happy to enlighten you."

"No thanks." She risked a full-on take of his gorgeousness. His traffic-stopping smile infected her with deep heat. In spite of herself, a smile grew from her heart and broke onto her face. "You were good, though."

The room buzzed. Alex was still on an adrenaline high. People had been patting him on the back and telling him he was wonderful for the last hour. Weirdly, Maggie's opinion was the one that counted most. She'd been there for him when he was Alex the wannabe. Her approval mattered above all others.

"How've you been?"

"Good." The conversation stalled.

She looked stunning. Better even than he remembered.

"You look different."

"Different good? Or different bad?"

"Different ..." Accosted by a couple of luvvy types, he lost the chance to find the right word to tell her that the moment he'd set eyes on her that evening a lightning strike of desire had torn through him and he'd been aching to be alone with her ever since.

"Alex, you were fabulous."

"Marvelous."

"Your Hamlet's wicked." A third girl joined the group drawn to Alex like bees to a tree in blossom.

Maggie didn't fade away. She stood her ground. Poised. Patient. She waited for the onslaught of hugs and kisses to subside.

"Come on. Let's get out of here. I need to talk to you – alone." He placed his hand low against her back. Sexual tension zapped him, like two planets colliding. He broke the connection and held the theater door open for her to step through, trying to convince himself that it wasn't his attraction to Maggie making him high, it was the first-night buzz.

Outside they walked in silence until they reached the Millennium Bridge and stood looking at the lights reflected on the River Thames, watched over by the spectral white shape of St. Paul's Cathedral dome lit up against the dark sky.

*By heaven! I yearn to kiss her.* It wasn't first-night euphoria after all, but he really should get out of character. He ached to pull her into his arms and kiss her beautiful lips until the sun came up over London. Or take her back to his penthouse apartment and make crazy, stupid love to her. Was that so impossible? It was, if he was to stick to his decision.

"I've been thinking." A chill October wind whistled across the bridge. He searched Maggie's face. Her brows knitted.

"Alex, why didn't you tell me you were donor-conceived?"

It was the barb that had lacerated his heart, the weapon his father used every time he'd threatened to disown his sons.

"Because I didn't want to dump my hang-ups on you. I don't

know who my dad is." He paused, wary of saying something to offend her. "It certainly isn't Drake."

"It takes more than an ejaculation to make a dad? You told me that."

"And I meant it. Except it doesn't apply where my father's concerned. He gave up being a dad the day he walked out on my mother. He was playing a part. It's as simple as that. We're his embarrassing secret."

"Don't you trust me?"

"No. It's not that." He'd been deliberately keeping it from her for good reason. "I didn't want to pour cold water on your plan. My parents aren't exactly great advertising for a sperm-donor family." He hesitated, uncertain about hitting her with things that pained him. "Do you want to know how I found out that Drake isn't my biological dad? You'd think sharing that information would be something parents planned out carefully, wouldn't you?" Maggie nodded, watching him carefully. "Well, I found out in an airport. I was thirteen. My mother was half-cut. And out it came. No build-up. No warning." Awkward silence hung in the air. Maggie opened her mouth to say something and no words came out. He'd thought having a broken-hearted mother and being rejected by a father who constantly put him down were his deepest scars. The bombshell of not being Drake's biological son ran deeper. "You know. Who told you?"

"Cassandra let it slip."

He was sorry he hadn't told her but he didn't want to talk about Drake and Cassandra. His years of trying to fix his mother's heart-break, protect his brother, prove himself to Drake were behind him.

"I need to talk about us." He wanted her to be happy. He'd watch from the wings, celebrate her ups, be there for her downs. He didn't know if he had it in him, but he planned to try. Maggie shivered. Her lovely face was tipped up, her eyes locked on his. "What I'm saying is … You can count on me. As a friend. Whatever you need, whenever you need it – help, money … Just call me and let me know, I'll do whatever I can for you." *Until you find The One.* How could he explain that he couldn't promise to love her because he couldn't risk hurting her? Them. "I don't want to let you down," he said simply. "But I'll be there for you – and the babies."

Maggie's expression was cool, her eyes fixed on the glistening dark water of the Thames below. "That won't work," she whispered.

He reached out his arms and wrapped her in a hug. Her hair beneath his jaw felt soft, lovely. She smelt delicious, kind of zingy.

He wanted her. His Maggie. With him. On tour. In his arms. In his bed. He wanted fun, colorful, lovely Maggie. She'd turned his world inside out. The complexity of what he felt shattered him. He didn't do complicated. He couldn't have what he wanted. Worse, much worse than that, he couldn't be what she needed. He was an actor. Make-believe was what he did best. He could pretend that Maggie's babies were his. He'd do it in a heartbeat. He wouldn't have to pretend. If only it were that simple. What he couldn't stand was for them to pretend that he was their dad. There was too much potential for heartache in that scenario. They'd be living a lie. He'd turned it over and over in his mind. He couldn't be a worse father than Drake. But what if he couldn't do any better? What if he broke Maggie's heart?

Maggie wriggled and he loosened his hold, so that she could slip out of the circle of his arms.

"I don't need your help, or your money, thank you very much." Her words were edged with sarcasm. "Believe it or not, my finances are in perfect order. I'd hardly have decided to be a single parent if they weren't."

"I didn't mean to imply that you were reckless," Alex cut in. He wanted her to understand that he was offering back-up, someone to rely on. "What I meant was …"

"I don't want to hear it." She held up the palms of her hands and backed away from him. "What do you expect from me? Do you want me to say that's really sweet? You can drift in and out of my life between girlfriends? Maybe even have the occasional shag? I can't do it."

"You've got it all wrong. I didn't mean some kind of friends-with-benefits thing. Just friends. Why not? We were friends before. We can be again." He spluttered it out, knowing it couldn't happen.

"I love you." Her arms hung limply at her side. The fury had gone from her face. "I can't be just friends anymore. I shouldn't even be here. I wouldn't be, if your brother hadn't interfered."

"What?" She loved him? Confusion clouded his mind. Nick and he were finally on separate career paths, leading different lives.

"Nick set us up." Her eyes narrowed and her chin jutted. "You mean he hasn't told you?" She shook her head despairingly. "He fixed for me to get hired to style you in Boston. And if he hadn't? None of this would have happened. I wouldn't have gone to New York. I wouldn't be here now. Face it, Alex. If you'd walked past me on a London street, you wouldn't have recognized me."

"Oh, I'd have recognized you." The shattering of his heart echoed in his voice.

"You don't have to look after me. I'm not your responsibility."

She spun on her heels and walked away. He hurried after her, following at a close distance, a pace or two behind, like her minder. When they were off the bridge, he hailed a taxi. He pulled her into his arms, held her tight, and pressed his forehead to hers. He ached to kiss her mouth. Instead he brushed her forehead with his lips and let her go. Cold as a marble statue, he watched the taxi's tail lights disappear. After it rounded a corner he remained frozen to the spot, utterly dispirited. He raked both hands into his hair, took two quick strides, aching to run after her, get her back. There was no point. No matter what she felt, he couldn't be her perfect man. He sucked in a deep breath and let it go in an anguished gasp. Accepting, finally, that this was goodbye, he turned and walked purposefully towards the theater.

Time to rejoin the party.

Alex was breaking inside.

Back at the theater he walked straight bang into Drake. He'd sent him an invitation to the first night, but he hadn't RSVP'd, so Alex had assumed he wasn't there.

His face beaming, the grey-haired actor grabbed Alex in a firm hug. "Well done, son," he said. "You knocked *Hamlet* out of the ball park. I knew you could do it." With that he swept out of the building to a waiting car.

The American expression coming from the English actor's mouth sounded ridiculously incongruous. He wasn't being facetious. He meant it. Alex had earned Drake's approval. It paled into insignificance. His heart hammered in his chest. The only approval he really needed was Maggie's love and he'd let that go.

Back in the bar, he hunted down Nick. He'd moved on from champagne and was sitting, looking bored and peeling the label off a bottle of beer.

"What did you do it for?"

"What do you mean?"

"You know. Setting me up with Maggie."

"Because if I'd said 'Hey, why don't you look up Maggie?' – you wouldn't have. It was a nudge in the right direction."

Alex's cheek muscle flickered. "You were out of order."

"Maybe, but the minute you heard she was our stylist, you got her an upgrade on the flight so that she could sit with you."

"That doesn't mean you were right." Tension ripped through Alex's body.

"I engineered a reintroduction." Nick shrugged and slugged his beer. "I'd say New York was a pretty good indication that I didn't get it entirely wrong." He grinned lopsidedly. "The rest is up to you!"

# Chapter Twenty

"I'm starting to look like a pot-bellied pig and I'm only twelve weeks. I'm eating like a prize porker too." Maggie picked up a blueberry muffin and took a bite.

Layla looked her over critically. "I don't think we need to build you a sty or buy you a trough just yet!"

Four weeks had passed since Maggie had left London for Cornwall. She'd started thinking about redecorating the cottage and the kitchen table was covered in drawings for her new venture – designing babywear. In a corner of the sitting room she'd set up her sewing machine. There was a big pile of colorful fabric samples stacked up beside it.

She was sitting in her kitchen with her best friend and next-door neighbor, Layla. Layla's unmissable dyed red hair lit up the room with color. She had boundless energy and enthusiasm. It was Layla who'd encouraged Maggie to have a go at designing, pointing out that if other fashion stylists could turn designer, why shouldn't she?

It warmed Maggie's heart remembering the hours she'd spent at the scratched rustic pine table as a child drawing and coloring and cutting and pasting. Her grandmother had been ever- patient with Maggie. She had helped her learn how to turn her creations into reality by showing her how to sew. Under her watchful eye, she and Layla had made a vast collection of clothes for their toys. They'd had the best-dressed teddies in the village.

Maggie sighed, her eyes resting for a couple of seconds on the kitchen notice board. She'd sorted out the shoebox under the bed and stuck up a photo of her teenage parents – happy, smiling, in love, in the moment. She wondered what would have become of her if her mother hadn't left her behind when she'd hightailed off to Spain. She'd probably have spent the last ten years pulling pints of *cerveza* in the Green Flamingo karaoke bar and serving up bacon and eggs to tourists. Her singing voice was rubbish. She'd be useless at karaoke. She shuddered. That was her mother's dream, not hers. She'd never fully understand what her mother had felt when she left, but she knew now she hadn't gone because she looked like her dad. She'd been emotionally defeated, moving forward, but not going anywhere. She hadn't left her behind because she didn't love her. She'd done it because she did.

As well as her designing project, she had an exciting new work prospect on the horizon. It had turned out that the television presenter who'd cancelled her for the awards show hadn't done so in a fit of pique over her rubbish leggings and I Heart NY tee in the press photos of Maggie in New York. Quite the reverse. The day-time television presenter had caught chicken pox from her three-year-old. She'd had to miss the ceremony altogether, so hadn't needed a stylist. But the "New York Cinderella" pictures had caught her eye. Then a "Who's The Daddy?" story, speculating about whether she might be expecting Alex Wells' baby, had got her noticed by a producer on the morning magazine program. They'd approached her about doing a series of maternity fashion items on the show.

She'd been quick to put them straight, make sure they under-stood that there was no man in her life, and that the Alex thing was a misunderstanding. The producer didn't seem bothered. She'd been intrigued by her go-it-alone approach to parenting, and they'd gone on to discuss a follow-up contract of regular slots doing yummy mummy makeovers, fashion advice and cool kit for babies and kids. It was a dream job and a great way to get exposure for her planned line of baby clothes. She aimed to create something fun and fashionable for little ones using funky hard-wearing fabrics. Her target market would be busy mums who wanted practical clothes with an emphasis on every child's unique individuality.

She hadn't settled on a brand name yet. Layla had lots of suggestions.

"How about 'No Mini Me's Allowed'? Or 'Minis by Magenta'?"

Layla sat with her foot up on a kitchen chair, resting a sprained ankle. She picked up one of Maggie's designs and studied it. "So what exactly happened in New York?"

"What happened in New York was meant to stay in New York." Maggie got up, went over to the sink and filled the kettle.

"Come on, Magenta." Layla started to tidy Maggie's drawings into a neat pile. "It's four weeks since you came home to Cornwall," she said sulkily. "I've tried the softly-softly approach and it's not working. There's only so long a person can go without dying of curiosity. It's high time you spilled the beans. I want details."

When she'd moved back to the village half the magazines in the local shop had had pictures of her and Alex somewhere between their covers. She'd been a hot topic of local gossip for about a week. Then the WI's Winter Fair and who'd be odds-on favorite to bake the best Victoria sponge cake took over. People lost interest and she went back to being the Plumtree girl.

Maggie looked out of the kitchen window. It was one of those lovely early-winter mornings before the frost killed the last flowers and the final golden leaves dropped. "There's really nothing to tell," she said, struggling to keep her tone even. "I met an old friend. We hooked up. Now we're getting on with our lives."

Layla narrowed her pretty, brown eyes. She watched Maggie's back analytically. "I'm guessing there's more to it than that. There's something you're not telling me." Maggie opened a cupboard and took out her grandma's old Chinese-patterned tea caddy. She got two flowery- patterned mugs and popped a tea-bag into each one. "You know your trouble, Magenta?" There was frustration in Layla's voice. "You're always pushing people away. And when you're not pushing them away, you're closing them out. You've been doing it for as long as I've known you, and let's face it, that's forever."

Maggie knew she was right. She didn't trust easily. She'd learned that being self-reliant was easier than trusting other people. Others let you down. She'd opened up to Alex, and he hadn't returned her trust, didn't tell her he was donor-conceived. She shouldn't have let him into her heart. Worse, she'd spilled out feelings that she should have kept in. She'd overstepped the boundaries and given him her heart. She turned and gave her friend a fragile smile.

"I'm sorry," she said. "I can't talk about it."

She hadn't the strength to let Alex be a friend. Because she loved him. That's why, this time, she'd been the one who had to leave.

She'd reconnected with him, and far from ending things by getting that spark of chemistry out of the way, the sex that she'd hoped would be a fun fling had deepened her feelings for him. That night on the bridge she'd finally accepted what she'd always known – he wasn't in love with her.

Layla wouldn't let it go. "This is me, remember? Best friends forever have rights."

Maggie laughed. "Stop fishing."

"Just tell me one thing. Was New York the start of something?"

"No-ooooooh." Maggie sighed out her denial on a long breath. Nights like the one they'd spent in New York didn't last forever. "Definitely not. It was an ending, really. Alex and I said goodbye." Maggie opened the fridge.

"In that case how come you went to his first night?"

Maggie briskly closed the fridge door. "I'm out of milk," she said, avoiding the question. "I'll run down to the shop and get some. Wait here."

Layla pointed to her bandaged ankle and made a face. "I'm not going anywhere."

Maggie grabbed some small change and took her coat from a peg in the hall. "I'll be back in ten minutes," she shouted.

"Good. Cos I'm not leaving until I get some answers!"

The cottage door banged closed.

A white-painted wood gate swung on creaking hinges in the breeze. Alex marched to the glossy blue front door and reached for the brass knocker. Overhead a seagull screeched. It settled on the chimney pot as if it had come to watch the show. He inhaled a lungful of fresh sea air. *Here goes.* He gave a sharp rat-a-tat-tat. The garden in front of the cottage was a riot of color. Orange and yellow nasturtium flowers, their trumpets peeking out from between flat, circular green leaves, clambered and tumbled over the low, whitewashed wall. A window box and a couple of terracotta pots by the front door contained red geraniums, poised to defy the winter weather.

Alex hooked his sunglasses into his top pocket. The snooty voice on his satnav had been taking him around in circles for what seemed like hours. The high Cornish hedges didn't help. Finally he'd arrived and there was no answer. Maybe she'd gone back to London. *Damn!*

*Hamlet* had been playing to packed houses for four weeks. Maggie had been right about everything. The Jago factor was attracting new audiences to Shakespeare. It hadn't taken him long to realize that as well as angsting on stage as the Prince of Denmark, he was angsting off-stage between performances, at all hours of the day and night, about Maggie. She'd been a nightmare to find. He knocked again.

The door swung open and a young woman with unnaturally red hair appeared, hopping on one foot. Alex opened his mouth to say he'd got the wrong address.

Layla cut him short. "Alex Wells, I presume. Magenta won't be long. She's gone to the village shop for a pint of milk."

Trying not to stare at the wild red hair Alex fixed on the red geraniums at his ankles. "She should bring those in. Before the first frost gets them."

"I take it you haven't come all this way to offer horticultural advice." Her lovely Cornish accent was a lot more pronounced than Maggie's.

"No." Alex laughed.

"So why have you come?" she asked, fiercely protective.

Alex was stumped. He didn't know exactly why he'd come. Except, he needed to see Maggie. Dog-tired from driving, stressing about what he planned to say, he ran a hand through his hair to the back of his head and threw a silent glance around his surroundings. He opened his mouth to reply, couldn't find words, and closed it again.

"Sorry. None of my business." The reception party mellowed. "I'm Layla, by the way. You'd better come in."

Alex held out a hand. "Pleased to meet you. I've heard a lot about you." *Although not about the hair.*

"Not as much as I've heard about you, I'll bet." A sheepish look crept across her pretty features. "From magazines and stuff. Not from Magenta. She's taken a vow of silence where you're concerned."

"I see." A track ran up the side of a hill behind the cottage to the right, and to the left a narrow lane wound down towards the sea between higgledy-piggledy houses. He'd parked his Smart car in the lane in front of the row of cottages. One perfectly plucked eyebrow arched, Layla glanced back and forth between it and him.

"Which way's the shop?"

"I think she took the cliff path." She pointed down the hill to the sea. "But if you want to catch her up, it's quickest to cut along the beach."

"Thanks." Alex called over his shoulder. He practically ran down the lane in his hurry to find Maggie. When he got to the beach he was struck by how beautiful it was. He could taste the salt in the air. He loved Maggie's home in an instant – the cliffs, the little harbor at the far end of the curve of golden sand, and the steady roll of the waves, breaking and washing up the beach. No wonder this was her retreat.

He'd missed her like crazy. The flames she'd lit in him in New York wouldn't die. He'd been an idiot. Maggie was the best thing that had ever happened to him and he'd let her go.

Drake had brought friends to see the play. It was a compliment. Afterwards he'd come backstage to his dressing room. It was a turnaround realizing that the king of the abysmal put-down was proud of him. He'd been right in believing that there was more to being a father than sperm, after all. The emptiness in his soul had nothing to do with not knowing himself, and everything to do with missing Maggie.

Another night Nick had come to see him backstage before he went on. He'd handed him a package. "That's for Maggie," he'd said mysteriously. "Go find her."

Nick had been clearing out some old stuff and found a children's book that he'd held onto. It was *The Little Engine That Could*. The tale of a blue railway engine that had to try and pull a long train over a hill, all the time the little engine kept repeating the words "I-think-I-can-I-think-I-can". Alone in his dressing room after the performance, Alex's heart thundered when he opened the package and found the worn copy of the book with his father's inscription inside. "You can! All my love, always, Dad". Holding the book felt bizarre. He realized that there must have been a time when his parents had wanted to get it right. Even when their personal lives crumbled, determination had driven them to succeed, and despite everything else they'd passed that determination on to Nick and Alex.

Nick and Cassandra had been pestering him about New York. His mother kept sending him texts saying things like "*How smitten were you with Maggie? Do something about it!*" Nick was blunt. The last one from him read, "*You wouldn't know a good thing if it walked up and grabbed you by the codpiece!"*

He had people who cared about him, but they didn't need him like they once did. Maggie had become the one person who mattered to him most in the world and he'd closed his heart to her magic. Her belief in him was what had pushed him to nail *Hamlet*. All she'd needed in return was his belief in her love and he'd let her leave, too afraid of what ifs to see that he was wrong.

What if he could take her by the hand and walk forward into the future, no looking back?

Everything in Alex's universe had clicked into place and all he wanted was to see Maggie again. She'd got so deep under his skin that she was like a part of him, a piece of himself that he couldn't live without, like his beating heart. He'd requisitioned the stage manager's Smart car, shoe-horned himself into it, and set off for Cornwall. He only had twenty-four hours to find her before he had to be back in theater-land.

Emotional paralysis set in as Alex strode along the beach. What if she didn't want to see him? Going by Layla's snippy reaction to him turning up out of the blue, she mightn't be pleased to see him. What if it was too late? What if she didn't want him? She had every right to send him packing. He'd hurt her. She'd told him she loved him and what had he done? He'd put her in a taxi.

He froze. A soggy, sandy dog came running up to him carrying a stick. It dropped the stick and ran off. Alex picked it up and started writing in the sand. He wrote his name. ALEX. Then he drew a great, big, enormous heart in the sand. Underneath he wrote MAGGIE. Alex heart Maggie. He stood back to look at it. Was that what he'd come to say? The dog came bounding back, ready to play. Alex threw the stick and the dog tore off across the sand, scuffing most of the letters in Alex Heart Maggie as it went. "You've ruined my handiwork," he called after it. "It looks like Alex Heart Maggot. Thanks for that."

He scrubbed away the letters with his foot and stamped out the heart, kicking clumps of seaweed over what remained to disguise it.

His gut churned. He wanted to hold her, touch her, love her. But how would he tell her? He was no good with words. Only ones he'd learned, rehearsed, repeated over and over. Improvisation wasn't his thing. He scowled at the empty beach. Where in heaven's name was she?

The dog reappeared at his feet. He threw the stick again. And again.

Just then he saw her. He looked up and there she was, standing on the cliff above the beach, hair flying in the wind, wearing the coat she'd had on the night he'd put her into a black taxi. Watching the tail lights leave with her on board, he'd felt wretched. His heart thumped. She waved and started zig-zagging her way down the path to the beach. She seemed to be taking forever, ambling across the sand, swinging her shopping bag and stopping every few feet to pick up shells and put them in her pockets. He gazed at the scene, as though she was his favorite film. Bracing himself to face her, he forced his legs to move, each step he took towards her more difficult than the one before.

Suddenly she was right there. She held out a square of opaque green glass. "Sea glass," she said, as if she'd been expecting him. "What's that?" Puzzled by the mess of seaweed and scrubbed out writing in the sand, she nodded to the cliff and added, "From up there it looked like "Alex heart Maggot".

"Blame the dog." Alex jerked his head at the wet animal. It was sitting, looking up hopefully, stick in mouth.

"Who's your new best friend?"

He wanted to say Ophelia, because the little dog reminded him of the actress who'd been relentlessly hanging around making eyes at him for the last few weeks, when all he could think about was Maggie.

He shrugged. "Dunno. Maybe it's a stray."

Maggie dropped her shopping bag. She knelt down on the sand and checked for a collar. Nothing. "She's skin and bone under all that fur." She searched the empty beach. "Maybe she's been abandoned."

Alex crossed his arms over his chest. "What should we do?"

"I'll bring her home with me, give her something to eat, and ask around, see if anyone knows who she belongs to." She stood up and dusted the sand off her hands. "I guess if no one claims her, I'll have to keep her." Their eyes locked and his heart missed a beat on impact. "Alex, what are you doing here?"

"I'm … Um … I came to say …" Small white-crested waves gently rolled and broke.  Pushing closer, the incoming tide swept up the beach and formed a perfect heart of foam on the sand. "I'm sorry." Alex looked down into the face he loved and laid himself bare. "Sorry I stayed in LA and didn't contact you. Sorry I didn't come back for you. Sorry I didn't say goodbye." He hesitated for a fraction of a second. "Sorry that I let you go twice."

"That's a lot of sorry." She stared at the place near her feet where the sea had made the foam heart and hugged her arms defensively across her body. "Is there anything you're not sorry about?"

Unnoticed, the little dog nudged open the shopping bag, chewed through a biscuit packet and chomped away at its contents. Alex's heart filled with hope. He should tell her that he wasn't sorry Nick had found her. He wasn't sorry about what happened in New York. Mostly he wasn't sorry that he loved her more than life itself and he wanted to spend the rest of his days with her.

"I'm not sorry that when I'm with you I know exactly who I am – who I want to be." Remembering the stupid strategy he'd come up with on the plane to Boston, he thought of a point five.

*Point Five: Scratch the strategy and marry Maggie.*

He circled an arm around her waist, pulled her close and tucked a knuckle under her chin.

"I'm not sorry that I want to marry you." He searched her eyes. She didn't try and look away. "If you'll have me."

He folded her into his arms, lowered his head, and kissed her for the longest time, exploring her soft mouth, reveling in having her close. Finally, he forced himself to break the kiss. It was harder than knocking a limpet off a rock with a stone. He wanted to go on kissing her and holding her until the tide came in. He held three lives in his arms. And he loved all of them.

In a crazy spin, Maggie reeled from his kiss. She ached to tell him that she was still in love with him. But did he love her back? Or was the marriage proposal more about being there for her? A rehashed version of what he'd offered her on the bridge that night. She needed to know, and there was only one way to find out.

"Do you love me?"

He put a big, strong, reliable arm around her. She gazed up at his face, the face she'd missed so badly, the face she'd wanted to forget. All stubble, and blue eyes, and heart-stopping smile, he was more gorgeous than ever. And he was hers. But only if he loved her. Melting with desire and love, she buzzed with anticipation.

"I love you." He rumbled out the words, dark and delicious. "I love you so much. And I plan to spend the rest of the day showing you how much."

He grabbed what was left of the sandy shopping and laced her fingers between his. Together they walked away from the beach, up through the meandering village houses, the little dog trotting contentedly behind. Maggie couldn't wait to be alone with Alex at the cottage. Hop- along Layla was waiting for a cup of tea. Maggie crossed her fingers that her friend would get the hint and make herself scarce.

Alex had told her he loved her and now she was the one who hadn't told him back. To get to the cottage they had to cross an iron bridge over a stream trickling down to the sea. Its green paint was rusty in places and somebody had attached a tiny lovelock to it, decorated with a bright-red nail color heart, a promise of forever love. Maggie stopped in her tracks. Her fingers interlaced with Alex's, she turned to face him. For the first time giving love wasn't a risk.

"Alex," she said, reaching up to wrap her arms around his neck. "I love you. You're The One."

# *Chapter Twenty One*

The chapel by the sea was picture-perfect for the Christmas Eve wedding. There were more fishing nets and lobster pots than holy crosses, but that was fine by Maggie. Hollowed into the cliff, it had been a sanctuary since the fourteenth century. Maggie had loved it to bits since she was a child. The church was at the heart of the community, a place where people gathered in happy times and in sad. Villagers in centuries past went there to pray for the safe return of their loved ones. When someone was lost at sea it was the quiet place where they went to cry.

Never in her wildest imaginings could Maggie have predicted marrying her dream man in tiny Saint Elisabeth's. Layla and her friends from the village had done a great decorating job. They'd twisted sprigs of mistletoe and holly into long green trails of ivy and dotted the church with pine cones, peppered in amongst the pebbles and seashells that were so much part of its charm. With enough candles to light a stately home, never mind a small chapel, and a tangle of fairy lights wrapped around the rafters, the place looked magical. Outside a fresh snowfall had turned the world white. It could not have been more perfect had it been a film set created in Hollywood.

Everyone Alex and Maggie cared about was there. Nick was exceptional as the best man and Layla an outstanding maid of honor. Cassandra shone in Parisian couture. Drake put in a super-polite appearance. Ella, no longer Nick's plus one, but still a friend of the brothers, flew in for a few hours, taking a break from filming on location somewhere fab. Maggie's mum turned up with her fiancé in tow. Delighted to be the mother of the bride, and thrilled that the happy couple were tying the knot on Christmas Eve, she was a tad disappointed that they'd declined to sell their wedding-photo opportunity to a glamorous magazine, but she was discreet enough not to make a fuss about it. Alex had traced Maggie's Australian grandparents and invited them. They couldn't make the wedding, but they'd promised to come the following summer to meet their granddaughter and the baby twins.

Maggie was every inch the stunning bride in a red-silk wedding dress. She'd been tempted to suggest that they put the wedding off until after the babies were born, but Layla had pointed out that if anyone was up to styling a still-comparatively-smallish bump it was Maggie. "After all," she'd enthused, "You're marrying the man you love, not trying to look like you belong in a bridal magazine." Although, given the fantabulous outcome, she wouldn't have looked out of place.

Layla had tried to insist that she wear a shade of purply pink that exactly matched her name, but Maggie was having none of it. In deep-forest green, a pretty contrast to Maggie, Layla, with her bright-red hair, looked fantastic. With superstitious leanings, she'd been a little bit concerned about the green, having heard somewhere that it was an unlucky color for weddings, but Maggie had been adamant that it was fine, and festive.

When Maggie arrived at the chapel and Alex turned to see her walk up the aisle, her heart was bursting with love.

"Do you Alexander Drake Wells take Magenta Sunrise Plumtree to be your lawfully wedded wife?"

Alex's eyebrows shot up. "Sunrise?" he mouthed.

She nodded.

"Me by Magenta Sunrise is the name of your baby collection," he whispered, halting the proceedings momentarily.

Things were moving full-steam ahead for Maggie. After the honeymoon, she'd be negotiating a deal with a big retailer. They were proposing to launch a new babywear range, offering her design input, and using her name to front the brand.

"It is."

The young vicar raised his hand to his mouth and gave a discreet "Ahem".

"It's also my … um … full name."

"I never knew that."

Alex gazed at his beautiful bride.

"Well, now you do."

"I do."

Seizing the moment, and eager to complete his first wedding, the triumphant vicar pronounced them husband and wife. "You may kiss the bride."

Alex banded one arm around Maggie's waist, drew her to him tighter-than-tight, and placed a possessive kiss on her lips.

A cheer rang out in the candlelit harbor chapel.

"You forgot the rings." It was an onlooker who drew it to everyone's attention, one of the ladies from the WI who'd squeezed in at the back to watch the Plumtree girl marry Hot Vampire Guy.

The inexperienced vicar blushed so hard that his ears complemented the wedding dress. Everyone laughed. Nobody minded. Certainly not Alex and Maggie. They couldn't have been any happier. Or any more in love. Alex took Maggie's hand in his. Her neatly manicured nails shone with natural polish. Gently he slid the wedding ring into place.

They'd taken over the local Manor House Hotel for the holiday weekend and all the family had stayed. When the last drop of champagne had been drained and the bouquet thrown like a beach ball straight to Layla, Alex and Maggie said their goodnights. Wrapped in each other's arms, moonlight streamed through the mullioned window of the bridal suite. Far below waves crashed onto rocks.

Maggie stood on tiptoe and kissed her husband lovingly. He scooped her off her feet into his strong arms. He carried her across the room and tumbled her gently onto the four-poster bed.

"I love you, Mrs. Wells."

Maggie brimmed with love and desire for her gorgeous husband. In the shadows, she reached out, ran her hands across his cheeks, down over his lightly stubbled jaw, and linked them at the back of his neck. The fingers of her right hand connected with the metal band on the ring finger of her left. A bubble of joy erupted inside her. She touched the soft, short hair at his nape and pulled him close, seeking out the mouth that he'd promised to her with a lifetime guarantee. Happiness filled her heart when he kissed her.

"You're The One. The only one. Ever," he murmured. He started oh-so-slowly to untie the crisscross laces in the back of her red-silk dress. She laughed softly. He loved her inside out. "You're the color of my love."

She didn't believe it was humanly possible to be this happy.

*If I am the color of your love, you are the color of my tomorrows.*

The thought was lost in his kiss. He was the man she didn't know she could have, the one to love forever. He enfolded her and she wrapped around him like a seam of soft rock melded with granite.

# *Epilogue*

June sunshine streamed into the penthouse apartment. The place had been transformed into a temporary photo studio. At the heart of the craziness were tiny twins Horatio Alexander Wells and Phoebe Rose Wells.

"We chose names from Shakespeare," Maggie explained to the journalist. "And Rose was my grandmother's name."

The babies had arrived three weeks early while Alex was in London to discuss a future directing project and Maggie was by herself in Cornwall. Her waters had broken at half past six on a beautiful May morning and the first thing she'd done was call Alex. Then she'd called the duty midwife, who'd reassured her that since she hadn't had any contractions it might be hours before anything happened but advised her to come straight in.  Luckily Layla was next door and she'd driven her to the hospital.

The midwife was right. It was a bit of an anti-climax at first because nothing happened at all. Left to her own devices, she and Layla read all the magazines, punctuated by cups of tea, pacing up and down the corridor, and the occasional check-up to make sure that everything was alright.

When it all kicked off without any sign of Alex her heart sank. She was in the middle of a contraction when news came via a student nurse that a helicopter had been given permission to land on the emergency helipad.

Shortly after, Alex's voice boomed through the maternity unit as if he was speaking to the back of a large theater without a microphone. He caused quite a commotion bypassing Reception and heading straight to the labor ward.

"I'm the dad!" She couldn't see his face, but she'd have recognized that dark, rumbling voice anywhere.

He'd arrived in the nick of time. Horatio was born first and little Phoebe Rose followed twenty minutes later.

Exhausted, elated, Maggie had never been happier.

And now she was showing the Wells babies off to the world.

With the babies dressed in colorful teeny outfits from her first babywear collection, Maggie sat next to Alex on the cream-leather sofa that she'd slept on all those months ago. With a backdrop of London and the River Thames spread out behind them through the wall of windows, Alex cradled Phoebe and Maggie cuddled Horatio.

Maggie smiled. She'd been apprehensive about her first in-front-of-the-camera photo shoot. She needn't have worried. She turned her head slightly as the camera clicked. Grinning from ear to ear, Alex's gorgeous smile said everything she needed to know.

The journalist was another story. "So tell me, guys," she probed. "Plans to extend the family?"

Maggie breathed an inward sigh of relief when Alex didn't tell her to get lost. His finger tightly held in Phoebe's grasp, he switched his gaze back and forth between his baby daughter and son with comedic timing.

"We need to get a bigger place."

"It sounds like you're planning on a full house," the journalist hinted.

Maggie smiled at Alex's careful answer and supplied one of her own, "A home full of love." With her husband at her side, she felt no need to hide, or avoid the direction of the question. "No plans just yet," she informed the journalist, "But I'm sure we'd like a brother or sister for the twins in the future."

Wherever they might live, whatever shape their only-just-started family might eventually take, it was their love for each other she counted on – far more than four walls and a roof. She'd never give up her tiny Cornish cottage, no matter how big her family got. Visits there might become a squeeze, but it would be the love inside that mattered more than anything.

A whole lot later, when the magazine team had gone, and the babies had had a flying visit from Uncle Nick and were tucked up cozily asleep in their cribs, Alex kissed Maggie, deeply, passionately. With one hand he tangled his fingers in her hair, with the other he circled the pad of a thumb on her cheek. Crushed so close against him that he felt like a part of her, she smiled against his kiss.

"I'm more in love with you than I ever could have believed possible," she whispered.

"I love you, Magenta Wells." His lovely drawl made her float on air. "Always and forever."